W9-BFZ-761

ISBN: 978-0-7394-8890-4

Published by B & H Publishing Group
Nashville, Tennessee

GILBERT MORRIS

B&H
PUBLISHING GROUP

Nashville, Tennessee

TO

Fran Hebel and Kathy Anderson—
the finest two Yankee ladies I know!

PART ONE

Temperance

Chapter One

SPRING HAD COME TO Oregon Territory, bearing its spongy odors, and the birds had returned, bringing their anthems announcing the end of winter. Their cheerful songs pleased Temperance Peabody as she drove the team at a fast trot along the trail that led to Walla Walla. The wind out of the north was still raw and chilling, and Temperance savored the rank smell of winter's breakup of rotted earth about to come alive.

Lifting her gaze, she took in the mountains. The noon sunlight gave the snow-capped peaks a brilliant glitter, and there was pleasure in the sight, for mountains always gave her a sense of exultation. She held the lines loosely but sat up straight, making a rather prim figure. She had a wealth of light brown hair and a pair of wide-spaced, well-shaped blue eyes, but she was not a beauty. Her face, strong rather than pretty, was marked by high cheekbones and a mouth too wide for stylish beauty. Her long, composed lips spoke of a temper that could charm a man or, at times, chill him to the bone. Her hands were square-knuckled and strong, and she was faintly full at the breast and narrow in the waist. Although she had just celebrated her thirty-second birthday, she had the figure of a much younger woman, though this was mostly concealed by a heavy wool coat.

As she approached the town, Temperance's attention centered on a group of wagons not drawn into a circle, obviously part of a newly arrived train. Drawing the wagons in a circle, she understood, was a protection against Indians, but the Indians in this part of Oregon Territory were not troublesome in the year 1850. She was not surprised to see the train, for Walla Walla was the jumping-off point for the last leg of the long journey from Independence, Missouri, to Oregon City. Walla Walla was seated close enough to the Columbia River that the immigrants naturally halted here to make their final decisions. There was no trail through the Cascade Mountains to the coast that wagons could follow, so the Columbia River itself was the only way for the seekers of land to reach the coast.

Suddenly Temperance drew the horses to a halt. Her eyes had touched on a small child sitting flat on the ground, crying and rubbing her eyes. Quickly she secured the lines, then jumping lightly to the ground, moved quickly toward the young girl.

"What's the matter, sweetheart?"

The child, no more than two, looked up with tear-stained cheeks and frightened eyes. "Mama!" she whispered faintly.

"Come along. We'll find your mama." Reaching down, Temperance picked up the child and held her close. At first the small girl resisted but then threw her arms around Temperance's neck and held on tightly. The embrace brought a clear thrill, of sorts, to Temperance. She had always loved children and as a girl had longed for her own family. No man had claimed her, so the dream had evaporated. Still, at times when she saw a small child like this, the old desire for her own children would return with a force that shocked her.

As she approached the wagons, a woman came running toward her crying, "Pearl, where have you been?" She stopped in front of Temperance and held out her arms. At once the child cried strongly, "Mama!" and grabbed the woman.

GILBERT MORRIS

"I found her sitting on the ground."

"I declare, this child is a wanderer!" the woman cried. She was a lanky woman with light hair and faded blue eyes—and worn by the rigors of the trail. "I'm so glad you found her. Thank you so much for bringing her back."

A tall, rangy man with a worried expression on his lean face hurried up, snatching his battered hat off. "We've been looking everywhere for Pearl. Appreciate you bringing her back."

"Oh, you would have found her, I'm sure. She was only a few hundred yards down the trail."

"Well, you know how it is when a child gets lost or something," the man smiled. He had a narrow face and a full, brown beard. He looked as worn and tired as the woman.

"My name is Josh Summers," he said. "This is my wife Faith and this is Pearl."

"I'm Temperance Peabody."

"You live here in Walla Walla, Miss Peabody?" the woman asked.

"No, I have a homestead five miles out of town. Did you just get in?"

"Yes, ma'am, just pulled in this morning." Summers took a deep breath and shook his head faintly. "It's been a sight of trouble getting here. We've been on the trail for four months."

"Have you been to Oregon City yet?"

"We were just starting to go when we lost Pearl. Most of the others have already gone."

"How far is it to Oregon City?" Mrs. Summers asked. Like her husband she was worn down to a thin edge. The trail, Temperance knew, did this to people. They came seeking free land, but the land was not really free. By the time they made the dangerous journey from Independence, Missouri, and arrived

5

on the land itself, there were still trees to be felled, cabins and fences to be built, and the land to be broken. A sudden feeling of pity rose in Temperance. "You still have a way to go, and there's no trail for the wagons."

Summers nodded. "I heard about that," he said. "The saying is that we have to take the river down to Fort Vancouver and then from there we can drive on to Oregon City."

"That's right. Some just abandon their wagons and take the trail over the mountains with what they can take on pack animals."

"We can't do that. We need the wagons, the stock, and the farming tools. We brought them all the way from Missouri," Summers said. "I reckon I can build a raft. Is it dangerous— floatin' down the river?"

"Well"—Temperance hesitated—"you should be all right. The worst of the spring floods haven't started yet."

Summers looked down at the ground and chewed his lower lip thoughtfully. When he looked up, there was discouragement in his face. "I wish we'd never left Missouri."

Mrs. Summers put her hand on his arm and smiled. "It'll be all right, Josh. This time next year we'll have a cabin built and the crops will be in."

The man smiled and put his arm around her. "I swan, you're a comfort, Faith, you purely are! Good to meet you, Mrs. Peabody."

"Just Miss. I don't have a husband."

Something about the statement caught at the couple. They looked at the woman as if trying to pick the heart out of her words. "Well," Mrs. Summers said, "you're a young woman yet. You'll find one, I'm sure."

e◦

AS ALWAYS WHEN TEMPERANCE approached the town, she felt a twinge of remorse that took the form of longing for the past. Walla Walla was not built for beauty, being a raw frontier town. The buildings were, for the most part, built of logs, although, since the sawmill had come in, there were now a few unpainted, framed buildings. There was a main street with a hotel, saloon, stable, blacksmith shop, and several stores, none bearing any marks of beauty. They were all utilitarian structures built to serve the farmers in the local area and the travelers reaching the final stretch of the Oregon Trail.

Temperance could not help comparing the crude dwellings with the small town in Maine where she had grown up. She remembered the straight, attractive streets with the strong, well-built houses of stone and brick, each with its little garden in the front and flowers around the house. She remembered her family's house, with its polished walnut furniture gleaming darkly with curving grace built by master craftsmen. She suddenly had a vision of the town with the white church, its spire lifting high into the sky, gleaming white in the sunlight, while out at sea the white sails of the schooners and the clipper ships dotted the blue-green waters of the sea.

The dreams of a more amiable town made a faint longing in Temperance, but she had learned to accept the rawness of the frontier. It had been difficult, but she made that transition. Other dreams were more difficult to control, and the ones that gave her the most difficulty were her girlhood dreams. From the time she was entering into her teens, she longed for what most women want: a husband, children, and later grandchildren. Now that first youth had faded, she had quietly put those dreams away, but at times they would return with a strength that troubled her.

Temperance shook her shoulders, and her broad mouth tightened as she almost forcibly rejected such thoughts. "Get up, Lucy—Alice," she said, and the team broke into a faster trot. Pulling up in front of an unpainted frame building with a sign "Satterfield General Store," she wrapped the lines tightly and got out of the wagon. She held her skirt high but was unable to avoid the mud that soaked her calf-high leather shoes. Reaching the boardwalk, she stomped her feet, and some of the mud fell off. She entered Satterfield's and at once was greeted by the owner.

"Wal, now, Miss Temperance, good to see you."

Silas Satterfield, owner of the general store, was forty-five years old. He had a shock of orange-red hair and a pair of piercing blue eyes. He also had a house full of children, eight at last count, and came forward at once, wiping his hands on his apron and smiling as he approached. "Looks like winter's 'bout over, don't it now?"

"I'm glad of it."

"So am I. Been a hard winter."

"There's part of a wagon train parked just outside of town."

"Yep, some of the folks have come in." Satterfield nodded his head. The two stood there talking, and finally Satterfield asked, "How's the Jackson family doing?"

"The children are fine, but Mr. Jackson is poorly."

Satterfield drew his hand down his face and shook his head in a gesture of futility. "Cholera's a terrible thing. It's like one of the Old Testament plagues."

"It is bad."

"Well, you're doing your bit helping sick folks. I don't—"

Satterfield broke off as a big man entered the store. He wore a pair of greasy buckskins, moccasins, and a round trapper's hat.

A gray beard covered his mouth, for the most part, but his eyes were quick and black. Although he was not a young man, somewhere past fifty, there was a strength and bull-like vitality about him.

"Howdy, Silas. How be you, Miss Temperance?"

"I'm fine, Marshal Meek."

Silas Satterfield grinned at the big man. "I wisht I was a federal marshal and didn't have no more to do than you do. If you did a day's work like I do here at the store instead of rambling all over the country, you'd be tired enough to sleep at night."

Joe Meek grinned and shook his head. There was a wildness in the man. "You don't know how hard it be catching up with these hard cases."

"Marshal, have you seen Burt Denton?" Temperance asked.

"Your hired hand? No, I ain't seen him in some time. Why? Did you lose him?"

"I saw him," Silas Satterfield said. "He came in here yesterday. Bought supplies and rode off. Said he was going prospecting."

Meek's sharp black eyes took in the expression that changed on the face of the woman. "Did he get to you, Miss Temperance?"

For a moment Temperance hesitated. "I paid him off, and he asked for an advance and I gave it to him."

"He never was no good," Meek grunted. "Wasn't broke out with honesty. I come near to hauling him in a time or two."

"He wasn't much of a worker either," Temperance said, "but he was all I could get." She hesitated for a moment and then said, "Do either of you know of a man I could hire for spring plowing?"

Meek laughed deep in his chest. He was a man who could not be still, and now his feet twitched and his shoulders moved as he slapped his meaty hands together. "I know of one, but he ain't no better'n what you had."

"I've got to have somebody. Who is he?"

"His name is Thaddeus Brennan."

"I don't know him. He's not from here?"

"No, ma'am. He's just a drifter. He got drunk and wrecked the Dancing Pony last night. Ain't got a cent to pay for it."

"You think he would work for me? You think he can plow?"

"I don't know about that, but he sure picked the wrong saloon. Judge Henry owns half of that place, you know. He was mad enough to hang Brennan, but I reckon he couldn't do that. If the judge set out to hang every drunk in the territory, there wouldn't be enough rope."

"I guess he's got him in the jail."

"Sure has, but he's going to make Brennan work out the fine at a dollar a day. I guess if you hired him though, the judge would be willing to work it out with you, Miss Temperance."

Satterfield suddenly grinned. "If he don't suit, you can hand him back to the judge."

Temperance hesitated and then said, "I've got to have somebody. I think I'll go talk to Judge Henry."

"Tell him I said it'd be fine with me."

The two men watched as the woman left, and then Satterfield shook his head sadly. "I feel right sorry for that woman. She's had a tough life."

"Was it some man done her wrong?"

"Don't think she's ever had a man. Never been married anyhow. She come here with her family eight years ago. Yankees, they were, Joe. Five couples came out here to start some kind of a religious settlement. Her pa was the leader."

"I heard about them folks. Real strict in their ways so I heard."

"Wouldn't eat an egg laid on Sunday, that bunch! It was downright hard on the girl. They wouldn't let her see any man at all. She did the teaching of the kids, and when her pa got sick, she had to take up the slack."

"What happened to them? They ain't around here anymore, are they?"

"No, that settlement kind of fell to pieces. Miss Temperance lost her parents, and the rest of the bunch wasn't as strong as her pa was."

"Well, I'll run down and tell the judge to give her a break—though I don't know if Brennan would be of much help. He's a whiskey bum as I see it."

"Do what you can, Joe. She's a good woman. Works herself into a frazzle helping all these sick folks around here. This cholera, it's going to kill off half the population!"

⌐

THADDEUS BRENNAN WOKE UP, lifted his head, groaned, and put it back on the thin, corn-shuck mattress. The hangover did what it always did, gave him a splitting headache. He cursed feebly, then pulled himself up and peered around the room with a dismal expression. As he did, the door opened, and Benny Watts came in. The jailer was a rather dim-witted young man with a long, skinny neck and a prominent Adam's apple. He had a tray in his hand and said, "I done cooked you breakfast, Brennan. I hope you like mush and fatback meat and coffee."

Staring bleary-eyed at the young man, Brennan spoke in a husky whiskey voice. "I need some whiskey. Go buy me a bottle."

"Buy you a bottle with whut?"

"There's money in the leather bag in my saddle."

Watts grinned broadly, and his Adam's apple joggled up and down as he said, "You ain't got no saddle nor no horse neither."

Brennan stared at the young man. "What are you talking about?"

"You wuz out cold when they had your trial."

"Trial? You can't try a man when he's unconscious!"

"I reckon you jist don't know Judge Henry, Brennan. When Marshal Meek drug you in, he jist laid you down on the floor right smack in the judge's office. The judge was sore as a boil that you wrecked his saloon. He claimed he wouldn't wait for no trial, so he found you guilty. Fined you two hundred dollars for wrecking the Dancing Pony."

Brennan stared at the horse-faced young man. He got to his feet, then swayed dangerously. "He can't do that!"

"He done it all right. Told the clerk to sell your stuff." Watts giggled. "And he sentenced you to work out the rest of the damages for a dollar a day, building roads. Take about a year," he said.

Brennan once had a fiery, uncontrollable temper that had gotten him into all sorts of trouble. Now at the age of forty-one, he had learned to control it. However, it broke out again. He reached out and slapped the tray from Benny's hand. The contents sloshed all over Watts, who stared down at the wreckage of the breakfast. "Well, there went your breakfast," he observed, then turned and left, locking the door behind him.

Brennan stared down at the food scattered on the floor. "That was a fool thing to do," he muttered thickly. He sat down on the rickety cot and felt so bad that he lay down again on the rank mattress. He felt as bad as he always felt when he was coming off a drunk, but when the door opened again he sat up. Watts was there, grinning foolishly, as usual. "This here lady wants to see you, Brennan. Her name is Miss Temperance Peabody." Watts turned to face Temperance and put his hand on the gun on his hip. "You want me to stay? This here's a dangerous outlaw."

"I don't think so."

"Well, jist holler when you're finished. I'll let you out."

As soon as the door closed, Brennan stared at the woman. His mouth was dry, and he had difficulty speaking. He cleared his throat, spat on the floor, and then said, "What do you want?" in his raspy voice.

"I want you to work for me."

For a moment Brennan could not understand the woman. "Work for you?" he said. "What are you talking about?"

"I just lost my hired hand. I don't have anybody to do spring plowing. I've got to have a man right away."

Brennan scratched himself and stared at her. He made a rough-looking sight, tall and lean but with broad shoulders. He had a wiry-looking, ragged beard and coarse, black hair that needed cutting. His heavy-duty features had two vertical creases beside his mouth that gave him an odd look. Everything about him was rough and durable, made for hard usage.

"I ain't working for no woman."

"I'll pay you four dollars a working day."

Brennan cursed, spat again, and threw himself on the cot. "Get out of here, woman! I ain't working for you and that's final!"

Temperance stared at the man and then raised her voice. "Jailer, open the door please."

The door at the end of the hall opened at once, and Benny stood there, grinning. "I heard whut he said. He wouldn't do you no good anyhow. He's jist a whiskey drunk."

Brennan cursed, reached over, and looked for something to throw but satisfied himself with cursing Benny and the woman.

Temperance moved down the hall and stepped into the marshal's office. She found Meek waiting there, his black eyes laughing at her. "I heard him cussing back there. I guess he turned you down."

"He says he won't work for a woman."

Meek chuckled deep in his chest. "Let me go talk to him. You go on home, Miss Temperance. I guarantee you'll have a hired hand before the sun goes down."

"I don't think so, Marshal."

"Leave it all to me," Meek grinned. "I'm going to make him an offer he can't refuse. He'll be out at your place later today. If he gives you any trouble, just let me know and I'll tend to it."

"Thank you very much, Marshal."

"I heard about another family down with the cholera. Their name is Dutton. You know 'em?"

"Yes, I know where they live anyway."

"They got a baby too. I thought you might like to go by and see if you could help."

"I'll do that, Marshal."

Meek waited until Temperance left the room, then winked at Benny Watts. "Come on and see how I handle that drunk, Benny."

The two men walked down the hall. Meek unlocked the door and stepped inside. "Well, Brennan, I hear as how you got an offer of employment."

"Who hit me over the head?"

"In the fracas at the Dancing Pony? That'd be Al Sharpless. He's a bad fellow to tangle with."

"I'm going to bust him when I get out of here."

"You ain't getting out of here—not for a year at least. Didn't Benny tell you? The judge said you're working out that fine at a dollar a day. May take more than a year. You'll be doing road building." Meek was enjoying the situation. He winked at Benny and said, "This man likes road building. Myself, I never cared for working twelve, fifteen hours a day, but Brennan here, he's a tough one."

"I never worked for no woman!"

"You never built a road for Judge Henry neither. Me, I'd rather eat cactus than work for that man."

"Who is that blasted woman?" Brennan said. His mind was not working at full speed, but he was at least alert enough to see that building roads for a year was not the most appealing thing in the world.

"She's a good Christian woman and she needs help, but the choice is up to you. I'll make you a deal. I won't sell your horse and your gear, and I'll get the judge to cut back on the fine. A couple of months' work won't hurt you none." Meek grinned at Brennan, adding, "But it's your say. If you'd rather bust rock for a year, that's fine with me."

Silence prevailed for a moment, then Brennan cursed loudly and said, "I'll have to do it, but it don't go down good."

"Well, now you're getting smart, but let me make this clear to you, Brennan. You try to soldier on the job, I'll be out, and you'll think the roof fell on you. You try to run, I'll run you down. You ask around town what Meek is like when somebody crosses him. You got me?"

Brennan took a step closer. He was an extremely tall man, two inches taller than Meek, who was a big man himself. "I'll do the work without any sermon from you, Meek."

"Now you're being smart. I'll work out the deal with the judge. You'll be out at the Peabody place in time to do the afternoon chores!"

Chapter Two

BRENNAN STEPPED OUTSIDE INTO the sunlight, followed by Joe Meek and Benny Watts. Meek gestured with a thick hand toward the livery stable. "Your stallion is there. I talked the judge out of selling him."

"That's good because I'd have to steal him back again," Brennan remarked sullenly. He started toward the livery stable, and Benny trudged along beside him. "That horse of yours bit Hank Avery. Took a plug out of his butt."

"Should have known better than to get familiar with a strange horse. He try to bite you too? His name's Judas. He tries to bite everybody."

"You took his name out of the Bible?"

"Worst man I could find, just like he's the worst hoss I ever had."

"Why do you keep him then?"

"'Cause he's the fastest and got more stamina than any horse I ever had, but he'd bite my arm off if he got a chance at it."

The two reached the livery stable, and Hank Avery, the black-smith and owner of the stable, scowled. "I ought to charge you extra for that plug this hoss of yours took out of my behind."

A rare smile lit Brennan's face. Dryness rustled in his voice as he murmured, "A man ought to be more careful around a Kiowa stallion."

"How in blazes am I supposed to know he's a Kiowa hoss?" Brennan didn't answer but entered the stable. Judas was in a stall, and his eyes fastened on Thaddeus at once. He lashed out with his heels striking the wall behind him like a thunderbolt.

"That's a good hoss! I'm glad to see you're in good humor today," Brennan remarked. He plucked the bridle off the nail and struggled until finally, after a heroic battle, he got the stallion bridled. "Open the gate there, Benny."

Benny looked askance at the horse whose eyes were white and wild. He opened the gate, then scampered out of the way. Brennan led the horse out of the stable into the yard and tied him to the hitching post. As he left to get his saddle blanket and saddle, Judas swerved around and made a kick. He missed Brennan by the most narrow of margins.

"If that hoss had kicked you, it would of broken your knee, brother," Avery remarked.

"Ain't no horse gonna kick me on Tuesdays. Nothing bad ever happens to me on Tuesdays. Monday is my bad day. Everything bad happens on Monday." As Brennan marched in to get his gear, Benny Watts said, "Why does a man want to have a horse that contrary for, Hank?"

"Match his own moods, I reckon. That Brennan's pretty much like that stallion. He'd kick anybody that gets in his way."

The two watched as Brennan returned. He kept the saddle in his right hand and eased toward the horse. Judas made an ineffectual effort to reach Brennan to take a plug out of him, but Brennan had snubbed the horse too tightly. Brennan laughed roughly, put the blanket over the horse, then the saddle, and drew the cinches as tight as he could.

"You're cinching up too tight," Avery remarked.

"No, he swells up. Then he can let his breath out and get some slack. This is the most intelligent horse I ever had."

"Oh, you want intelligence in a horse? Not me!" Avery shook his head. "I want a stupid horse that will just get me from one place to the next."

"He shore is a beauty though," Watts said. "Where'd you get him? I bet you paid a pretty for him."

"I stole him from a Kiowa war chief. They chased me half-way across the territory."

Leaving Judas snubbed to the post, Brennan turned and headed toward Satterfield's store. "You gonna leave him all tied up like that?" Benny demanded.

"Yep."

"Well, he'll be uncomfortable. Might make him mad. He'll try to bite you."

"He always tries to bite me whether he's comfortable or not. I'd stay away from him if I was you."

Stepping into the store, Brennan looked around. He reached into his pocket and pulled out what money he had there and said to Satterfield, "I'll get my necessities first and then the fancy frill."

"What'll you have, Brennan?"

"I'll have a gallon of raw whiskey, the meanest you got."

Satterfield frowned. "Miss Peabody don't allow no drinking out on her place during working hours."

"That's her policy, is it?"

"That's it."

"Well, she'll just have to readjust her rules. Trot that whiskey out."

Reluctantly Satterfield produced a jug of whiskey and then at Brennan's direction added three plugs of chewing tobacco, a pouch of smoking tobacco, and two boxes of snuff. "You use all of these?"

"A man ought to get what enjoyment he can out of life while he's able. What else do you have? I want some of that sweet, hard candy, a sackful of it."

"You got a sweet tooth, have you?"

"It goes with my personality. I need some ammunition for this hog leg." He pulled a huge Navy Colt out of his holster, checked the loads, and then slipped it back in the holster. "I need some cartridges for my Henry rifle."

When Satterfield totaled up the bill, it came to fourteen dollars.

"I ain't got but ten. Put the rest on Miss Peabody's account."

"Why, I can't do that, Brennan."

"Yeah, you can. I'm working for her. She'll pay for some of the supplies. Go on and charge it. You can fuss with her over it."

Reluctantly Satterfield jotted down the amount and watched as Brennan left the store. His wife came up and said, "Is that the man that's going to work for Temperance?"

"Well, he's headed that way. I don't know if they'll make a match or not. He's pretty rough-cut."

"He doesn't look like a man that would make her happy."

"Well, she ain't marrying him, Helen. He's just going to do the spring plowing and the chores, but you're right. They wasn't made for each other."

Brennan moved out to where Judas was tied to the snubbing post. He filled his saddlebags with the candy and tobacco and tied the jug onto his saddle horn. Keeping his eye on the stallion's heels, with a swift movement he put his foot in the stirrup and swung aboard, catching him off guard. He grinned.

"Caught you that time, didn't I?" Leaning down, he undid the rope, recoiled it, and put it over his saddle horn. Turning the stallion, he started out of town.

But when he got even with the Dancing Pony, he saw Al Sharpless standing outside, grinning at him. Sharpless was a big, bruising man who considered himself the toughest man in the territory. It galled Brennan that Sharpless had hit him with a pool cue and brought him down. For a moment the temptation was strong to get off his horse and go whip the man, but he saw Meek standing down the street, watching his movements carefully. He nodded at Sharpless and said, "I'll be seeing you later, Mr. Sharpless. We'll have a few things to talk about."

"Come on in any time, drunk. We never close," Sharpless laughed.

"Which way to perdition, Marshal?" Brennan asked as he came even with Meek, leaning against the wall of the apothecary stall.

"Go straight down that road for four miles, take a left, and just keep going until you see it on the right. A big log cabin. It'll be neat, which is different from most around here."

"Sure appreciate your kindness and courtesy."

"You just mind your manners. You treat that woman right, or I'll put you where the dog won't bite you."

Once again Brennan was challenged. The marshal was a burly, strong-looking man, well known as a terrible roughhouse and saloon fighter as well as a deadly shot with rifle and six-gun. Brennan studied him, and the eyes of the two men met. Joe Meek had the gift of mind reading, it seemed, for he said, "You don't want to take me on, boy. You just go on out and do your plowing. In a couple of months, you can get out of here and go your own way. Don't make me come after you."

"Wouldn't think of it, Marshal." Brennan turned his horse down the middle of the road, but his mind was still on Meek. *Why, I could whip him if I had it to do. He's big, but he's bound to be slow. If I had to, I could take a pool cue to him like Sharpless took to me. Always a way to whip a man if a fellow knows just the right way.*

As he cleared the town, Brennan passed the wagon train that was made up there. He carefully studied the children and the settlers. As always, when he saw families like this, he felt sadness. He had been a loner all his life, but the sight of a family touched a nerve in him that he could not understand. Since he had never known the joys of home life, it was mostly a dream. Watching the children play ring-around-the-rosy, he was tempted to stop. But he was a man who didn't waste time on dreams that could never come true. Kicking Judas in the side, he said, "Come on, you handsome devil, get me out of here!"

Judas snorted, tried to turn his head to bite Brennan's leg, and was jerked roughly back into place. To get his revenge, he broke into a dead run. Brennan laughed and said, "Go on. Run yourself to death. See if I care."

❧

THE HOUSE WAS BUILT with logs, all exactly the same size. They were fitted together so tightly that the house needed practically no chinking. Many of the cabins in Walla Walla were roughly built with the corners fitting so badly the mud used for chinking fell out and the wind whistled through. But as Temperance moved about the kitchen, a sudden memory came to her. She remembered her father and the other men of the group taking great pains with all of the cabins. They were the finest cabins in the settlement—snug, strongly built, and able to survive anything except a fire.

Temperance looked at the tintype in the oval frame on the wall. It featured her father and her mother looking deadly serious, her father sitting, her mother standing beside him with her right hand on his left shoulder. Something tightened in her throat, and she moved closer remembering them. *I wonder why they never smiled for pictures? You'd think they were miserable.* She knew that was the way portraits were made, a totally serious business. She turned back to check the dinner, which was finished except for frying the chicken. She liked to do that last and to get it fresh out of the hot grease.

Sitting down in the rocking chair beside the woodstove, she picked up her Bible and began to read. She rocked back and forth, and finally her cat Augustus, in one smooth easy jump, landed in her lap. "Gus, you shouldn't sit on the Bible." She pulled the Bible from under the huge cat and stroked his fur. She had found him when he was merely a kitten, and he was the strangest-looking cat she had ever seen. He had tufted ears, enormously long hind legs, and a mere stub of a tail. His eyes were golden, enormous, and his mouth was red as flannel. He had long, silky, gray-black hair that he loved to groom. At night he shared her bed, forcing her to the edge at times, demanding a space of his own.

For a time Temperance stroked the silky fur, and soon Gus was purring, making a noise like a muted engine. He also gave off heat like a furnace. She was stroking his fur and wondering about the man she had hired. Something about him disturbed her, but there was no way she could get out of the situation now. Gus lifted his head and then leaped from her lap. Going to the door, he looked through the screen and began to growl low in his throat.

"What is it, Gus?" Rising from her seat, Temperance went and stood at the door. She saw Brennan riding a fine-looking horse. She also spotted a jug of whiskey tied to the saddle horn. "We'll have to talk about that!" she said, biting off the words.

He rode up to the house, got off, and dodged the horse who tried to bite him. He snubbed the horse tightly, tying the reins three times. "I see you found your way here," she said pleasantly. She waited for him to reply, but he didn't. His hat was pulled down over his face, and the smell of whiskey was strong as he stepped up on the porch. "I'll show you where you stay." He still had not spoken, and she took him to the barn. Opening the door, she led him to the room her father had built for the hired men. It was actually a comfortable room with a good bed, a real mattress, a washstand, and an old chest of drawers that had belonged to her grandmother. The room was filthy now, because her last hired hand had left it a total wreck.

"I hope you're a better housekeeper than my last man."

Brennan gave the place a careless look. He threw the remains of a cigarette on the floor and didn't bother to step on it. "I never set myself up or made no claims about keeping house." He spoke in a surly way, and his speech was slurred.

"You can come and wash up now. I'll have supper on the table when you get cleaned up." She waited again for him to respond, and when he did not, she turned and left. Anger touched her. *It seems I'm going to have to put up with a sullen drunk. Not what I would really like!*

AS SOON AS BRENNAN entered the house, Temperance saw that he had not changed his clothes and had not washed. She knew he was trying her out. "Brennan, get out on the back porch. There's a wash basin and a pitcher of fresh water. Wash your face and hands and comb your hair. If not, you can do without supper."

Brennan glared at the woman. She was not tall, and he towered over her. But she was not intimidated by the difference in size. "I guess I'm clean enough."

"You might be clean enough for that jail, but you're not clean enough to share my table. I've got chicken, beets, green beans, fresh biscuits, and I made a sweet potato pie. You don't get any of that unless you act like a human being. Which will it be?"

Brennan was strongly tempted to turn and walk away, but the delicious smells from the kitchen weakened him. "All right," he muttered, cursing under his breath. He slammed the door and went out, which caused Temperance to smile. "Slam the door all you want, but you're going to do what I say."

Five minutes later Brennan came in. His face was red from the exertion and his hands were clean, and he had evidently used his fingers for a comb. His coarse, black hair was too long, and she made a note of that. "You can sit right there. I'm not going to have this discussion every time we eat. If you want to eat at my table, you'll wash first."

Brennan opened his mouth to argue, but then the smell of the food got to him and he nodded in a surly fashion. As soon as he seated himself, he reached for the chicken, but her voice caught him. "We'll thank the Lord for the food, Brennan."

Brennan stared at her, then slumped down and refused to shut his eyes. Temperance shut her eyes and said, "We thank

Thee for this food and for everything which You provided. In Jesus's name we're grateful. Amen."

"Is it all right if I eat now? Or are you gonna preach a sermon and take up a collection?"

"That will do!"

Brennan loaded his plate until it would hold no more. It looked like a small mountain. He worked his way through the food, eating like a starved wolf, and his manners were the worst Temperance Peabody had ever seen. He snorted and groaned and grunted and even paused once to spit something onto the floor. Twice she started to call his attention to his manners, but then she decided any hope she had of improving this wild man would come slowly.

She tried to carry on a conversation, asking him about his past, but got only monosyllable answers and grunts or shakes of the head. Finally, when he had demolished half of the sweet potato pie and washed it down noisily with coffee, she said, "Come on. I want to show you the work to be done." He got up and followed her outside. She watched as he rolled a cigarette expertly. He did it with one hand, it seemed, licked the middle, and twisted the ends in one smooth motion. Pulling a kitchen match out of his shirt pocket, he lifted his leg and struck it on the outside of his thigh, then threw the match on the ground. "All these fences are going to have to be repaired. They all need work. The troughs are leaking. Tomorrow you can work on that, but the main thing is spring plowing."

She turned to him and saw resentment in his eyes. Something had painted shadows on his face and had laid silence on his tongue. It had branded his solid face with rebellion and loneliness. "You do know how to plow, don't you?"

"Spent the first ten years of my life looking at the hind end

of a mule. Thought I'd seen the last of it, but here I am again."
He drew on the cigarette, blew a perfect smoke ring, then
dropped the cigarette and ground it into the earth with his
boot heel. "Here I am doing what I said I'd never do."

"One more thing," she said. "I don't like my help drinking
during working hours."

Brennan turned to face her, looking down at her with a
strange expression on his face. "You ever been married?"

The question caught Temperance off guard. "Why—no, I
haven't."

"I didn't figure so. Easy to see why."

His words angered her. "You shouldn't talk like that."

"You like to push at a man, Peabody."

"Most of the men I've seen need pushing."

Her words touched him, and there was a feral wildness in
him. For a moment something like fear came to Temperance.
She was alone with this man who had a violent streak in him.
Her eyes widened, and she had to resist taking another step
backward. He was a limber man with amber eyes half-hidden
by the drop of his lids. He had a looseness about him, and the
sun had scorched his skin, putting layers of tan smoothly over
his face. All his features were solid, and his shape was the flat
and angularly heavy build of a man turned hard by time and
effort. She could not read his eyes for they were empty mirrors
looking out at nothing. He made Temperance nervous, and she
said, "Breakfast will be on the table at five o'clock. Remember,
I'll expect you to do no drinking on the job."

Brennan watched her go and, when she was out of hearing,
muttered a curse. "What you expect and what you get might
turn out to be two different things, you dried up old maid!"

TEMPERANCE HAD COOKED BREAKFAST, but no Brennan came to eat it. She waited ten minutes, then left the kitchen. Going at once to his room, she banged on the door and heard a muffled voice cursing. Shoving the door open, she saw he had the covers pulled over his head. "Get out of that bed, Brennan. You're late for breakfast."

Brennan came out cursing. He had been sleeping in his underwear, which was dirty and filled with holes. The hair on his chest curled through the front of it. "Get out of here!" he yelled.

When Brennan plopped back down and closed his eyes, Temperance picked up the pitcher of water from the washstand and poured it over his face. Brennan sputtered and cursed. He came out of the bed, and she saw that the bottom part of his underwear was in worse shape than the top. He started for her angrily, but she did not move. She looked up at him and said, "If you're not cleaned up and ready for work in half an hour, I'll have Marshal Meek come and see what he can do with you." Without another word she whirled and left the room.

Brennan glared after her and more than anything he had wanted in a long time, he wanted to get dressed, ride out, and never see this woman again. He knew, however, that he was in a bind. "Building roads," he muttered, "can't be much worse than her." He knew better, however, and began pulling on his pants.

❧

THE BREAKFAST WAS HUGE. Brennan ate six eggs, so runny he had to eat them with a spoon, and fried ham and biscuits seemed to flow down his throat. He used the fine, fresh butter to layer the biscuits, dumped the peach preserves on them, and washed it all down with fresh milk. Finally, when he was so swollen he had to undo his belt, he looked over and said reluctantly, "That was a good breakfast."

"My mother taught me to cook, Brennan."

She had eaten probably a fifth of what Brennan had eaten, and now he seemed to be in a receptive mood, at least for him. "What about your people?"

Brennan took a swig of coffee, then pulled the makings out and made a cigarette. He was half expecting her to tell him he could not smoke in the house, but she said nothing. He twisted the ends, lit it, drew the smoke deeply into his lungs, and finally shrugged his shoulders. "Don't know."

"That's sad."

"Things happen."

"Who raised you?"

"I did."

The two sat there uneasily. Conversation with this man was merely impossible, and finally Temperance said, "I'm going to see a family that's been hard hit by cholera. You can start the plowing. I'll be looking to see how much you've done by the time I get back."

"Better stay away from the cholera. It's a good way to get sick yourself."

"I trust God to keep me from that."

"Well, God sometimes makes mistakes, or so I hear."

"Who told you that?"

"A Pawnee war chief."

"He didn't know God."

"He knew his god."

Temperance did not want to get into an argument over the differences between the god the Indians knew and the God she knew. She got up and said, "I'll clean up the dishes. You can go on and start on the fences. I warn you, Brennan, you'll have to work even when I'm not watching."

"You're worse than Marshal Meek!"

∾

TEMPERANCE HAD MADE THE Duttons as comfortable as she could. Their cabin was poorly built, and the wind sifted through the crevices and cracks between the logs. She had brought food, had done their washing, and now she was holding two-month-old Timothy. She loved children, and Timothy was a charming baby, fat and healthy with an unexpectedly cheerful smile at the oddest times.

"Aren't you a handsome one?" she said. Timothy gurgled, reached out and caught her finger, and stuck it in his mouth. She let him bite it for awhile and then got the store-bought nipple that his mother had used. Martha Dutton was a small woman and did not have enough milk for the baby, so she kept goats for milk, which seemed to satisfy Timothy. The two women sat together, and before long, as she had expected, Martha began expressing her doubts. "We should never have come to this awful place. I never wanted to come to Oregon. It was Clyde. He had this dream of owning land, but we would have been better off renting it back in Missouri."

"You're going to be fine. You've got a good place here."

Martha looked toward the single bedroom the cabin afforded. "Clyde's so sick." Fear washed across her face. "What will happen if he dies? I couldn't take care of my baby or myself."

Temperance knew this woman was not strong in body or in will. She belonged back East where life was more settled. For a long time she encouraged the woman and finally said, "You've just got to trust God. Clyde's going to be all right. I'll come early tomorrow and get the rest of the clothes washed. I'll cook something that Clyde will like. You just rest and try not to get sick yourself."

As she left the cabin and headed back to her own homestead, she was wondering how long the woman would last. Clyde Dutton looked like a dead man to her. She had had enough experience with cholera to recognize the final stages of it, and she would not be surprised if Clyde was one of those who didn't make it.

When Temperance got home, the late afternoon shadows were already beginning to draw their long shapes outside the cabin. She made a quick tour and found that most of the fences had been fixed. Part of the field next to the cabin had been plowed, but the animals were put up now and there was no sign of Brennan. She went at once to his room, calling out, "Brennan, are you there?" But when she looked inside, she saw that his things were there though he was gone. Returning to the barn, she noticed that his horse was missing. A disgust came to her. "He's probably gone back to town to get drunk."

The struggle to stay alive in Oregon country in 1850 took all the strength a man or a woman had. It was hard on any human being, and Temperance was not as strong as some of the pioneer women. Now as she went to the house, she suddenly found it difficult to climb the steps. She made it to the top and then sat down in one of the white oak rockers her father had made. She began rocking, and Gus came at once and jumped into her lap, purring like a steam engine. She rubbed his chin, which he loved, and murmured, "I wish I didn't have any more worries than you, Gus."

Gus responded by digging his claws in and releasing them. He loved to trample her, not that he ever punctured her with his huge claws, but it seemed to give him pleasure to shove them down and back and forth.

The struggle of life caught up with Temperance Peabody. She was tired, exhausted. She was seeing sick people every day, knowing that many of them would not live. Her family was gone, and she had the sense of total isolation. Now her hired hand was probably in town getting drunk, probably would quit, and she had no one else to help.

She was not a crying woman as a rule, but she could have cried as she sat there. Finally she heard the sound of a horse approaching. Eagerly she looked up and saw Brennan on his stallion. It was getting dark, but she saw that he had a large deer tied down on the horse. He pulled up, and she said, "I thought you'd gone to town."

"There you go, always thinking the worst of me." He came off the horse and gestured toward the buck. "I hit him but not dead center. Had to run him down."

Quickly, she tried to think of something pleasant to say. "Some fresh venison would go down good. I'll show you where to dress him."

"I seen the place. I'll go cut off some steaks, and you can cook 'em while I do the rest."

He started to turn the horse away, and she said, "I thought you had run away."

Brennan somehow found that amusing. He smiled, and when he did, the two creases beside his mouth became more prominent. "Peabody, I've run off from more places than you can think of, but I'll let you know when I run off. I won't sneak off in the night."

She thought this was a strange thing, but she didn't ask any more questions. She walked out with him and watched while he strung the deer up and quickly cut the two steaks out. He said, "We'll save the hide. It might be a good rug."

"You can always use another rug." She hesitated, then said, "I saw the fences. They look good."

"Ain't hard to fix a fence."

"The plowing looked good too."

"You know I didn't mind it as much as I did when I was a boy. I'd hate to do it for the rest of my life though. Go cook the steaks."

Temperance turned and headed back toward the house. When she was inside, Gus was pawing at the raw meat. "Well, Gus," she said, a smile softening her features, "at least he didn't run off."

Chapter Three

BRENNAN DECIDED TO SHAVE, and then he decided not to.

For a moment he stood looking at the mirror over the washstand, taking in the shaggy, coarse, black hair and the whiskers that in two weeks had become more than just stubble, and felt a perverse sense of satisfaction. Ever since he had come to work for Temperance Peabody, he had deliberately remained filthy and unshaven merely to aggravate his employer.

"I reckon I'm just about pretty enough to make her happy," he spoke to the mirror. He had a habit of speaking not only to animals as if they could understand but also to inanimate objects. Now he nodded toward the fly-specked mirror and grinned. "Another two or three weeks of this, I'll be just about ripe enough for that psalm-singing preacher woman."

He moved across the room to a small table, picked up the jug, and tilted it. Only a few trickles were left, and with a curse he slammed the jug down and grabbed his hat, which hung from a nail on the wall. He took one look around the room and was satisfied that it was about as disreputable as he could make it. He knew this irritated Temperance Peabody, and he spit on the floor and said, "There! That ought to put the finishing touches on it."

Brennan left the room and saddled Judas after the usual titanic struggle. He waited for him to try to kick him, and said loudly, "Why, you'd be good for a month just to get a chance to bite me once." Cautiously he put the saddle blanket on, then when Judas swung his big head around, teeth bared, Brennan rapped him sharply in the nose with his fist. "There, you spawn of Satan! Try to bite me again, I'll bust your teeth out!" He waited to see if he would respond, but the stallion merely quivered his withers. Brennan, with satisfaction, slapped the saddle on, cinched it up, and then went through the usual difficulty of getting Judas to accept the bridle. "You better not mess with me today, Judas. I'm just in the mood to kick the daylights out of anything that moves and you're closest." The horse knew the tone, evidently, for he allowed Brennan to slip the bridle on.

Stepping into the saddle, Brennan rode out of the barn and was headed for town when he heard his name called. "Brennan!"

With a sigh he turned and saw his employer standing on the front porch. "Well, Judas, she caught us. I guess we'll get another sermon now." He did not dismount but simply rode within ten feet of the porch and asked grumpily, "What do you want?"

"Where you going?"

"I'm going to town and buy some whiskey." He knew this would anger her, and it pleased him inordinately when he saw a cloud pass across her face.

"You didn't finish plowing the south field."

"No, I didn't, and I ain't going to."

"Why not, may I ask?"

"Because it's Monday."

"What does that have to do with it?"

Patiently, as if speaking to a child, Brennan said, "Why, didn't you know Monday's a hard-luck day? Shucks, I thought everybody knowed that."

"Don't be ridiculous. It's just another day like the other six."

"Not for me it ain't. Everything bad that's ever happened to me in my life happened on Monday."

"That's ridiculous."

"No, it's not! Let me tell you something, lady. I was walking down the streets of Mobile, Alabama, one time, and I got shot. And guess what day it was? Monday! That's what it was."

"Who shot you?"

"Oh, I disremember his name. He was a dentist and he was drunk."

"Why'd he shoot you?"

"Oh, I didn't say he was aimin' to shoot *me*. There was a lawyer named Simmons who was sleeping with this here dentist's wife. I don't mean when he shot me, I mean on a regular basis, and it aggravated that dentist. So he got his pistol out and waited outside the lawyer's office. Wouldn't you know it was just my luck to come along right then. Now, if it had been Tuesday, I'd have been gone. Or if it had been Sunday, I'd probably been in church." Brennan grinned at this and waited for her to protest, but when she was silent, he shrugged. "If bad luck's going to happen, it's going to happen."

"That's silly."

"Silly! Why, he shot that lawyer, and the bullet went plum through him and hit me right in the leg. Laid me right up for a month." Brennan shifted his weight and shook his head sorrowfully. "I felt so bad I couldn't go see that sorry dentist hung."

"Monday didn't have a thing to do with that. It could have happened any day!" Temperance insisted.

"That's what *you* say. Every time I've had a bad time, it come on a Monday. Once I was out with the dragoons and a

36

whole mess of them sorry Cheyenne surrounded us, and they kilt all our horses. Before we left, I tried to tell the lieutenant that Monday wasn't no day to be trying to tackle a Cheyenne war party, but he wouldn't listen. Durned fool didn't believe me! I guess he believed me when he got an arrow through his gizzard. Why, we had to walk away that night, and we was lucky to get out with our skins. No, Monday I try to be as quiet as I can so that bad luck don't fall on me."

Temperance had learned that Brennan could tell a tall tale, especially when he was trying to get out of work. She put her hands on her hips and stared at him. "You make your own bad luck, Thaddeus Brennan, and Monday has nothing to do with it." A thought came to her, and she nodded firmly, "I'm not giving you any money for whiskey."

"Didn't ask for none."

"Well, you're not getting any. Go by the store and get what's on this list." Reaching into a pocket of her apron, she came out with a slip of paper. He was not going to dismount and come for it, so she walked up to him.

"Stay away from that horse's head. He'll bite you."

"No, he won't. He's a nice horse," Temperance said. "You're mean to him. That's why he tries to bite."

With disgust Brennan snatched the paper and stuck it in the pocket of his filthy shirt. "You don't know nothing about horses. This is the meanest horse west of the Pecos!"

Temperance reached up and stroked Judas's nose. When the horse whinnied slightly and nudged her, she said, "See? He's a nice horse. I'm going over to the Dutton place and help them, Brennan. When you get those things from the store, bring them by their place."

"Not me. I'm not going near that cholera, not on Monday."

"You do it or I'll tell Joe Meek."

Brennan stared at the woman, and a hot reply rose to his lips. He had discovered, however, that nothing he did could get her goat, as he put it. It irritated him, for he was accustomed to having his own way with women. "I'll bring it, but I ain't going into the house," he shouted as he whirled Judas around and left the yard at a dead gallop.

When he was out of sight of the house, he pulled the bay down to a walk and then, as was his habit, began thinking of what had happened. It preoccupied him, and at such moments as this he forgot that Judas was a treacherous animal. He was caught off guard when suddenly the horse humped his back and flung himself sideways. Making a wild grab at the horn, Brennan managed to stay in the saddle. He fought the animal to a standstill and realized he was lucky not to be thrown.

"Well, you thought you had me that time, didn't you?" he said loudly. "Well, you didn't. You're about the sorriest, meanest, no account hoss that ever lived!" He continued to berate the animal and finally nodded, saying, "But you ain't as mean as Miss Temperance Peabody. What she needs is a man to take a belt to her. That's what she needs. Well, Judas, I may be just that hairpin to give it to her! There ain't no law that says a man can't take a switch to a single woman—when she needs it, that is."

All the way to town Brennan talked on and off to his horse. "And another thing," he said as they turned down the main street, "I'd run off and leave her, but I gave my word." A smile crossed his rugged lips and he chuckled. "I'd like to give that Joe Meek a run for it. He'd never catch me, not in a hundred years! I'd run him until he wore his legs off to the knees. Why, he thinks that badge makes him some pumpkins, but he ain't. I can clean his plow anytime. But you know," he said confidentially, "I can't leave until I whip Al Sharpless for parting my hair with a pool cue. As soon as I get enough money to pay off that blasted fine, I'll tell that preacher woman off, and then I'll whip Al and maybe Joe Meek too. Then I'll ride out and laugh at the whole bunch of 'em."

The sun had passed the meridian and was slowly beginning to sink to the west as he turned down the main street of Walla Walla. He made straight for the Dancing Pony. He dismounted, avoiding a feeble attempt on the part of Judas to bite him. He slapped the stallion on the nose and said, "You just wait. I'm going to teach you a lesson if you don't stop that!"

He stepped inside the saloon, and at once Al Sharpless turned to face him. Sharpless was wearing one of the most colorful floral vests on the market, and his black hair was laid flat with grease. He had small dark eyes that he fixed on Brennan. Then he grunted, "Whut you doing in here?"

"Why, Al, I just come into town. Thought I'd stop by for a friendly visit."

"You make any trouble, I'll shoot you."

Brennan shrugged his shoulders, walked over, and stood at the bar, facing Sharpless. "Why, Al, that ain't no way to talk to a friend."

"I don't consider you my friend. Not after you wrecked my place."

"Well, I'm paying for it, Al, and I just stopped in to buy a jug of whiskey."

Sharpless stared at Brennan, then suddenly laughed. "How you like working for a woman, Brennan?"

"Well, Al, I'll tell you what," Brennan said, "Honestly, I just love it! It's the best job I ever had. I don't think I'll ever leave."

Several loafers engaged in a poker game had been listening to the interchange. One of them, a tall lanky man named Simon Gee, laughed the loudest. "You won't leave because you know Joe Meek would run you down and whip your tail."

Brennan turned to face the speaker. "Why, Simon, that ain't so. Me and Joe Meek have got to be real good friends. Why, shucks, I may even hire out as his deputy."

Sharpless stared at Brennan. "You'd rather lie for credit. Just tell the truth for cash. Now what do you want?"

"Like I said. I want a gallon of whiskey."

"You got the money?"

"Just put it on my tab, Al. You know I'm good for it."

"Not likely," Sharpless said. "Now get out of here before I throw you out."

For a moment it seemed Brennan would take up the challenge. Sharpless saw something in the face of the tall man that made him take a step backward, but Brennan merely laughed and said, "When I'm rich and famous, you'll wish you had sold me that whiskey on credit, Al. I'll see you gentlemen later."

Leaving the Dancing Pony, Brennan unhitched Judas, swung into the saddle, and rode down the street. He stopped in front of Satterfield's General Store. "Well, Judas, you better wish me luck. I've got to have something to drink on. I'll have to get it out of Satterfield, I reckon."

He dismounted, tied Judas to the hitching rail, and then entered the general store. Silas, he saw, was grinding coffee beans, and the rich aroma of coffee filled the air. "That shore does smell good, don't it now, Silas?" Brennan greeted the owner breezily. "Nothing smells better than coffee being ground, I don't reckon."

"Hello, Brennan. What can I do for you?"

"Got a list for things to get for my boss." Brennan fished in his pocket and came out with a list. Satterfield glanced at it and then cocked his head to one side. "Miss Temperance tells me you're not a bad hand at plowing."

Brennan leaned on the counter and pulled a piece of candy out of a glass jar. "Is this here penny candy?"

"On the house, Brennan—the first one anyway."

Brennan popped the candy into his mouth and talked around it. "About that plowing. You know a man does well with whatever he loves doing, don't you know, and I always loved plowing. Nothing I'd rather do than stare at the back end of a mule for, oh, ten—twelve hours a day."

Satterfield laughed. He was disgusted with the big man, but there was something likable about him at the same time. "Yeah, I loved it, too, when I was growing up." He listened to Brennan talk as he filled the order, then said, "Anything else?"

"A gallon of whiskey please."

"You know I'm not going to give you any whiskey."

"Why, Silas, I'm surprised at you."

"Miss Temperance would never forgive me. You're liable to get drunk and bust up the saloon again or ride off until Joe Meek hauls you back."

"You hurt me deep in my heart, Silas," Brennan said. "Why, Miss Temperance has gone over to help that poor sick Dutton woman, and she wants this for medicinal purposes, and you won't even give her the medicine she needs. Here I thought you was a Christian man, Silas."

Silas Satterfield stared at the face of Thaddeus Brennan. "I don't ever know whether to believe you or not."

"Why, it's gospel truth. That's where she's gone—over to the Dutton place. She sent me to get this stuff."

"Why didn't she put it on the list?"

"She forgot it, but she called out to me to get it as I left."

Silas Satterfield struggled for a moment, then threw his hands apart with an impatient gesture. "Well, I'll give it to you, but it's on your head. She'll see it on the bill."

"Why, of course she will." Silas moved down and leaning under the counter came out with a brown jug. He put it on the counter and said, "I'm not sure I'm doing the right thing here, Brennan."

"Oh, it's fine. You know she drinks herself."

Silas was startled. "Who drinks?"

"Why, Miss Temperance. She gets drunker than Cooter Brown after it gets dark, but I don't want you to tell nobody. She's downright ashamed of it. Put that stuff in a sack for me so I can tie it over my saddle horn, will you? I'll carry the jug."

Five minutes later Brennan was on the road again. The first thing he did when he cleared town was uncork the jug and take several long, deep swallows. "I forgot to make a toast, Judas. Here's to that psalm-singing woman who thinks she's my boss. She's paying for this here drinking whiskey and mighty nice of her, I might say." He began to sing a ribald song, and by the time he was halfway to the Dutton place, it was all he could do to stay in the saddle.

ல

PULLING THE LAST OF the worn diapers off the line, Temperance dropped them in the basket, then moved back toward the house. She had been thinking of Brennan as she loaded the basket. She had become absolutely sick of the man. He was filthy, refused to bathe, shaved only on occasion. He did his work but was sullen and critical of her, especially of her religion.

"I'll be glad when he's gone," she muttered. "He's the most trifling man I ever saw in my life."

She moved inside the house, quickly folded the diapers, and went to the cradle where the baby lay sleeping. She reached out and gently touched the blond hair and then straightened up and moved across to the stove. She filled a deep bowl with broth and, plucking a spoon from a box, moved into the bedroom.

Martha Dutton lay on the bed, her thin form outlined by the cover. Her eyes were sunk back in her head, and her lips seemed to have shriveled up.

Her husband had died a week earlier, and she had been too sick to attend the funeral, a fact that grieved her greatly.

"Well now, Martha, you've got to eat something."

"I'm not hungry, Temperance."

"You've got to keep your strength up." Temperance put the bowl on a table beside the bed, sat down in a cane-bottom chair, and filled the spoon. Martha, however, turned her head away. "I can't eat," she whispered. Her voice was thin and reedy and seemed like an ethereal sound from somewhere outside herself.

"Martha, you've got to eat."

"I'm going to die, Temperance." Martha Dutton turned, and her face was like a death's head. Pity ran through Temperance, for she remembered how pretty this woman had been before the cholera had struck her down. She and her husband had been one of the finest-looking couples in the area, and now Clyde was under the sod and Martha, in all probability, would be there soon.

Tears ran down Martha's face, and she whispered, "I couldn't even go to Clyde's funeral."

"You were too sick, Martha. Clyde would have understood. I think he does understand."

"You think people in heaven know what's going on on Earth?"

"I'm sure they do." Actually Temperance was not certain of her theology, but she would say anything to give this dying woman some assurance.

"Why does God let bad things like this happen? We weren't bad people."

"Of course you weren't." Temperance had gone through this before with others who had had loss. She quoted several Scriptures and laid her hand on the woman's brow. Martha's face was like a tiny furnace, and as she leaned down and pulled a blanket over her, Temperance said, "You've got to sweat this fever out."

Martha Dutton lay still for what seemed like a long time. Her eyes were closed and her lips were moving. Temperance could not understand her, and she leaned forward. "I can't hear you, Martha."

"My sister—Kate."

"What about Kate?"

"She and her husband, Tom Blanchard, they—"

The words trailed off, and Martha passed into a semi-conscious state. Quickly Temperance got cool water and a cloth and began to bathe the sick woman's face. "Can you tell me about Kate?"

The water seemed to have revived Martha. She opened her eyes, and there was a haunted look in her expression. "Kate and her husband tried to talk me and Clyde out of coming to

Oregon, but Clyde wouldn't listen. They don't have any children of their own. They had two, but they lost them."

"Where do they live?"

"In St. Joseph, Missouri."

Suddenly Martha reached up and grasped Temperance's hand. "Please, Temperance, they'd take my Timmy for their own. Promise me you'll take him!"

Temperance Peabody did not make promises lightly. She took each one of them as a sacred vow, and for that instant she pictured the immense distance and the terrible difficulties that lay between Walla Walla in Oregon Territory and St. Joe, Missouri. She looked down and tried to think of some way to deny the woman, but Martha Dutton's eyes begged her; and almost despite herself, Temperance took the woman's hand in both of hers. It felt frail; the bones were like fragile bird bones. "I promise I'll take Timmy to Kate."

For a time they sat there as Martha thanked her and then finally she heard a horse. "That's Brennan coming with things from the store," she said.

She left the sick woman's room and opened the door, but instead of Brennan it was the Reverend Cyrus Blevins. He took his hat off and stepped inside, saying, "How's Mrs. Dutton?"

"Not well at all. I think you'd better pray with her, Reverend."

The two went back to the room, and Blevins laid his hand on the sick woman's head and prayed a fervent prayer. When he ended, Temperance said, "She's asleep. Come along. I'll fix you something to eat."

The two left, but Blevins said, "I don't have time. This cholera is getting worse. I don't think Martha's going to live."

"She may."

"Of course, God could work a miracle. That's what it would take, I think." He ran his hand through his thinning hair and said, "Did you hear about the Abbotts?"

"No, what about them?"

"Same old story," Blevins said wearily. "But it happened so quick. Cholera got both of them."

"Oh, Pastor, how terrible!"

"It is terrible. Vance was a deacon in the church. Virginia was one of the finest women I ever knew. Always cared for everybody."

"When did it happen?"

"Yesterday. They got sick three days ago, and it took them like a whirlwind. They died within six hours of each other."

"And the children. Where are they?"

"The Johnsons have taken them in for now."

"How old are they?"

"Billy's two and Rose is six. Billy doesn't really understand but Rose does, I think. It's hard to tell children about things like this."

"What will happen to them?"

"Virginia's parents live in Fort Smith, Arkansas. They left a note begging for someone to take the children there. I don't know how in the world we'd get them there, Temperance."

For a moment Temperance hesitated, then she said, "I promised Martha that I'd take Timothy to her sister. They live in St. Joe, Missouri."

Blevins was startled. "Why, Temperance, how are you going to do that?"

"I don't know, but I'll have to. We'll have to find a way. I gave my word."

"Well, that's three, all babies really. If they were older, it might be possible to get them with a freighter, but no freighter's going to take three babies like that."

The two talked earnestly about a way when suddenly Blevins lifted his head. "Somebody's coming."

"Probably Brennan."

The two stepped out on the porch, and Brennan pulled his horse up. He dropped the sack on the ground and said, "There's your groceries. The stuff from the store."

"Brennan, I need to talk to you."

"I ain't coming in that house."

"Well, go home then, but I want you to feed the stock, gather the eggs, milk the cows. Do all the chores. I'm going to stay here."

"If you want to be a crazy woman, that's fine with me," Brennan shouted. He turned Judas around and galloped off.

"He's drunk, isn't he?"

"I expect he is, Pastor."

"How do you put up with him?"

"I try to talk with him about God and he curses me. But he's all I've got." Temperance shrugged her shoulders helplessly. "I'll have to stay here with Martha and take care of Timothy."

"We'll have to pray about a way to get these children where they can be taken care of. I'll have my wife come out and help you with Martha."

"She's got plenty to do with two children. I'll make it fine."

❧

BRENNAN WAS PLOWING WHEN he looked up to see Temperance pull up in front of the house with the wagon. He tied the mules off, walked over, and saw that she was taking something out of the seat beside her. When he got closer, he saw an infant.

"What's that?" he demanded.

Temperance turned and he saw that she was disturbed. "It's a baby. Timothy Dutton. Martha died this morning at two o'clock."

"What in the cat hair are you going to do with a baby?"

Temperance Peabody had an even temper as a rule, but suddenly all of the fatigue and the worry over Martha and Clyde and the care of the baby seemed to make her boil over. "Don't you have an ounce of goodness in you?"

Brennan stared at her. "No, not an ounce. That kind of thing can get people into trouble."

"You're hopeless, Thaddeus Brennan!" Turning around, she walked into the house.

Brennan watched her, then walked slowly back to the mule. "She's crazier than I thought. She'll probably take that baby and raise it." He unwrapped the lines and began plowing again, but the scene had troubled him. "I guess I can feel for people as well as anybody," he addressed the mules. "What does she want me to do—make my voice quiver and bust out crying?" He slapped the mules with the line, cussed them, and the startled animals broke into a stumbling trot.

⌒

THE FUNERAL OF MARTHA DUTTON had been one more in a long series. Temperance had stood beside the open grave and watched as the casket was lowered. The men had uncovered the wooden coffin of Clyde Dutton, and she had watched as they had wedged the coffin containing his wife beside him.

The March wind was cold as she stood there, holding Timothy, who grew fussy halfway through the closing remarks. Looking around the small crowd that had gathered, she realized how the cholera had decimated the community, the whole area it seemed. People who would have been there were now under the sod themselves. Others were home taking care of the sick.

When the service was over, Pastor Blevins asked for a meeting of the men to discuss the fate of the children. They went to the church, and Temperance attended the meeting along with the pastor's wife. They were the only women there. She listened as Pastor Blevins outlined the situation and explained that now there were three children who had to be taken back East.

"Couldn't we find someone here to take them in?" Joe Smedly said. He was a short, barrel-shaped man who had lost two of his own children to cholera.

"Not Timothy," Temperance broke in. "I promised his mother I'd see that he got to her sister."

"Well, I don't know how you're going to do it." Smedly shook his head. "Who'd take on a chore like that?"

"That's right," Pastor Blevins said. "The trains are all coming this way, not going back. The only wagons going that way are freighters. Mule skinners are a rough bunch."

Joe Meek had attended the funeral, and he listened for a time, then said, "Well, I hate to tell you about this, but Sadie Overmeyer died last night."

"Poor soul," Blevins said, his voice tinged with compassion.

Indeed, the Overmeyers were both poor souls. Everyone in the room was thinking about Fess Overmeyer, who was serving a life term in prison for murder and would never see a free day.

His wife, Sadie, had always been a rough woman and turned to prostitution. She had three children.

"What about those kids of hers?" Smedly asked. "How old are they?"

Meek shrugged his shoulders. "There's one girl just a year old. The boy is six and Rena's the oldest at twelve."

"Nobody's going to take them in," Tom Finley said. "The oldest two are wild as outlaws."

"Sadie left a note. Said she's got relatives in Louisiana, a sister and her husband. Name's Maude Slaughter; husband's name is Ed. They live in Baton Rouge."

"Might as well be on the other side of the world," Smedly said. "It looks like we're just going to have to farm those kids out."

No one had any solution, but as Temperance left the meeting, she had a burden such as she had never felt before. *Six children—all orphans, all needing to go thousands of miles away. God*, she prayed, *I just can't do this thing!*

Chapter Four

SILAS SATTERFIELD LIFTED HIS flyswatter, took dead aim, and brought it down with a resounding thump. He examined with satisfaction the mashed remains of the fly he had annihilated, then his attention was caught as the front door slammed. Turning, he saw Judge Phineas Henry had stepped inside and was advancing to the counter where Silas waited.

"Good morning, Silas." Judge Henry was a short, rotund individual of fifty-two. He had a red bulldog face, a pair of hard gray eyes, and a thatch of salt-and-pepper hair neatly clipped with a roughly chopped beard to match. "You got my cigars this morning?"

"Sure did, Judge. They just came in." Satterfield moved down the counter, reached under it, and came up with a box. He laid it before Henry and shook his head. "I'll never understand why a man spends so much money to burn dead leaves and then suck smoke into his lungs."

"You have no appreciation of the finer things of life, Silas."

"Breathing smoke from dead weeds don't seem very fine to me."

"To each his own poison. Life has few enough pleasures and this is one of mine. What's yours?"

Silas Satterfield stopped for a moment and thought hard. "I guess gluttony would have to be my favorite sin, Judge."

Henry laughed shortly. His round belly shook, and he opened the box carefully and pulled out a cigar. Closing the box, he removed a small knife from his pocket, cut the ends off, licked the cigar hungrily, then chomped down on it with his teeth. He took a kitchen match from his inner pocket, struck it, and drew mightily on the cigar. He watched as the purple smoke rose, then sighed with satisfaction. "Well now, I sure hope they've got Havanas in heaven."

"You're bound for that place, are you, Judge?"

"That's my intention."

"Doubt if they got cigars there."

Judge Henry studied Satterfield, then laughed shortly. "I guess we'll find out. How's that fellow Brennan doing? Giving Miss Peabody any trouble?"

"He's just ornery, I expect." Satterfield shrugged his thin shoulders and rubbed his chin thoughtfully. "He does his work though. Has he been paying his fine?"

"Miss Temperance pays it. We don't let him have any money." He puffed thoughtfully on the cigar for a moment, then said, "He's what we've got too many of in this country—broken-down whiskey bums."

"I guess he is, but I don't know what Temperance would do without him."

"Why don't that woman get a husband? She's got a nice farm out there."

"Maybe men want more than a farm when they go looking for a wife."

Judge Henry blinked with surprise. "I thought you had more sense, Silas. You never heard of a man marrying a rich woman just to get her money? Seems to me I have a time or two."

"She ain't rich, Judge."

"No, she's not, but she should be married. How old is she?"

"Around thirty-two, I think."

"She ain't no beauty, but she might be if she'd redd herself up a little bit. She ought to be married."

"I guess most men are scared off by her religion. She's got enough to load a boat."

Henry and Satterfield spoke for some time until finally they came to the subject that everyone had to speak of every day: the cholera epidemic.

"Seems like that cholera leaves and then it comes back stronger than ever. Have you found out any way to get those children back East to their families?"

"No. Men are too busy making money to do that."

"I was in Portland recently, Silas. I talked to Captain Charles Beckwith. He owns the *American Eagle*. He said he'd take them around the Horn on his ship, but somebody would have to go along and be responsible for the kids."

"Why, that might be an idea. How much would it cost?"

"Nearly a thousand dollars for seven passages."

Silas whistled a low note and shook his head in despair. "Nobody's going to pay that. Did you ask him about children's rates?"

"You don't know Captain Charles Beckwith. He wouldn't give his own mother a better rate."

"Well, something's got to be done. The preacher and his wife are keeping those wild Overmeyer kids, but they're too much of a handful. They're driving the preacher's wife crazy. When does the *American Eagle* leave?"

"Not for three weeks at least."

"We've got to do something before then, Judge. I declare I just don't know what."

TEMPERANCE MOVED SLOWER THAN usual as she fixed break-fast. She had been up most of the night with Timmy, who had been fussy, and the dark circles under her eyes gave evidence of her weariness. The work on her place, which was already heavy, had been augmented when she had taken the Abbott children. Billy was two and Rose six, and she was shocked at how much work two small children, along with a two-month-old baby, could create.

Boots sounded on the porch, and she looked up to see Brennan, who came in looking shaggy and unshaven as usual. "Is breakfast ready?" he grunted.

"Sit down."

Billy and Rose were already at the table, Billy sitting on a box placed on a chair and Rose beside him. Temperance ladled out large spoonfuls of mush, filled Brennan's bowl, set it in front of him, and then added a plate full of fried ham.

"What's this?"

"It's mush."

Brennan picked up a spoon, mined the bowl, and then tasted it. "A man can't plow all day on mush, woman."

"Then you cook your own breakfast. Go out and collect the eggs, and I'll scramble them for you."

Timmy began to cry, and Temperance rocked him in her arms, looking down in his young-old face. He was really an attractive baby, but he was the first that she had ever had to care for full time. She had held other women's babies but handed them back almost at once. Now a sense of despair came to her as she thought of the task she had taken on.

Brennan began to eat noisily. He deliberately magnified his indifferent table manners because he knew it irritated her. He made slurping noises and was pleased when he got a disgusted look from his employer. He stopped suddenly and said, "What's that I smell?"

"It's Timmy. He needs changing. You want to do it?"

Brennan stared at her in disbelief. He went back to his mush and cramming his mouth full of ham and washing it down with large swallows of the black coffee.

Rose had been watching Brennan carefully. She had watched him from the beginning as if he were some kind of dangerous wild animal. Rose was small for her six years but had a maturity that many young children lacked. She fixed her eyes on his face and forgot the breakfast before her.

"You're going to have to milk the goat, Brennan," Temperance said. She had been thankful that she had a goat because Timmy evidently had a delicate stomach, and without mother's milk, goat's milk was the only thing that agreed with him.

"I ain't milking no goats!"

"Yes, you are!"

Rose suddenly piped up. "Why are you so mean?" she demanded, looking up into Brennan's face.

Brennan glared at her. "I like being mean. It keeps kids from expecting me to be nice." He got up abruptly, kicked his chair back, and left the room.

"I don't like him," Rose said. "Why don't you make him go away?"

"Believe me, Rose, I'd like to, but I have to have a man around to do some of the work."

For the next fifteen minutes Temperance tended to the children. She had put Timmy in a dishpan filled with warm water, and he chortled gleefully, splashing water all over her. This amused her despite the wetness of the situation. Rose and Billy watched, and Billy said, "No bath!"

"Yes, you get a bath, you dirty little boy."

"No bath!" Billy shook his head firmly.

Brennan came in the door, bearing a small pail. "Here's your blasted goat milk." He put the pail down with unnecessary force and glared at Temperance. "What else you want done?"

Temperance felt her nerves giving way. She thought suddenly, *I never used to get nervous at all, but now all this is getting to me.* She had struggled with the problem of the orphans for weeks, and she wanted to scream at Brennan, who had told her she was crazy. But, instead, to her horror she suddenly felt tears forming in her eyes. She tried to hide them by turning away quickly and muttering in a thick voice, "Just—just *leave*, Brennan! Go do something useful."

Brennan stared at her silently. He had seen the tears, and they were something new. Temperance Peabody was not a crying woman, he knew that well enough! She had scowled at him too many times for him to miss the acid side of her character. Now he saw that her shoulders were trembling, and he said loudly, "That's just what I need, a squalling female." He turned and stomped out again, kicking the chair as he went and sending it over backward.

Blinded by tears, Temperance picked up the pail. Her hands were trembling as she filled the bottle, heated it, and affixed the nipple. She had to shift Timmy in her arms to do this, but when she started for the chair, Rose said quickly, "I can feed him."

"Can you, Rose?"

"Sure I can. Just let me get in the chair." Rose plopped herself in the chair, and Temperance put the infant in her lap, then handed her the bottle. She watched as the girl stuck the bottle into Timmy's mouth and had to smile when he began to suck greedily on it.

"You make a good little mother, Rose."

"I like babies. I helped tend to Billy when he was born and I was only four. Why are you crying, Temperance?"

"Oh, I'm just not feeling too well today. Don't worry about it." She began to clean up after Billy, who usually made a complete wreck of his side of the table. He protested strenuously as she took a wet cloth and began to wash his face. "No wash!" he cried out, beating at her with his fists. "No wash!"

"Yes, wash, you dirty little pig." She helped him to the floor. He went at once to the side of the kitchen where he had blocks he had built into incomprehensible forms.

Temperance started cleaning the kitchen and inwardly she was praying, *Oh, God, I can't do this. Please help me!* It was not the kind of ordered form of prayer that she most often prayed, but she found out she was in quicksand and sinking deeper every day.

Looking out the window, she could see Brennan had hitched up the mules and was plowing. She watched him for a time and, as usual, had the same struggle to like the man. He was one of the most unlovable humans she had ever seen, and his attitude was rotten. She had to admit that he could *do* things well. She knew plowing was not easy, but he moved the team easily. Despite her feelings, she had come to admire the way he made hard jobs look easy. There was a grace in the man at such times that belied the shambling walk he usually affected.

She went about her work, but thirty minutes later she heard a buggy. Going to the screen door, she saw the pastor, Brother Blevins, unfolding his thin, gangly form and getting out of his buggy. She saw him wave to Brennan, who ignored him point-edly, then he turned and came up on the porch. Temperance opened the door and said, "Come in, Pastor." She noted as he came in that his face was thinner than usual and that he had a drawn look. *It's those Overmeyer kids,* she thought. *I've heard how bad they are. They're probably wearing his wife out too.*

"Sit down and let me fix you something to eat."

"I've already eaten. A cup of coffee would go good though." Blevins sat down and she joined him. They sipped the coffee, talking about the various illnesses, and he gave her a report that was at least partly good. "Only been two deaths this week. Maybe this thing's about over. I pray it is."

"I'd gladly pray that, Pastor," Temperance said. "Have you had any success finding somebody to take the children back East?"

"Well, the judge talked to the captain of the *American Eagle.* It'll be leaving in about three weeks to go back around the Horn. Trouble is, it'll land in New York. That's almost as far from Missouri and Arkansas as we are here. Besides that, it'd cost a thousand dollars."

"Surely we can't afford that."

"No, we can't. These are hard times, Temperance."

"Maybe we could find somebody." In her heart she was begging God to provide that somebody for she was vaguely feeling that God wanted her to do this thing. She had never challenged God, but many times during these days she had wanted to say, *God, You're making a terrible mistake here. I can't do this. I'm only a woman.* She buried those feelings and said, "Surely we could hire somebody."

"Hire who?" Blevins asked gloomily. "Married men are afraid to leave with this cholera like it is. Besides, no man could take care of six small children."

Doubts had been plaguing the Reverend Cyrus Blevins for some time. His theological views had been badly shaken by the way person after person had been taken out of this life without so much as a warning. Many of them were good Christian people. He had watched the believers die among the unbelievers and struggled with the age-old question: Why did bad things happen to good people? His faith was shaken, but he carefully concealed it from Temperance. "Don't worry, sister," he said gently. He supposed that she was simply going to help find a way and perhaps help pay for the expenses.

"God will help us, Pastor." At that instant Temperance was strongly tempted to tell Blevins how God had spoken to her heart. She had told him her promise to get Timothy back to his relatives in the East, but she had not told him that she was thinking of doing the job personally.

Blevins finished his coffee and then got up wearily. "I've got to get over to the Masterson place. They're both going to make it, but they needs lots of help."

"I wish I could go help—"

"You've got plenty to do with these three children. It's pretty much of a chore, isn't it?"

"I didn't know how much work children are." A plaintive note touched Temperance's voice, and he saw a strange expression in her face. "You know, Pastor, the only thing I ever really wanted was a husband and children—a family, you know. But it was all kind of an idealized dream." She laughed self-consciously. "I saw myself in our nice house back East with everything in place and the children all well behaved and the husband making money. There we were with everything going fine."

"You didn't dream about dirty diapers or measles, I take it?"

"Oh no! My dreams were much more sanitary than that."

"Well, you'll find out one day, I hope, that it's worth the trouble."

"That time's past for me, Brother Blevins."

"I'd not be so quick to say that."

Temperance was disturbed by the conversation and said, "Let me know if I can do anything."

⁀

BRENNAN WAITED UNTIL THE preacher left. He avoided preachers whenever possible, but as soon as Blevins drove off, he drew the mules to a stop and came to the house. He stepped inside and found Temperance holding the baby and rocking. "When I was in town yesterday, I met a man named Wilson. He owns three sawmills. Rich fellow."

"What about him?" Temperance saw that Brennan looked nervous, which was unusual for him. He was one of the most unnervous men she had ever seen.

"Well," Brennan cleared his throat and said, "he offered me a job running a sawmill down in Oregon City. He'll be paying me three times what you're paying me here. I could have my fine paid off in a month."

"You said you'd work here."

"I agreed to work here until my fine is paid off, and now it's all down to the word I gave you."

"You led me to believe you'd stay." Temperance felt suddenly that she was going to begin crying, and she couldn't bear for him to see it. "I suppose you'll be leaving then?"

"I'll finish this last field today. That's all the plowing. A man's got to look out for himself, Peabody." He stood there for a moment and then said abruptly, "You never want to trust people, Peabody. They'll let you down. I ain't the only one. Everybody does it."

She looked up, and her lower lip was trembling. "You're the most worthless man I've ever seen."

"If you was a man, I'd bust you for that. I didn't agree to work in no nursery. Kids make me nervous. I can't stand them! I'll be leaving as soon as I plow the rest of that field." He turned without another word and stalked out.

Temperance passed her hand across her face and by sheer force of will kept the tears back. "Go on then," she said. "It's all you're ever good for, running away or getting into trouble. Who needs you?"

c~

BRENNAN DISMOUNTED, SLAPPED AT Judas—who halfheart-edly tried to bite him—tied the horse up, and then walked up to the door of the judge's office. A handwritten sign in pencil said: "Gone. Back at four o'clock."

"Why don't that worthless judge stay in place?" Brennan turned disgustedly and walked down the sidewalk. He had come to town to make arrangements with the judge over his fine. Wilson had agreed to pay the fine off and would take it out of his pay. Brennan was highly pleased, for he knew sawmills and though it was hard work, he told himself, *At least there wouldn't be a holier-than-thou preacher woman and a bunch of snot-nosed kids around to put up with!*

He passed by the door of the Dancing Pony, hesitated, and reached into his pocket. He found two silver dollars he had stolen from a stash Peabody thought was well concealed. Not enough to get drunk on but enough for a drink.

He shoved through the door and saw three men playing poker at the table. Two more rough-looking individuals headed for the mines were at the bar. Al Sharpless was behind the bar, watching Brennan cautiously. "What are you doing in town?"

"Came to see the judge, but he's gone."

"If you got any money, you can have a drink."

"Let's have it then, Al." He took out one of the silver dollars, put it on the bar, and Sharpless poured him a full glass. "The best liquor you're likely to get around here."

"It's tolerable, but I don't reckon it ever won any medals."

"What do you want to see the judge for? To beg off of that fine? You're wasting your time."

"No, I ain't begging the judge for nothing." He started to tell Sharpless about the job with Wilson, but then he remembered he promised himself to whip Sharpless before he left town. He studied the man with anticipatory delight. It would be a joy to pound Sharpless into the floor of his own saloon. He didn't want any more fines, though, so he'd catch him away.

Ignoring Sharpless, Brennan turned and saw Ed McAfee playing solitaire. He was a gambler who dealt faro and blackjack. An impulse came to Brennan, and he took the silver dollar out of his pocket. Holding his drink in his right hand, he walked over and said, "How about a hand of blackjack? I got one dollar."

"I always like to take a man's last dollar," McAfee grinned. He had a thin face and a pair of penetrating black eyes, and he manipulated the cards like a magician. It was hard to cheat at blackjack, so he didn't like the game much.

Brennan sat down and McAfee dealt the cards. Brennan looked at the king on top and said, "I'll play these."

"You don't know what you've got. That may be a two or a three under there."

"I'm riding my luck, McAfee."

McAfee said, "I'll take one."

He threw the card down and grimaced. "Busted!"

"Well now, I've got two dollars. Let's get down to some serious gambling."

Ten minutes later Brennan had run his luck up and had forty dollars in front of him. That was the way cards ran for him sometimes. "You know why you're losing, McAfee? You don't go to church. That's why."

"I suppose you go to church yourself."

"I never miss a Sunday." He scooped up the money, and McAfee protested. "Aren't you going to give me a chance to get even?"

"No, I'm going to win the money from all those fellows in that poker game."

Brennan rose, and walked over to the poker table, and looked down. He knew two of the men, rough-looking sorts, but one was a small fellow dressed in fancy Eastern clothes. His hair was pompadoured, and he had a thin handsome face. "You fellows need another player?"

"You got any money, Brennan?"

"I got forty dollars here."

All three nodded and one of the miners said, "This here is Brennan. He's a vicious criminal, Simons."

Simons grinned then. One of the saloon girls was sitting beside him, running her hand down the back of his neck. "Well, we'll take that vicious criminal's money. I'm Frank Simons."

"Thaddeus Brennan. Glad to know you."

Brennan sat down and began playing. His luck was running high, and he saw at once that Simons was a short-tempered individual. Every time Brennan won a hand, he got a cutting word from Simons, but he ignored it.

The saloon girl, the woman sitting beside Simons, began to tease him. "You going to let this dirty fellow take all your money, Frank?"

"He's not taking everything," Simons said. The pot was big in front, and Simons said, "I'll just raise that ten dollars."

"I'll call," he said, and the other two players dropped out. The pot continued to grow, and the woman was urging Simons on. "You promised me that necklace, Frank."

"It's in this pot right here as soon as I beat Daniel Boone."

"Daniel Boone. That's good," Brennan said. "I always liked Daniel." He had shoved practically all of his money out and said, "I'll take two cards." He dealt the cards, looked at them, and said, "I raise you ten."

"You're bluffing, Brennan."

"Cost you to find out."

Simons cursed and put the money out and then turned his hand over. "I've got a flush."

"Not good enough, old son. This is what they call a royal flush. Don't see these very often, do you?"

The woman squealed, "You lost my necklace, Frank!"

"I ain't lost nothing," Simons said. "You cheated, Brennan."

A silence fell across the saloon, and every eye turned toward Brennan. He sat loosely, his hands on the table. He had reached out to bring in the pot, but he now froze. "Nobody cheated you, Simons."

"I saw you. You dealt from the bottom of the deck. You're a liar and a cheat!"

Suddenly Simons's hands darted beneath his coat. He came out with a Derringer, and Al Sharpless, who was watching, could not believe the speed with which Brennan drew the Navy Colt at his side. The two shots sounded almost at once, although Sharpless felt that perhaps Simons's shot came first. The slug whistled past Brennan's ear, but Brennan's own bullet took Simons in the chest. It drove him over backward, and he let out a wild cry and then lay still.

Brennan dropped the Colt back in the holster and looked around the room. "You saw it," he said. "He drew first. He drew on me."

"If I was you, Brennan, I'd get out of here," one of the miners said.

"What do I want to run for? It was a fair fight."

Sharpless said quickly, "He's right, Brennan. If you got a horse out there, get on him and ride out."

Brennan stared around him and saw the same shock on every face. He reached out, picked the money up, and stuck it in his pocket. The girl was kneeling over Simons's body. "He's not dead," she said.

"Quick," Sharpless said, "let's get him to the doctor."

"Well, I'll help you."

"You'd better get out," Sharpless warned.

"I'm not running from no law, not when this fellow drew on me first."

The doctor's office was just down the street, and Brennan was one of the four who carried the inert body. He saw that his bullet had struck Simons somewhere high in the chest, but the man was still breathing.

The doctor opened the door, took one look, and said, "Put him on the table."

Brennan and the others deposited the limp form of Frank Simons, and then he turned to go. He was met by Joe Meek who, without warning, reached forward and pulled Brennan's gun from his holster. "I've got to arrest you, Brennan."

"Arrest me! For what?"

Meek made a big form in his tight buckskins, his muscles bulging. "You ought to be more careful who you shoot, Thad. You killed the son of a senator. Senator Harlan Simons is pretty small game even for a senator, but he's got pull. The next time you shoot somebody, be sure he ain't got no important relatives."

"But he ain't dead!"

"You better hope he's not. If he dies, you'll hang. If he don't, my guess is you'll be doing ten or fifteen years in the federal prison."

Brennan stared at the man. "But he pulled first."

"You think anybody's going to testify on your behalf? You're nothing but a two-bit hoodlum, Brennan. A prisoner working for a woman. He's the son of a United States senator. Who do you think the jury's going to believe?"

Brennan stood there, staring at Meek. Finally he said, "This is Monday, ain't it?"

"Yeah, what about it?"

"I knew something bad would happen as soon as I woke up this morning. Nothing good ever happens to me on Monday."

"Well, nothing good happened today. Come on. I've got to lock you up."

Chapter Five

"BE STILL, RUTH!" TEMPERANCE leaned her head against the goat's rough hide and continued to drain milk into the tin bucket she had placed on the ground. Ruth usually was a placid animal who did not object to being milked, but on this day she was nervous and irritable. She bleated, turned around, and stared at Temperance. The goat's eyes had the strange vertical slit that gave them an evil look somehow or other. Ruth, however, was the gentlest of all goats and produced kids and milk with equal fecundity.

"There. That's enough. Thank you very much, Ruth."

As Temperance rose and started for the house, she looked down the road toward the sound of hoofbeats. She had excellent eyesight and made out the bulky form of Marshal Joe Meek mounted on his huge iron gray stallion. It took a big horse to carry a big man like Meek, and as the stallion pulled up, Meek stepped out of the saddle with a grace unusual for a man his size. His face had a fine layer of dust, and taking out his handkerchief, he wiped it, first taking off his hat. "Howdy, Miss Temperance."

"Hello, Marshal. What are you doing out here?"

"Well, I reckon I'm the bearer of evil tidings," Meek said. A disgusted expression crossed his blunt features, and he looked down at the ground for a moment and seemed reluctant to speak.

"What in the world is it, Marshal?"

"Well, to tell the truth, Miss Temperance, it's your hired hand, Brennan."

"Oh, my! Did he get drunk and wreck the saloon again?"

"No, ma'am, it's a little bit worse than that this time. He come into town yesterday, went into the saloon, and got into a card game. There was a disagreement, and he shot a man called Frank Simons. I'm having to hold him in the jail."

Temperance's hand went to her breast, and she asked quickly, "Is the man dead?"

"No, he's alive, but he ain't in good shape. Brennan will be tried, of course, for attempted murder unless the fellow dies. Then it will be for murder."

"I'm sorry to hear it. He's an aggravating sort of person, but he didn't deserve this. What do you think will be the outcome of the trial?"

"Oh, I never speculate on that. One thing I never bet on is horse races and juries. You'll lose every time." Meek jammed his hat on top of his head and said, "I got a couple worthless loafers in jail. They got no money for their fines, so instead of them working the judge's road, I'll bring them out and they can do Brennan's work."

"That would be kind of you, Marshal."

Meek gathered his reins and stepped into the saddle. The horse groaned under his weight, and Meek reached out and slapped him on the neck. "You know, he ain't a bad fellow—him."

"You mean Brennan?"

"Yeah, he reminds me of myself when I was younger."

"I can't believe you were ever like Brennan."

"I was a pretty bad cat. Like I said, I feel sorry for him." He pulled his hat down over his forehead and shook his head. "He's finished now though. The best he can hope for is ten years or maybe fifteen in a federal pen. That takes it out of a man. Myself, I'd rather die than go there. Well, I'll bring them fellows out early tomorrow morning, Miss Temperance."

Temperance watched the marshal ride out, then turned to go back into the house. She moved slowly, for her mind was occupied with the news she had just received. It was bad news all the way around, but a sudden impulse came. "I've got to go see him," she said aloud. Going into the house, she began to make preparations. It was not the same as when she was alone. All she had to do was put on her bonnet and hitch the team. Now she had three children to get ready. Rose was excited about getting to go into town, and with her help they were soon on their way.

Rose was silent for a great part of the way, and finally she said, "I miss my mama and daddy."

Quickly Temperance cast a glance at the girl. It was the first time she had mentioned the parents she had lost. Temperance reached over, put her arm around the girl, and drew her close. "I know you do, honey. I miss mine too."

"Were you a little girl when they died?"

"No, I was a grown woman."

"Sometimes," Rose said in a small voice, "I cry when I'm in bed after it gets dark."

"It's all right to cry, honey," Temperance said and leaned over and kissed the girl's forehead. "I do it myself sometime."

℘

BRENNAN WAS SITTING ON his cot with his head down in his hands, listening to Benny Watts, who had come into his cell to practice on his guitar. His excuse was that he needed an audience, but that was the last thing he needed according to Brennan's thinking.

"I'm going to Alabama with my banjo on my knee." Benny attacked the guitar with all of his might, squeezing the neck and striking the strings with his callused thumb. He had a high-pitched voice and seldom managed to get through a song without butchering it. When he finished, he said, "How was that, Thaddeus?"

"Well, Benny, I'd have to say you never missed a wrong note."

"Why, thank you, Thad! Mighty nice of you to say so. What would you like to hear now?"

Actually Brennan wanted to hear nothing, but Benny's company was better than none at all. He had spent the night thinking of the prison where he'd be spending the next ten or fifteen years. He had a vivid imagination and saw himself coming out of prison an old man, broken and sick, fit for nothing, with life all passed by him. "How about 'Oh! Susanna'?"

"Oh, yeah, I got that one down real good." Benny launched into "Oh! Susanna" and finally Benny's company was outweighed by his off-key singing.

Brennan looked up and said, "I guess that's enough serenading for awhile, Benny."

Benny grinned at him foolishly. "You know, you'll be an old man when you get out of the slammer, Thaddeus."

"Nice of you to come in and cheer me up, Benny. You ever been in prison?"

"Not a federal prison. I knowed some fellows that went there. It'll drive some men crazy," Benny said cheerfully. "Lots of them kill themselves before they serve their term. Why, I remember one fellow whose name was Roscoe Yates. He was—"

Suddenly Benny lifted his head. "Hey, somebody's coming." He left the cell, locking the door, then moved down the hall and closed the door.

Brennan did not move but sat on the cot and tried to make his mind blank. Every time thoughts came to him, they were bad, and he was afraid in a way he never had been before. Even a bunch of screaming Cheyennes hadn't put the fear in him that he felt now. He could face a Cheyenne's arrow in his belly, but the idea of being locked up like an animal gave him the shakes.

"Got a visitor for you. As a matter of fact, got four visitors for you."

Brennan looked up to see Temperance enter the room. She was carrying Timmy in one arm, and behind her Billy and Rose Abbott trailed along. Billy's eyes were big as saucers, and Rose was staring at him in a strange fashion. "I told you," she said, "if you was mean, something bad would happen to you."

"Thanks, Rose," Brennan said, getting to his feet. "You're almost as cheerful as Benny there."

"You folks visit all you want to. You want me to brang you a cheer, Miss Temperance?"

"No, that's all right, Benny. I won't be long."

Brennan backed up against the wall and folded his arms. "Well, this make you happy?"

"Of course it doesn't, Thaddeus," Temperance said quickly. "Why would you think that?"

"Well, you were mad because I was leaving you."

"I was upset, but I didn't want this for you. I wouldn't wish this on any man."

"Have you got to stay here forever?" Rose piped up.

"This or someplace worse."

"Maybe they'll let you go," Temperance said.

"Not very likely. I hear the federal judge is a hanging judge."

"They couldn't hang you, could they, if the man lives?"

"No, just a way of talking. He hands out the stiffest sentences he can think up. Anyway, this is all your fault."

Temperance's head jerked up, and she stared at him with astonishment. "What do you mean my fault? I didn't shoot that man."

"If you hadn't gone into town to get some hired help, you would never have heard about me, and I would be out bustin' rock, building a road for Judge Henry. Instead of that, you find me and I'm going to the penitentiary now and it's your fault."

Temperance shook her head. "Your reasoning is wrong there. Look, I brought you a cake." She slid the cake on the floor, and he looked at it with disdain. "I don't want none of your cake." Temperance had tried to talk to Brennan about God on more than one occasion. He had been less than receptive, telling her more than once to mind her own business, but now she knew she had to say something. "I know things are bad, but God can do all things. Don't give up on God, Brennan."

"I've already done that. Now I wish you'd leave."

Temperance started to speak, but seeing the set features of the tall man, she said quietly, "All right, but I'll be praying for you." He did not answer, so Temperance moved back toward the door of the sheriff's office.

Benny reentered and stared down at the cake. "She brought you a cake."

"I don't want her old cake."

"Well, give it to me then."

Brennan shoved the cake out with his toe, and Benny at once gathered it up and began breaking off chunks and cramming them into his mouth. He mumbled, "I reckon getting hung spoils a man's appetite. But you ain't dead yet. Maybe that Simons fellow will live, and they'll let you go."

"No, they won't." A gloom had descended on Thaddeus Brennan. He lay down on the cot and closed his eyes. "It's all up with me, Benny."

❧

BRENNAN MUST HAVE REMEMBERED his words in the days that followed: "It's all up with me." He had expected to be kept in jail for weeks, maybe even months, until Asa Witherspoon, the territorial judge, came by. As was his luck, Witherspoon appeared three days after the shooting and opened his courtroom the next day. Since Brennan had no money to pay for a lawyer, Witherspoon appointed an elderly, senile ex-lawyer named Leon Clark to defend him. Clark barely knew his own name, and when he came for his one visit, he had listened to Brennan's side of the story and said in his cracked, high-pitched voice, "Son, you just got to plead guilty and throw yourself on the mercy of the court."

"There were witnesses that he drew first."

"Look at yourself, boy. You're a dirty, shiftless criminal, and who was the man you shot? The son of a United States senator. If you got any sense at all, boy, you will know who that jury's going to believe. Don't even try to convince them. I'm not going to try."

Nothing Brennan said could shake the old man, and finally when he went into the courtroom, he already knew the outcome, and he was not wrong. He pleaded not guilty, and Witherspoon glared at him with icy blue eyes. "Your plea is registered. The prosecution may present its case."

The prosecution called three witnesses. Al Sharpless was one of them, and the other two were the miners who had been in the card game. They all three testified that Brennan had drawn his gun first.

Brennan rose in indignation, but the judge said, "Sit down! The prisoner will sit down! Mr. Clark, keep your client in line."

Clark grabbed Brennan's sleeve. "Son, do what I told you. Don't do to argue with this judge. Just hope that he ain't feeling especially mean."

But Judge Witherspoon was feeling mean. The trial itself lasted no longer than twenty minutes for, of course, Clark called no witnesses. He simply tried to present Brennan as an innocent bystander.

The jury was out for only ten minutes, and Brennan wondered bitterly why it took that long.

When the jurors came back, he saw his fate written on their faces.

"We find the defendant guilty of attempted murder, Judge."

Witherspoon said, "The prisoner will rise."

Brennan stood up, and his eyes locked with Witherspoon's. "You've been found guilty of attempted murder. I sentence you to ten years in the federal prison. Mr. Simons is still in some danger. If he dies, you'll be brought back from prison and tried for murder. Take the prisoner away, bailiff. Next case."

Joe Meek had attended the trial, and now he came over and put his hand on Brennan's shoulder. "I'm sorry, Thad. It ain't right. Those witnesses were intimidated. Sharpless don't even spit unless Judge Henry tells him to, and Judge Henry and Witherspoon are old cronies. You didn't have a chance, Thad."

"No, I didn't."

"Let this thing die down. I'll try to get you a retrial when things cool. Simons is going to be all right. When he gets well, I've got some friends in Congress who can talk to the senator."

"I appreciate that, Joe, but it won't do any good."

"Don't give up, son. Never give up!"

TEMPERANCE HAD NOT ATTENDED the trial. It would have been too difficult with three small children. She got the word from Reverend Blevins, who came to her farm. As soon as he stepped onto the porch, Temperance said, "They found him guilty, didn't they, Pastor?"

"Yes, I'm afraid so."

"What was the sentence?"

"Ten years."

"It's so unfair."

"Justice isn't always done in this world, but I've been talking to Marshal Meek. He says as soon as it cools down, he can get Brennan a new trial. In the meanwhile he's going to talk to the witnesses and threaten them if they don't tell the truth for the next time."

"Does he really think there's hope?"

"So he says."

"I'm sorry for it," Temperance said.

"So am I. Prison is a bad thing for any man." As he turned to leave, he said, "I'm still looking for somebody to take the children back East."

⟡

AS USUAL, BY THE time Temperance got into bed, she was exhausted. She went to sleep almost at once, but then in a manner very unlike her usual habit, she suddenly awoke. It was as if someone had spoken in her ear. The immediacy of it frightened her, and she lay very still, thinking at first that someone was breaking into the house.

The house was silent, however, and she heard nothing, then finally, as her custom was, she began to pray. She had gone to bed thinking about the problem of getting the children to their families, and now she began to argue with God. *God, do You really want me to take Timmy and the rest of these children back East? You know I couldn't do it alone.*

For a long time she prayed, but nothing came from heaven. Not a voice, not a thought, not an impulse. She didn't want to wake the children, but she prayed fervently, whispering in a passionate way.

She was bending down to pull the covers up when suddenly a thought pushed its way into her mind.

There was no other way to describe it. The thought actually pushed its way in! It was as if she were in a room and the door had opened and a stranger had come in and placed himself before her. She fell silent and waited for the thought to leave, but it persisted.

For twenty minutes she struggled, and finally she remembered how Jacob had struggled all night long with an angel. She remembered, too, that the Bible said Jacob struggled so hard he was injured in the wrestling match.

The struggle was fierce though not physical; and, finally, by the time dawn began to lighten the line of hills in the east, she knew she had heard from God. Her face was marred with tears, and she said, *God, I don't understand any of this, but I'm going to do my best to obey You no matter how foolish people think it might be.*

e

BRENNAN LOOKED UP FROM where he was lying on his cot. He had not slept at all the previous night, for thoughts of prison weighed heavily on him. He heard Benny saying something but paid little attention, but when Temperance spoke to him, he slowly got to his feet and walked over to look down at her. "What do you want?" He saw that her face was pale and that her hands were not steady, so unsteady in fact that she laced them together to keep them still.

"I've come to ask you something."

"What would you have to ask me?"

Taking a deep breath, Temperance looked him in the eye. Even in his misery, he was aware of something, not for the first time: She was not beautiful, but she had a great deal of vitality and imagination—although she kept those qualities under restraint. He knew she was a strong woman, and suddenly it occurred to him that she was capable enough to draw a gun, shoot a man, and not go to pieces afterward. She had, in fact, the courage and simplicity of action that, at this moment, seemed nearly primitive. "What do you want?"

"What would you give," Temperance asked, keeping her voice steady, "to get out of this place?"

"You mean to escape?"

"Yes."

"Just about anything."

Temperance clasped the bars and put her face close to them. Her voice was driving and insistent, and he saw her earnestness. "If I get you out of here, will you take me and the children back East?"

Brennan blinked with surprise and then snorted, "Are you crazy, Peabody? You can't break me out of the jail."

"Yes, I can. I've got a plan."

"I don't know what it is, but it'll never work."

"But if it could work, what would you do?"

"To stay out of the pen? I'd do anything."

"I think you're a man without honor." She reached into her reticule and drew a thick, black Bible out. "Will you put your hand on the Bible and swear to me that you won't leave me and the children? That you'll get us over the trail somehow?"

Brennan shook his head. "That Bible don't mean anything to me, but I'll give you my word. As far as I know, I haven't broke it since I've been grown."

"Put your hand on the Bible and swear."

Brennan put his hand out. "What do you want me to say?"

"In your own words promise me, on your soul, that you'll get us back if you can."

"I promise you that I'll get you back East and the kids, too, if it kills me doing it."

The two stood looking at each other, and somehow both knew they had stepped over some kind of a line. They could never be the same toward each other as they had been before. Taking a deep breath, Temperance nodded. She put the Bible back in her reticule and asked, "Does Benny sleep here?"

"Yeah, but he's got a gun. He sometimes gets the idea that he's tough, and he'd shoot you if you tried to bust me out."

"I know that. You just be ready to go sometime before midnight."

"I think you've lost your mind, Peabody. This ain't never gonna work."

"Yes, it will, Thaddeus. God will get you out of here, and we'll get these children to their people!"

Chapter Six

TEMPERANCE TOOK THE GOLDEN brown chicken out of the grease, laid it on the towel, and let it drain. She looked out the window and saw with satisfaction that there was only a thin sliver of a moon. It looked like a tiny shell that had been washed by the tide as it hung over the sky.

A glance at her clock showed her that it was past ten o'clock, which meant she would get into town about eleven—exactly what she planned. Turning her attention to the chicken, she put it into a basket on top of a white covering and then put the smaller basket into a larger one. She added a jar full of potato salad and carefully stacked biscuits wrapped in napkins.

Going to the lower cabinet, she pulled out the jar of hard cider she seldom used. It was as potent as any liquor and had a delicious taste. Her father had taught her to make it back in Maine, and she kept a milder form of it for use at the table. But this had the kick of a mule. She removed the lid from a quart jar, filled it half-full of the cider, then set the jug down. Reaching on the top shelf of the cabinet, she pulled out a large brown bottle holding a pint of liquid. This was laudanum, the potent drug used by all frontier people for killing pain. Carefully she added three more spoonfuls, but then stared uncertainly at it. She didn't want to kill the man, but she did want him rendered unconscious. Satisfied that she had added enough of the drug,

GILBERT MORRIS

she capped the bottle, put it back, then added the spiked cider to the large basket. She closed the lid and took it outside to the wagon. She had already made pallets in the back for the children for she would have to take them with her.

Going back inside, she went into the bedroom and leaned over saying, "Rose—Rose, wake up."

Rose woke up and opened her eyes sleepily. "What is it, Temperance?"

"We've got to go to town."

"Is it daytime?"

"No, it's night, but we've got to go. Can you get Billy dressed while I get the baby ready?"

"Yes."

"It's still a little cool out, so wear something warm."

Fifteen minutes later Temperance shut the door and walked quickly to the wagon. Timmy was protesting slightly but went right to sleep under the warmth of the covers she wrapped around him. She put him down on the floorboard in a box she used whenever she took him to town and then reached down and picked up Billy. Rose scrambled to the seat and pulled Billy over beside her.

"Why we going to town, Temperance?"

"There's something I have to do there. Why don't you get on the pallet? You can go back to sleep."

"I think I will. Come on, Billy."

Temperance watched the two crawl under the blankets and cover up. Then she spoke to the team. The two horses stepped forward, no doubt wondering where they were going at such an unusual hour. As they left the yard, a coon looking like a bandit with its black mask came cautiously down from the pecan tree in the front yard and watched the wagon as it left.

THE STREETS OF WALLA WALLA were dark as Temperance drove into town—which was what she had hoped. She had not been to town this late at night before, and as she drove the team down the street, she could hear the tinkling sound of a piano coming from one of the saloons and the off-key voice of a woman trying to sing. She pulled the team down to a walk, hoping that no one would notice.

No one came out of the saloon. As she glanced in the window, she saw that a man and a woman were dancing, and she wondered what it was like to go into a saloon and drink whiskey. It would be something as foreign to her experience as going to the moon.

She stopped the wagon on a deserted street before she got in front of the jail and glanced down to see that Timmy was sleeping soundly. Another look showed her that both Rose and Billy were asleep. Breathing a prayer of thanks, she stepped out of the wagon, picked up the basket, and went to the door. She knocked gently, and there was no answer. From inside the jail there was no sound and only the faint light of a lamp.

She knocked louder and finally heard someone speak.

"What do you want?"

"Is that you, Benny?"

"Yeah, it's me." The door opened, and Benny stood before her, blinking owlishly. "Why, Miss Peabody, it's you."

"May I come in, Benny?"

"Why, shore you can. Come on in." Benny stepped back. "Whut you doing out this time of the night?"

"Oh, I had to make a late visit. I had some food to take to a family, but it didn't work out. I thought I might leave it for Brennan." She paused and smiled. "Unless you'd like some. I don't guess you're hungry this time of the night."

Everyone, including Temperance, knew that the jailer's appetite was a natural calamity. The rumor was that he had a tapeworm or a disease, for he would still be eating when everyone else was pushing back from the table.

"I made up way too much fried chicken and potato salad and fresh biscuits. Would you like some, even though it's late?"

"I shore would, ma'am!"

She handed him the basket and said, "I didn't know if you were a drinking man or not, but I brought some cider my daddy taught me how to make back in Maine."

"Why, nothing I like better than good homemade cider!"

"You be careful now. It's pretty strong stuff."

Benny laughed. "Stronger the better I say. Here, you set yourself down and eat with me."

"Well, I believe I will have a bite."

Benny quickly cleared off the desk, and Temperance began to unload the basket. "You go ahead and start," she said. "You have some glasses we can put this cider in?"

"Shore do." Benny eagerly found two mismatched glasses and sat down. At once he began eating the chicken, and Temperance sat down and began to eat rather daintily. She was not hungry, but she was pleased to see that Benny washed the chicken down with huge swallows of the cider.

"This cider is good. Got kind of a different taste to it."

"It was my father's secret remedy. You better be careful or you can get too much of that and—"

"Can't get too much of a good thing, I always say."

Temperance was highly nervous; she had no idea who might come in the door at any minute. She could still hear the tinny sound of the piano, but she saw with satisfaction that Benny had drunk at least half of the quart of cider. She herself pretended to drink out of a glass but merely sipped at it. It made her shudder as the tiny swallow hit her stomach. She could not imagine what it was doing to the jailer's! She felt bad about this, but she had been unable to think of any other way to do what God was leading her to do.

Benny was slowing down. His speech was becoming slurred. He was digging at the potato salad with a spoon and his eyelids drooped as he said, "Best . . . meal . . ." He tried to finish the sentence and said, "Don't know what's . . . the matter. Doggone . . . I'm sleepy!"

"You probably missed a lot of sleep, Benny."

Suddenly she heard Timmy crying out in the wagon. "Oh, there's the baby crying. You go ahead and finish. I'll go get him and bring him in."

"Can't hardly . . ."

Quickly Temperance ran out and lifted Timmy from the box. Turning, she went back inside, and when she stepped through the door, she saw with a mixture of relief and fear that Benny was slumped in the chair, his head back and his mouth open. She was afraid she may have killed him, but when she got closer, she saw the rise and fall of his chest, and he was muttering something in his sleep.

Holding Timmy with one arm, she plucked the key off from one nail. She had seen Benny do the same thing on a previous visit. Opening the door, she stepped inside the corridor. It was so dark she could hardly see, but a candle burning at one end threw its pale, feeble light.

"Brennan, are you awake?"

"Yes."

"I've got the key here." She had trouble fitting the key in as dark as it was and trying to hold the baby with one hand. Finally she found the keyhole and turned the key. To her relief the door swung open at once.

"What did you do to Benny, stab him?"

"No, I fed him drugged liquor. Come on. We've got to get out of here. Somebody could come at any minute."

The two stepped back into the office, and Brennan took one look at Benny. He leaned over and said, "He's dead drunk."

"We'd better take all this back. We don't want to leave any of the food or my basket. Somebody might recognize it."

They gathered everything together, and she reached down into the bottom of the basket. "Here's an empty whiskey bottle. I thought we'd leave it. They'll think he drank himself into a drunken state."

Brennan was moving around behind the desk. He opened the lower drawer and pulled out his gun belt. He checked the loads and strapped it on.

"We've got to leave," Temperance said.

"You go on back to the house."

She stared at him. "Aren't you coming with me?"

"I'm not leaving without Judas. That's the best horse I've ever had. Besides, if he's gone, they'll think I've taken off for the coast or else back over the trail."

"How will they think you got out?"

"Benny came back and played checkers and practiced his guitar in my cell. Everybody knew that." He stared at her and shook his head. "I didn't think you could do it. I've got to hide for a few days. You sure you want to do this, Temperance?"

"Yes. God told me so."

"All right. You go on home. I'll come in later and we'll figure out how to do it."

❧

TEMPERANCE LOOKED UP, AND when she saw Marshal Joe Meek coming on his iron gray stallion, fear touched her. She covered it quickly, however, and when he stopped, she smiled and said, "Why, Marshal Meek, what are you doing out so early this morning?"

Meek was disturbed, she could see. His face was trapped in a scowl. "I'm out chasing a man."

"I've got something to eat if you're hungry."

"I'm so hungry I could eat a skunk."

"Come on in," Temperance said. She led him inside the house, and he glanced over to where Timmy was lying in his box and on the other side of the room Rose and Billy were playing with the blocks. "You still got the younguns."

"Yes, I have. Here, sit down." She put out meat, a huge cut of roast, potatoes, and fresh bread and filled his coffee cup. He looked at her oddly and said, "You hear about Brennan?"

"What about him? The last I heard he was in jail."

"He broke out last night."

"Broke out!" She managed to assume an astonished look. "How could he do that?"

Meek shrugged. There was a look of disgust as he took a big bite of the pork roast. "Benny ain't much. He got drunk, and he was always careless about leaving the cell doors open." He chewed thoughtfully and said, "He had a terrible hangover this morning. He thought you was at the jail last night."

"Me? Why would I be there? I have three children to take care of."

Meek drank a huge draft of coffee. "Well, Benny was pretty drunk. I thought you might have been there earlier to visit."

"In the middle of the night?"

Meek looked embarrassed and finished his meal. Finally he said, "I had to let Benny go. Now I got to run Brennan down. I want to look at the room he stayed in, Miss Peabody."

"Why, of course, Marshal. It's out in the barn. I can't go with you for I can't leave the children."

"I'll find it."

"It's right in the back."

Temperance went over and picked up Timmy, walking the floor to conceal her nervousness. She sang a little song to him, but Meek was back almost at once. "Nothing in there to tell where he might have gone. He didn't have much."

"No, he didn't."

Meek grabbed his hat and jammed it on his head. "I'm thinking he took off for Portland, hoping to get a ship out. That's where a lot of fugitives run to. Thanks for the meal, Miss Temperance."

"You're welcome, Marshal." Temperance watched the big man mount his horse and leave at a dead run. She should have felt easy, but she did not. She had expected Brennan to come in last night after she had gotten him out of jail, but he had not appeared, and now it was getting late in the afternoon. Doubt took her, but she said aloud, "He swore he would help me. I've got to believe it!"

ⅽ

A THIN SLICE OF the moon was high in the sky, and Temperance watched as a small cloud drifted toward it. She tried to guess whether it would hit or miss the moon. Finally it missed the moon, and the silver crescent seemed to shine even brighter.

"Well, I'm back."

Temperance gave a huge start for she had not heard a sound. She jumped out of the chair and saw Brennan standing beside her on the porch. Her heart was beating fast, and she said, "I didn't hear you."

"You weren't supposed to. I need something to eat."

"I've left stuff to warm on the stove. Come inside." She led him inside and he sat at the table. She took the coffeepot off and watched him as he drank two cups while she heated the food. She put part of the pot roast on the table, the same Meek had shared, and she mentioned that to him. "Marshal Meek was by here looking for you."

"Did he suspect you?"

"Benny said something about my being there, but I think the marshal thought he was just drunk. Where have you been?"

"I had to stake Judas in the deep woods. I found a good spot. People know that hoss, and if they see him, we're dead." He threw himself into the meal, and she sat down and watched him sip from a coffee cup. When he was through, he pushed the plate back, and she asked, "When can we leave, Thaddeus?"

"I've been thinking about that. You're going to have to buy some oxen and a good wagon."

"Won't our wagon do?"

"No. We've got to have a Conestoga wagon in order to make the trail."

"I don't even know what that is nor how to buy oxen."

He leaned forward and studied her. "I want you to wait two or three days. By that time the noise about my escape will die down some. Then you go to that preacher and some of the rest of the men that have been trying to get these kids back East. You tell them that you've located a man to take you back."

"Well, they'll want to know who it is."

"Just tell them you got a man that was well recommended to you, but that he won't be here for a few days."

"I don't want to lie."

"I don't want to go over that trail back East with a bunch of kids either, but I'm doing it, ain't I?"

"All right. I think I can convince them."

"They'll be glad to help you. They all have been worried about getting those kids back. They might even help pay for it. Be sure you get four of the best animals that can be bought and a first-class wagon."

"All right, Thaddeus, I'll do it."

He sat there for a time holding the coffee cup in his big hand. She studied him carefully, for this was the man in whose hands she had put her life and the lives of the babies she wanted to get to their relatives. He was a man roughly thrown together, like a machine, it occurred to her. There was no fineness or smoothness about him. His mouth was wide and was expressive only when he smiled, and his heavy nose swelled somewhat to accommodate wide nostrils. His hair was black and rough, and his eyes were a strange shade of blue-gray she had not noticed before. He looked up and saw her studying him and said, "What's the matter?"

"Nothing, Thaddeus. I'm just anxious to get started."

"Don't you realize we could all get killed on this trip?"

"No, we won't."

"God tell you that, did He?"

"In a way. He wouldn't lead me into all this just to get me killed."

"Well, I'm proud you've got God for a friend. We're gonna need a friend like that on the way." He got up and pulled his hat down squarely. "I'll come in tomorrow night."

e⁓

TEMPERANCE WAITED THREE DAYS, and during that time she was aware the excitement over the jailbreak had faded. Jailbreaks were not uncommon. As soon as she sent word to the pastor that she wanted to see him, Blevins came by, and she said, "I found a man, Pastor."

"You mean somebody to take the children?"

"Well, I'll have to go with him to take care of the children."

"Who is he?"

"Just a man I heard about. He's on another job right now, but he comes well recommended."

"Has he ever been on the trail? What do you know about him?"

"Like I say, he comes well recommended. Yes, he's been over the trail several times." Quickly, to take the preacher's mind off the mysterious man, she said, "He asked me to get the men in the community to help buy good oxen and a Conestoga wagon."

"Why, that won't be any trouble at all. There's always travelers who leave their wagons and animals here and go by raft. I'll get the men together, and, Temperance, I think I could even raise some of the money for the outfit."

"That would be fine, Pastor."

"Are you sure you want to make this trip? It's rough."

"It was rough coming here, but God has told me to get Timmy to his relatives, and I've got to do it."

As soon as Blevins left, Temperance stood there for a

moment. Finally she muttered, "Well, Lord, I guess that was as close to a lie as I can come without actually lying, but You'll have to forgive me for it."

❧

ONLY TWO DAYS HAD passed since Temperance had talked to Blevins, but the men had gotten together and bought six of the finest oxen she had ever seen and a sturdy Conestoga wagon. Blevins and some of the other men brought them to her house. The pastor had been pleased beyond measure. "We've got it all stocked up with food. Everything you need for the trail. Silas wouldn't take any money for it. He says this trip's on him."

"I could never thank you enough."

"When do you leave? When is this man coming? I'd like to meet him."

"I'm not exactly sure, but we'll have to leave quickly. I want to get this trip over with."

"Well, bring him by when he comes. And don't worry about your place. I talked to the oldest Henderson boy, Todd. He's only seventeen, but he's responsible. He'll come and stay here until you get back. I'll see to it that your crop is made. You try not to worry."

Although she had no intention of worrying, Temperance said, "I'll try, Pastor."

That night Brennan came in and saw the stock. He went over the oxen in the moonlight and lantern light and looked at the wagon.

"Why, those fellows have done right noble," he said. "Fine a stock as I've ever seen. And I've gone over the wagon. It's just full of food and everything you'd need."

"Come in the house. There's something I want to tell you."

Brennan followed her in, and she turned and took an envelope out of her apron pocket. "I'm going to pay you five hundred dollars to make this trip, Brennan."

"You don't have to do that."

"I don't trust you."

"Good! You're learning. Don't trust anybody."

"Like you say, I'm learning to look out for myself."

"Well, we're probably all going to get scalped by Cheyenne anyhow, but I don't mind a little extra money."

"We won't get scalped," she said. She looked young and vulnerable, and at that moment he was surprised by the smoothness of her face. She had acquired confidence the hard way, and he could only guess at what cost. No woman could display so much pride without having to suppress great emotions. She kept her lips together, and as he watched her, he got an impression of her spirit. He felt something stir within him in spite of his determination to not like this woman. "Well, I say we leave at dawn. What about your place here?"

"The men are going to take care of it, watch the stock, until I get back."

"That's good. Well, I'll go get Judas and we'll leave at first light."

She watched him as he left. Fear came to her, but at the same time a challenge such as she had never known. "I'm going to do Your will, God," she said aloud, "and You'll just have to keep us safe." She looked in the darkness where Brennan had disappeared. "And I pray that You'd save that man's soul. He needs You bad!"

For a long moment she stood there peering into the darkness, and then she smiled and turned back to enter the house.

PART TWO
Thaddeus

Chapter Seven

THE SUN HAD ALREADY begun to etch a fine line on the tops of the Blue Mountains as Temperance drove the team along the road toward the Benton place. She was still upset over the altercation she'd had with Brennan earlier. He had wanted to be on the road before daylight, but there was no way that she could pick up the Overmeyer children any earlier. Her lips tightened as she thought of how profanely he had spoken, and even as she saw the Benton house, she tried to calm herself.

"What do I care what he says?" she muttered through stiff lips. "He doesn't care anything about anybody but himself!"

Glancing over her shoulder, she saw that Billy and Rose were still asleep on the pallet she had made for them. Rose was holding tightly to Timmy, with an overdeveloped maternal instinct. Temperance had suggested that Brennan keep the children while she went for the others, but he had merely glared at her and stomped off without even giving an answer.

Pulling up in front of the log house, she saw Carl Benton standing outside, waiting for her. She knew him slightly and nodded, "How are you, Mr. Benton?" Carl Benton was a thickset man with blunt red features and a shovel beard that gave him a rather dignified look. He helped her out of the wagon and for just a moment held her hand. "Miss Peabody, I'm going to warn you one more time. This is a foolish thing you are doing."

Temperance was not surprised. She had spoken with Benton before, and he had been dead set against her making the trip. She managed a smile despite the turbulence in her breast. "It's all right, Mr. Benton. I prayed about it, and God will be with us."

Benton was a Christian himself but also a man of practical instincts. "There's such a thing as having faith in God," he muttered as the two of them walked toward the door of the cabin, "and then there's such a thing as being mule stubborn. Everybody I know of in the community says you're crazy for going on this trip."

"Well, I'm glad they finally agreed on something."

Benton gave her a startled look, then snapped with obvious irritation, "It ain't nothing to jest about, but I see your mind's made up."

"Yes, it is."

Before they reached the cabin door, Elmus Benton stepped out, herding the three Overmeyer children. She had a harried look of fatigue, and Temperance guessed it was from caring for the children after taking over for the pastor and his wife. The youngest, Bess, was only eleven months old and would be no trouble, but Bent Overmeyer, at the age of six, had the look of wildness about him. He had bright red hair, green eyes, and freckles sprinkled across his face. He was a thickset youngster, not fat, merely firm even at his youthful age. He was staring at Temperance as if she were an enemy of some sort.

Rena Overmeyer, age twelve, had an even more resentful and rebellious look on her face. She had the same red hair and green eyes as the others, but even at the age of twelve was already maturing. She wore a gray linsey-woolsey dress that was shapeless, tied together with a string around the waist, and there was a look of total defiance on her face.

"Hello, Rena and Bent, and you, too, Bess." Temperance managed to smile. "Are you ready to go?"

"I don't wanna go nowhere," Bent said flatly.

"I don't either," Rena said.

"Now, that's no way for you two to talk," Carl Benton said. "Here Miss Peabody's going to all this trouble to get you to your uncle and aunt, and you ought to be more grateful."

Quickly Temperance said, "We've got to hurry. We're getting a late start as it is. Do you have your things ready?"

Rena glared at Temperance and, turning quickly, went back into the cabin followed by Carl. Elmus Benton stared at the door and shook her head in despair. "I declare I've seen stubborn, rebellious children before in my life, but never a pair like this! They're going to drive you crazy, Miss Peabody."

"Oh, I expect we'll get used to each other. I want to thank you both for taking care of them. I know it must have been hard."

"I'd rather take care of a bunch of wild apes," Carl muttered. "You better think again about this trip." Benton was still arguing when the two came out carrying bulging feed sacks.

"Just put them in the wagon, children. Here, let me take the baby."

Bess woke up as Temperance took her, took one look up, and began squalling at the top of her lungs.

"She don't like strangers," Rena said coldly as she reached over and took the youngster. "Come on, Bess."

Temperance made her final remarks to the Bentons, who both warned her again she was making the worst mistake of her life. They almost had her convinced, but as she climbed back into the wagon and glanced back, she saw that the two older Overmeyers were sitting bolt upright staring at her.

"Why don't you come and sit with me on the seat? Plenty of room."

"This is good enough for me," Rena said defiantly.

"I don't want to ride with you neither," Bent echoed.

"All right. We're going to go pretty fast, so hang on."

Temperance drove the team at a fast trot, hoping that one of the two would speak, but they kept a flat silence. Billy and Rose woke up, and Rose stared at the three newcomers. "My name's Rose Abbott. This is my brother, Billy. Who are you?"

"None of your business," Rena said coldly.

"Don't be mean, Rena," Temperance said, turning to glance over her shoulder. "This is Rena Overmeyer, her brother, Bent, and her little sister, Bess. You're all going to be great friends on the trip."

That had been all the conversation until finally, when they were almost in sight of the farm, Temperance turned and said, "Do you remember your uncle and aunt at all, either of you?"

"Bent don't. He was too little, but I remember them," Rena said. "They're meaner than snakes, both of them."

"Oh, I'm sure you just don't remember well."

"I remember 'em. My uncle beat me with a stick, and my aunt, she just laughed when he done it. I ain't gonna stay with them. We're all running off."

There seemed to be no answer for that, so Temperance tried not to think about traveling nearly two thousand miles with two outlaws like this in her company.

⌒

BRENNAN LIFTED THE JUG in the crook of his arm, tilted it, and drank four healthy swallows. The liquor bit going down. He grinned sourly as he put the cork back in the jug, thinking of how Temperance Peabody had argued with him about carrying liquor on the trip.

"This ain't no temperance meeting, Peabody," he had told her. "Either I get the liquor or I don't go a step."

Brennan put the jug back under the wagon seat, then walked to stand beside the lead oxen. "Well, Babe," he said, "we got a far piece to go. I sure hope you don't play out." He stroked the large beast that turned to look at him soulfully. "One thing about it, if you quit on me, we'll have to eat you, so you watch what you're doing. All right?"

He had already looked over the wagon carefully and despite himself had been pleased with the sturdy construction. It was one of the better samples of a Conestoga, having been built in Pennsylvania. The wagon was important because it had to be light enough not to place undue strain on the oxen pulling it, yet it had to be strong enough not to break down under heavy loads or under the rough terrain it would have to cover. Most of it was made of maple, hickory, and oak; because of weight, iron was used very sparingly.

He leaned over and examined the undercarriage, which was always the most difficult part of the wagon to maintain. The undercarriage was composed of the massive wheels that were three inches wide with bands of steel about them. He checked over the axle assemblies that included the reach, which connected the two axle assemblies. The hounds fastened the rear axle to the reach and the front axle to the wagon tongue. He shook the bolsters that supported the wagon bed and gave a grunt of satisfaction.

Moving to the back, he opened the lid of the grease bucket, dangling from the rear axle, and he satisfied himself that it was full. The grease was used to lubricate the wheels. Moving to the front, he opened the jockey box and checked the tools he had carefully selected, including an ax, hammer, augers, king bolts, linchpins, chains, heavy ropes, and other necessary equipment.

Fastening the top of the jockey box, he walked around the wagon. The cover was made of new canvas and was supported by frames of hickory bows. The canvas, tied to the side and extended beyond the bows at either end of the wagon, could be closed by drawstrings. Clambering up in the back end, he checked the food supplies. These included flour, bacon, coffee, baking soda, cornmeal, hardtack, dried beans, and dried fruit. Peabody had added other things he considered unnecessary, such as molasses, vinegar, pepper, and eggs packed in jars of sand. There was also a plentiful supply of rice and tea.

He had argued with Peabody about the cooking utensils; she had insisted on bringing a Dutch oven, kettle, skillet, coffee grinder, a coffeepot, butcher knives, and tableware.

"Fingers is good enough for travelers," he had insisted, but she had ignored him and packed the things anyway.

Brennan moved then to check the weapons, which he figured were more important than the coffeepot. He had taken the double-barrel percussion-lock shotgun that had belonged to Temperance's father. He had also added another rifle, a fine .44 Henry, a knife, gunpowder, lead, bullet mold, powder horn, and a bullet pouch. "A fat lot of good these'll do us if we get jumped by a bunch of crazy-drunk Cheyenne," he muttered.

He checked the blankets, ground cloths, and pillows and sneered at the tent with the poles, stakes, and ropes the woman had insisted on taking. He had argued that they could sleep in the wagon or on the ground, but she had fought him on this and then had her own way.

The sound of a wagon coming caught his attention, and he waited until she drove in.

"You're late," he said.

"I'm sorry." Getting down from the wagon, Temperance gave the names of the Overmeyer children, but Brennan gave them a sour glance, saying only, "I've got to unhitch the mules." He grabbed the harness and led the team off, and Temperance saw that he was even drunker than usual. He wore buckskin pants and a pair of black boots that looked ready to be thrown away. His wool shirt was torn and unbuttoned halfway down his chest. A black felt hat was settled firmly on his head. He drove the wagon to the barn, turned the mules loose, and stomped back to say, "Get in the wagon."

Temperance had gone to get Ruth the goat. She was tying her to the back of the wagon when Brennan came up with Judas and fastened the horse with a long line. "That goat," he grinned, "won't make it, but we can eat her when we can't get any other grub."

"We're not eating Ruth!"

Brennan snorted, "If you're going, you better get in that wagon because I'm headed out." Without another word he started toward the front of the line of oxen. He did not look back, and Temperance said hurriedly, "All you children get in." They scrambled into the wagon seat, and Rena said angrily, "I don't like him."

There were no lines to the oxen, a fact that had surprised Temperance. She was accustomed to animals being harnessed and controlled by lines, but Brennan had told her that oxen had to be led by somebody astride the lead ox or walking along-side. Now she watched as he slapped Babe on the shoulder and said, "Git up, Babe!" The big animal lurched forward, and the others followed suit. The wagon swayed with the weight in it, and as they left the yard, Temperance, who had picked up Timmy, turned and stared at the house that had been her home for so long. A startling thought came to her.

I may die on the trail. Lots of people do. This may be the last time I ever see this house. The thought troubled her, and she watched the house until the wagon turned around a group of trees that shielded it. She pulled her gaze away with an effort, and looked ahead, watching as Brennan sauntered alongside Babe, weaving somewhat drunkenly and singing a ribald song he had learned in a saloon. Turning, she looked at the children. Her voice was not quite steady as she said, "Well, we're on our way to Missouri."

$\backsim$

THE TRAVEL WAS SLOWER than Temperance had expected. The oxen plodded along in what seemed like a slow walk, and Brennan informed her they were slow but steady. "They can keep going when mules and horses quit, but when they're played out, they just lay down and you can't get 'em up with a pitchfork. They're good beasts though." He added, "I like 'em better than mules."

They had been on the road for two hours, and Bent said loudly, "I've got to go."

"Me too," Billy echoed.

Temperance called out, "Brennan, stop!"

"What for?"

"The children have to go to the bathroom."

"They'll have to hold it until we get to Missouri. If we stop every time they want to do business, we'll never get there."

"You do what I tell you, Thaddeus!"

Disgustedly, Brennan put his hand on Babe's head and said, "Whoa now, Babe." He slowed the beast and said, "Well, hurry up and get it done."

Temperance took the children into the bushes where they relieved themselves, and as they moved back toward the wagon, she said, "Rena, aren't you a little bit excited about your new home?"

"No, I don't want to go there."

Temperance shook her head. "You're lucky to have somebody to go to."

"No, I ain't. They're, both of them, meaner than the devil, and I ain't gonna stay with them. And I'll tell you something else." Rena stood upright and glared at Temperance. "I ain't gonna be your slave on this trip, so you might as well forget it if that's what you got on your mind."

"I didn't expect you to be."

"I ain't your slave either," Bent said, coming to stand beside Rena.

"There are no slaves on this trip, but it's going to take work by all of us. Come on. Let's go back."

"Yeah," Bent said, "the drunk will be getting nervous."

They climbed on the wagon, and Brennan glared. "Well, your majesty, will it be all right if we make another couple miles before we have to have another break?"

"Go on, Brennan. That's enough talk."

For the next three hours the wagon moved ahead steadily. Brennan came back once and took the jug from beneath Temperance's feet. He grinned at her, took two swallows, and then turned. "You kids want a little whiskey?"

"Stop that, Brennan! Put that jug back."

He laughed, wiped his mouth with his filthy sleeve, and wove his way back toward the head of the line. The oxen had kept on going at their usual pace, not even slowing up.

Finally, after what seemed like a long time, Brennan drew the oxen to the side, turned, and said, "You got anything to eat?"

"Yes. Everybody out."

Brennan had stopped beside a small stream, and Temperance pulled the basket out. She had cooked everything she could that could be carried, and they all feasted on fried chicken and biscuits, the last batch she would make in her home. Brennan sat cross-legged, staring off into the distance. Rose edged up closer to him and said, "Where are the Indians?"

"Indians? There ain't no hostiles around here, not any we need to be worried about anyways."

Rose continued to fire questions at him, stopping with, "Were you in jail for doing something bad?"

He answered in a voice slurred with liquor. "They don't put people in jail for doing good things. Now shut up about it! Get away from me 'cause I'm tired of your fool questions!"

"Why don't you be nicer?" Rose said.

"I don't like to be nice. It disturbs my indigestion. Besides, this is Monday. I ain't ever nice on Monday."

"I bet you ain't never nice no time," Bent said. "Can I shoot your gun?"

"No. Be just my luck if you shot me."

Rena laughed. "Wouldn't do you no good to shoot it, Brennan. You're so drunk you couldn't hit the ground with it."

"That's what you think. If you kids all shut up, I'm trying to enjoy my chicken."

Temperance had wondered about Indians. She had heard stories of the terrible torture they inflicted on their captives when she had made the trip West with her parents. They'd seen few Indians on that trip, but she had heard of the horrors that happened to many settlers attacked by the savages. "There's bound to be some danger from Indians," she said. "Everybody knows that."

Brennan finished gnawing the meat from the chicken bone, then tossed it over his shoulder. "When we get a little farther, we'll have to be a mighty careful. Everything north of us on the trip is Pawnee country. No danger there."

"Aren't they savages?"

"Not to me. I'm a blood brother to Little Bear, their war chief. I lived with him for a couple of years. We'll be all right with them if they give us a chance to talk before they kill us."

"What about other Indians?"

"Well, down south there's the Cheyenne. Now, that's a different story. They don't like me."

Rena snorted and glared at him. "Nobody likes you, Brennan."

"Well, they like me even less than most. And don't be uppity. It ain't fittin' for children to speak that way to their elders."

"Why don't they like you?" Temperance asked.

"When I was living with the Pawnees, we had a brush with them. We'd gone down to steal some of their horses, and in the fight I killed the son of Black Eagle, their war chief. Ever since then, they've been sort of put out with me." He got to his feet saying, "I'd just as soon not run into any Cheyenne for that matter. Come on. Let's get going."

They all got in the wagon except Bent. "I'm tired of that wagon."

"You want to ride one of the oxen?" Brennan asked.

"Yes!"

Brennan went over, picked the boy up, and set him astride the ox next to Babe. "There. Don't fall off."

"I want to ride too," Rena said.

"Wouldn't be ladylike. Besides, you've got to take care of that baby sister of yours."

The trip started again, and the hard seat began to wear on Temperance. She got one of the blankets, made a bolster, and sat on it. Rose grinned up at her, "That seat's hard on your bottom, ain't it?"

"It sure is and it's a long trip."

An hour later Temperance was surprised when Brennan led the oxen off the road toward a group of trees a quarter of a mile away. She said, "Where are you going?" But he did not answer. Finally, when they had reached the trees, Rena said, "Look, there's a wagon train coming."

Looking back, Temperance saw, indeed, there was a wagon train. Brennan came back to get a drink of whiskey, and Temperance said, "Why are we off the road?"

"I don't want anybody noticing us. They'd remember me, and I don't want to wake up some morning with Joe Meek standing up over me."

"You're going to dodge people all the way back to Missouri?" Temperance demanded.

"If I have to. This trip's going to be bad enough without having Meek on my trail."

⁀

IT WAS LATE IN the afternoon. The shadows were growing long when Brennan pulled the oxen to a stop. "We'll camp here for the night," he said. "You, kid, what's your name?"

"Bent."

"You go find some firewood, and you help him, girl."

"My name's Rena, not *girl*. I ain't working for you."

"You want to eat? You're going to have to work, both of you."

"Better do as he says, Rena. We're all going to have to work. You find some wood, and I'll cook up something fresh to eat tonight."

Rena shook her head with disgust but then said, "Come on, Bent, they're going to make slaves out of us. I can see that."

"Rose, you watch out for Bess. You're the nursemaid."

"I'll do that."

The Overmeyer children quickly found enough wood to get a fire started, and by the time Brennan had unhitched the animals, Temperance had a pot over it. Brennan leaned over and sniffed at it. "What you got to eat there?"

"Some stew. I brought the meat and the vegetables along."

"If there was any Indians around here, that fire would sure bring 'em."

"You mean we can't have fires on the way?"

"Sure we can. Just means a better chance of getting scalped." He grinned at her and then sat down. The stew was soon ready, but dark had fallen. The children were fussy, and by the time they had eaten the stew, most of them were ready for bed. "Rena, do you want to give the baby his bottle?"

"No. I don't care nothing about babies. He ain't no kin to me."

"Why do you—" Temperance broke off suddenly. The girl was determined to be unpleasant, and there was no help for it.

Brennan had uncorked the jug and was taking a long drink. His voice was thick as he said, "You ain't never going to get a husband, girl. You're sour as a pickle."

"You shut up!" Rena snapped. "At least I ain't a drunk like you!"

Brennan laughed. He looked down at the fire and said, "You better enjoy that fire. There'll be long stretches we won't have any wood."

"What will we cook with?" Temperance asked.

"Buffalo chips."

"I remember that from my trip over. I was young, but I remember having to collect them."

The darkness had closed around the wagon, and the fire made a cheerful, orange dot in the blackness. The children drew close to it, but finally they grew tired and went off to bed. Temperance saw to it that they all were down, and when she came back to the fire, she saw Brennan was drawing something.

"What are you doing, writing a letter?"

"No. I'm making a map. You want to see?"

Curious, Temperance walked over and sat down beside him. He turned the map so that she could see it by the flickering light of the fire.

"Where are we now?"

"Right here. Next civilization we get to will be Fort Boise."

"When will that be?"

"One week. Two. Depends on how rough the trail is. Might have a rainstorm and bog the wagon down. Who knows?"

She leaned closer, and he said, "Here's the way we'll go. We'll go to Fort Boise, follow the Snake River on down to Fort Hall. Then we get to the South Pass."

"The South Pass? What's that?"

"It's kind of a gap in the Rocky Mountains. About the only place wagons can get through. And by the time we get there, we'll be almost a third of the way, maybe a little better. You see

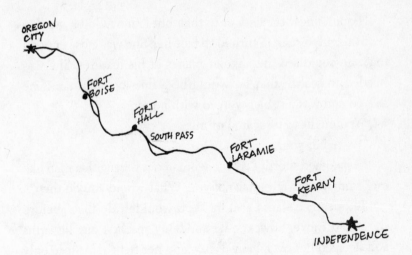

this?" He put his finger on the map. "That's Fort Laramie. From then on we follow the Platte River. Pretty easy going all the way into Fort Kearny, and then if we ain't scalped or don't die of cholera or fall in a well, we'll get to Independence."

"When will we get there, Thaddeus?"

"Middle of July, if we're lucky."

"What if we're not lucky?"

"Then we'll be dead. That'd simplify things, wouldn't it?"

"Why do you have to have a map if you know the way?"

"Just like to draw maps."

Temperance was sitting closer to him than she had ever been, soaking up the fire. She was so tired she could barely sit up. She glanced up and saw the brilliant stars overhead. "You know the Bible says the heavens declare the glory of God. Every time I see them, I think of what a great God He is to make all those stars."

"Well, they're mighty pretty, but lots of stuff ain't pretty. If God made them pretty stars, why does He make cholera to kill little kids?"

"I don't know the answer to that, but I know God is good."

Suddenly Brennan turned to face her. She was close enough that she could see the angular planes of his features. She was startled to realize that he would be a fine-looking man if he shaved and was not bleary-eyed with liquor.

"You ought to be scared of me."

"Scared of you, why?"

He laughed shortly. "A lone woman out here with a man like me? I might take advantage of you. What would you do then?"

Temperance stared at him. "You wouldn't do that." Before she could move, however, he suddenly reached out his arms and dragged her over. He was hugging her tightly, his face only inches from hers. She could feel the strength of his body and knew that he was conscious of her as a woman. She did not struggle, however, knowing it was useless. For a long moment he held her, then he laughed and released her. She got up at once and stared down at him. "Why did you let me go, Thaddeus?"

Thaddeus Brennan looked up at her and said thoughtfully, "Why, it's real simple, Peabody. You just ain't enough woman for me."

The answer struck Temperance, and she whirled and went at once to climb into the wagon. Without bothering to undress, she pulled a blanket over her, found a place beside Billy and Rose, and lay there in the darkness. Her face was flushed, and she could not help but remember the strength of his muscular body. *You're just not woman enough for me*, he had said. That troubled her, and she went to sleep thinking of ways to respond.

Chapter Eight

OVERHEAD, THE AZURE SKY seemed hard enough to scratch a match on. Across the horizon drifted soft, white, fleecy clouds that moved gently from east to west forming beautifully shaped columns that rose up like pristine castles. The air was cool and refreshing, as clean and pure as any air could be. From far off came the sounds of children talking, and over all the landscape peace seemed to come dropping slow . . .

But the dream faded when Temperance came awake, clawing at her stomach, and as the dream faded, all the harsh realities of more than a week on the western section of the Oregon Trail came rushing back. Gus was digging into her, treading on her stomach, and she shoved him away. "Stop that, Gus!" The big cat stared at her, then stalked away. Temperance scratched at her stomach through the linsey-woolsey nightgown, wondering if she was being attacked by bedbugs or chiggers, but decided that it was Gus's claws that brought on the irritation.

The darkness inside the wagon was complete, blacker than a hundred midnights, and she reached over and touched Timmy, who she kept close beside her. He made a soft mewing cry, and she drew him close in the crook of her arm. The smell of the trail dust was in her nostrils, and no matter how many times she blew her nose, it always seemed to be clogged up. With only a single wagon that seemed impossible, but it was true enough.

Cautiously, after a time, she moved her arm and sat up. Rose and Billy were sleeping toward the front of the wagon. She did not want to wake them yet. Her muscles creaked as she crawled awkwardly across the blankets covering the jumble of boxes, tools, and supplies that filled the wagon to the top of the sideboards. Rena moaned in her sleep as Temperance made her way between the Overmeyer children. She opened the draw-string, and throwing her legs over, she lowered herself to the ground. She had put her clothing at the back of the wagon, and now quickly glancing around, she proceeded to remove the nightgown and put on one petticoat and one cotton dress. As she moved, her body felt sore. Sitting on the hard wagon seat made her discover muscles she didn't know she had.

Glancing toward the east, she saw a pale opalescent line on the horizon breaking the empty blackness. A night bird com-plained softly somewhere to her left. All throughout the night she had heard the plaintive cries of the coyotes. Slipping into her half boots, she squatted awkwardly and laced them up, then paused, ready to start the regimen of the day.

As she moved toward the remnants of the fire, she was pleased to see there was still a faint glow in the ashes. Brennan had taught her how to put a large chunk of green wood on, before going to bed, and now there would not be the problem of starting a fire from scratch. He had also taught her to keep small and medium-sized sticks handy for starting the fire. These she now applied, blowing them until the smaller ones burst into a yellow flame that scored the darkness. As she nursed the fire into life, she thought of the difficulties of the trail and how different it was from what she had expected.

When Brennan had told her that they would follow the Snake River, that sounded pleasing. She had had a vision of a beautiful mountain stream, blue and clear, but it had not been like that. She quickly discovered that the Snake River was as ugly a river as its name. The river sank deep into a gorge, and the cliffs high above were scattered with boulders. Just getting water to drink meant lowering herself in the gorge, a torturous journey, filling up the water bags and cooking pots, and struggling back up. By the time she reached the top, she usually needed another drink. Temperance had not remembered this on her journey years ago when she had been a girl and had been filled with glowing aspirations and hope of a better life. Now she was older, and most of her youthful dreams had been extinguished.

Twice, over rough terrain they'd had to unload the wagon almost completely, unhitch the oxen, and let the wagon down foot by foot by means of ropes. Even now as she put the skillet over the flame, she felt the rawness of her palms cut by the effort. Getting up, she stretched her aching back and for that moment tried to pray. She had discovered that praying was not as easy as it had been in her cozy cabin back in Walla Walla. There had been a time and comfort, a warm fire in the winter, going out onto the porch to get the cool breeze, a place to meet with God. Now her prayers seemed as dry as dust, and the words seemed to catch and hold in her mind like a logjam in a river. She found herself unable to do more than say, *Lord, I wish I had more faith, but I don't. I know You hear prayers, but it seems to me that the heavens are made out of brass. So, Lord, I guess You'll just have to take me just as I am.* The prayer was dry and unsatisfying, but she doggedly kept at it.

Finally, as the darkness turned to a lambent milky color, she went back to the wagon where Thad was rolled up in a wool blanket. He never undressed and did not even take his boots off to sleep, another mark of his carelessness and lack of personal hygiene. "Thaddeus, get up." He did not stir, nor did she expect that he would. Reaching out, she shook one of his feet. "Get up, Thaddeus. It's late. We've got to get started."

After what seemed an excessive amount of speaking sharply and shaking Brennan's boot, he groaned, rolled over, sat up, and belched loudly. "What is it? What do you want?"

"It's time to get up."

Brennan had removed his hat, his one bedtime habit. He clawed at his coarse hair, digging with his fingernails into his scalp. He yawned enormously and then crawled out.

"You wouldn't be much help if there was an Indian attack," Temperance observed acidly.

Coming to his feet, Brennan stretched, then turned to face her. His eyes were bleary and bloodshot, and she could smell the raw alcohol on his breath. "Indians ain't gonna attack, not here anyway."

They had had this argument before, and Temperance had given up. "I want you to milk Ruth."

"I got other things to do. I ain't no milkmaid."

"I've got to cook breakfast and feed the baby."

"Get that Overmeyer brat to do it," he announced and abruptly turned and ambled off in the direction of the oxen grazing to his right.

There was no arguing with Brennan in times like these, so Temperance moved to where the Overmeyer children were all together in a clump. Rena was in the middle holding on to Bess, who had her head under the blanket, while Bent, on the other side, was mumbling and kicking at something, having a bad dream.

"Rena, wake up."

Rena awoke instantly, sat up, and said, "What do you want?"

"I need some help. Will you milk the goat for me?"

For a moment Temperance thought the girl would refuse. She often refused to do even the simplest chore out of a sheer rebellious spirit, it seemed. There was in Rena Overmeyer a contradiction that Temperance could not solve. The girl, at times, revealed a flash of goodness, surprising and indeed amazing. Considering that her mother had been a prostitute and her father a professional criminal, it was almost a miracle to see any sign of virtue. Still, it was there, although it was rare and one had to watch for it. *It's as if,* Temperance thought, *a beautiful violet grew up amid a garbage heap.*

"I guess so," Rena said. She got up and eased herself out of the blankets and went at once to milk the goat. It was one of her generous moments, and Temperance was grateful.

By the time Rena had milked Ruth and Brennan had yoked the oxen, Temperance had cooked a breakfast of mush, two-day-old biscuits, and antelope steaks. Brennan had shot the antelope the day before and had dressed it. The little creature was tough and stringy, but at least it was fresh meat.

"Breakfast is ready," Temperance called out, and the little band gathered itself. Rose came with two pans and got meals for herself and for little Billy. The two sat down and ate at once. Temperance noticed that Rena got the mush and put some sugar and cream in it for one-year-old Bess. Bess sat down, and Rena shoveled the mush into her mouth before eating herself.

Bent, on the other hand, ate like a starved wolf. He downed his mush then chewed on the tough biscuits and the even tougher antelope steak. "I can't hardly chew this," he complained.

"That's cause you didn't say no grace," Brennan grinned. He himself appeared able to digest scrap iron and filled his plate a second time.

As usual, he had a hangover, and Rose, who had some sort of fascination for the tall man, watched him eat. "You don't have no manners at all, Brennan," she said.

"Ain't important. Mind your own business."

"What were you like when you were younger? Were you as mean as you are now?"

"I was shorter," Brennan said testily.

He looked at the empty plate and said, "Ain't there some way you can make some sawmill gravy or something to loosen up these biscuits? You could use them to fire out of a cannon."

"Why don't you ever shave?" Rose persisted. "You look like an ol' porkypine."

Brennan turned and studied the young girl. Even at the age of six, she had an overdeveloped maternal instinct and watched out for her two-year-old brother constantly. She was a small child for her age but not delicate. The days on the trail had brought freckles out across her nose and tanned her skin into a summer darkness. Her dark hair caught the gleam of the morning sun with just a touch of red in it, and her eyes were a solid dark blue. "I'm afraid to shave," Brennan snapped at her crossly.

"Why? Afraid you'll cut yourself?"

"No. When I shave, I'm so pretty the women won't leave me alone."

Rose stared at him and finally announced loudly, "That's a lie."

Temperance had to smile, for it amused her that Rose, at her tender age, could get the best of Brennan. He stayed as far away from the children as possible and refused to have anything to do with the care they required.

"Where are we, Brennan?"

"We're out in the middle of the desert, can't you see?"

"I mean show me on the map." She had begun keeping the map that he had drawn, and he glanced at it with bleary eyes and poked with a dirty finger. "Right here. We'll be at Fort Boise sometime today, I reckon."

"That's good. I'd like to have a chair to sit down in."

"I ain't sure they even got chairs in Fort Boise—ain't much of a place." Abruptly Brennan got to his feet. "Let's get going if we're going. We're burning daylight." He turned and said, "When we get to Fort Boise, we'll have to buy some trading goods."

"Trading for what?"

"We'll try to trade the Cheyenne and the Pawnee some beads and maybe a knife or two."

"And what will they give us?"

"They'll let us keep our scalps if they're in a good humor." The effect of Brennan's words on the others seemed to please him. He laughed abruptly, then turned and said, "Everybody needs to take care of their personal needs. I don't want to stop every ten minutes on the way to Fort Boise for all of you to dribble."

❧

BY TEN O'CLOCK THE hard seat of the wagon had produced about the same effect on Temperance's bottom as if someone had beat her with a thick wooden paddle. The wagon had no springs, and every pothole and gully caused the seat to hit her like a blow. Finally, they stopped at noon and ate a quick meal. When they were ready to go, she said, "I'm going to walk, Brennan. Teach me how to lead the oxen."

Brennan had been about to go back to his position beside Babe. He turned now and studied her. Suddenly humor gleamed in his dark eyes. He took time to roll a cigarette, lit it, then grinned broadly. Every time he grinned, two parallel creases appeared at the sides of his mouth barely visible under the dirt and the whiskers. "I know why you want to walk. Your bottom is sore."

Temperance glared at him. "Don't—don't you talk to me like that!"

Brennan grinned even more broadly, "You always like to fool yourself. You think if you don't mention something it don't exist. Women got bottoms just like men."

"I don't want you talking about my anatomy."

"Anatomy?" Brennan grinned broadly at her. "What part of you is that?"

"Never mind! Just teach me how to lead the oxen."

Highly amused for once, Brennan said, "I reckon even a holy woman like you can lead oxen. The trail's marked out. Come on."

Brennan led her to the big ox Babe, who turned and looked at Temperance with liquid brown eyes. "Get acquainted with Babe. He's the brains of the outfit."

Temperance reached up and put her hand on the big animal's shoulder and stroked it. It was an enormous beast but placid and never showed any ill temper.

"Just say hup and start out, and Babe will go with you."

"How do I stop them?"

"Just stop and say whoa. That too hard for you?"

"No, I can do it."

"Who's going to take care of the younguns?"

"Rose can take care of Timmy, and Rena will take care of her sister."

"Good. I'll get to ride a horse."

"Ride a horse where?"

"Maybe I can shoot something, or I'll ride ahead and kill off all the bloodthirsty Cheyenne just lusting to have a nice, juicy white woman like you. They'll sure enough like your *anatomy*." He moved to the back of the wagon, mounted Judas, and a few minutes later shot past Temperance. A sense of fear came to Temperance as he grew smaller and disappeared around a curve. Here she was in the middle of the wilderness with six defenseless children, and between them and safety lay a dangerous trail with Indians, sickness, and disaster possibly every mile.

Putting the fears aside, Temperance slapped Babe on the shoulder and said, "Come on, Babe, let's go. Hup!"

The huge animal moved forward against the oxbow. The other animals followed suit and Temperance, pleased by the response, walked along. Actually walking was much easier than riding. From time to time she would glance back at the wagon to see that the children were all right. As long as they didn't fall out, nothing could happen to them. She knew that Rena would take care of Bess, and Rose was a youthful mother, in effect, taking care of Timmy.

An hour later she was looking rather anxiously for Brennan, who did not appear. He was right because there was no way to get lost. The trail followed the winding gulch with the Snake River bubbling beneath. Ahead, the Rocky Mountains lifted themselves in an irregular line, and she was eager to see signs of Fort Boise.

As always, her mind came back to Thaddeus Brennan. Putting up with him had been as difficult as any of the hardships of the trail. He absolutely refused to help with the children, but she had expected that. What she had hoped was that the gentleman hidden behind the rough exterior with manners crude beyond belief would step out somehow.

By now Temperance was convinced that Brennan deliberately aggravated her. On the second day of their journey, he had started to relieve himself in front of her and the children. Temperance had lit into him with her eyes flashing, and he had stood there looking down at her almost as if she were a relic in a museum. Finally he had shrugged and said, "That ain't the worst thing you're gonna see on this trip."

Thirty minutes later, she saw Brennan emerge from behind a small ridge. He came toward her, riding loosely in the saddle, and when he got there the first thing he did was go to the wagon without speaking, pull out the whiskey jug, and take several long swallows. He plugged the jug and turned to face her. "Fort Boise is right up ahead."

"Good."

"Better watch out. One of them traders might take a hankering to you. They don't see too many women along here."

"I can take care of myself."

"I expect you can, Temperance Peabody. Nope, no man's going to run off with you."

"I don't need a man!" Temperance snapped defensively.

"Most women do. As a matter of fact, most of them will do almost anything to catch a man."

"I'd have no man I had to catch."

Her remark amused Brennan. He reached into his pocket, pulled out the makings of a cigarette, rolled it, and considered her thoughtfully as he lit it. "Well," he said, "that's good news. I won't have to be afraid of you running off with a mule skinner." The thought amused him, and he dismounted then pointed forward. "Get 'em started, Peabody. My liquor's running low."

Chapter Nine

RENA SHIFTED HER WEIGHT uncomfortably, for riding in the wagon was a misery for her. She hated the hard seat and tried padding it with various things, but the jolting seemed to shake her all the way down to her bones. She had tried making a level area of the tools and supplies in the back, but somehow there was always a sharp corner punching at her from beneath the blankets she used for padding.

"What's the matter, Rena?"

Looking up, Rena saw Rose holding Timmy in her arms. The young girl seemed friendly enough, but Rena had become so suspicious of strangers that she had not made a friend of her. "I'm sick and tired of this wagon. It's shaking my brain loose."

"Well, aren't you excited about going to your new home?"

"No," Rena said sharply. "It won't be any better than what I had."

At that moment Bess began to cry. She had cried most of the night, keeping Rena awake, and now impatiently she shook her head. "I don't know what's the matter with this youngun. She's so fussy."

"Let me hold her. Here, I'll lay Timmy down. He sleeps like a rock." She laid the baby down, reached over, and took the one-year-old from Rena. "She's such a pretty girl. Look at that red hair! I just love red hair."

"I hate it," Rena said flatly. "Everybody teases us because of it."

"Well, I think it's pretty." Rose put her finger into the baby's mouth and exclaimed, "Why, this is what's wrong with Bess. She's cutting a tooth." She laughed and hugged the girl close, leaving her finger in Bess's mouth. "She just wants something to chew on. She'll be better when it comes through."

Rena stared at the young girl, so mature for her age. "I heard you crying last night," she said suddenly. "Were you scared?"

Rose dropped her eyes, tilting her head forward. She kissed Bess's red thatch of hair. "No, I wasn't scared. I just got to think-ing about my mama and papa, and it made me sad. You know how that is, Rena."

"No, I don't."

Rose lifted her eyes, for she could not understand this. She said, "You don't miss your ma and pa?"

"Why should I miss them? They never did a thing for me except beat on me when they were drunk. I never got a kind word from either of them." The words were harsh, and Rena's mouth was a thin line of bitterness.

"It'll be better when you get with your aunt and uncle."

"I don't think so. It's not good to expect anything, that way you never get disappointed." She shrugged her shoulders and said, "I'm going to walk for awhile. Can you take care of Bess?"

"Sure I can."

Rena crawled to the rear of the wagon, which was lurching along over old ruts, and was practically shaken out. She caught her balance, however, and started walking. The first thing she saw was her brother sitting astride the rear oxen. He looked tiny as he sat atop the large animal.

"Bent, what are you doing up on that ox? You get off of there right now."

"Thad said I could. He put me up here," Bent said defiantly. He turned and gave her a gap-toothed grin. "It's fun. Come on up."

"I don't want to ride on any old ox."

Rena plodded along for awhile, casting her glance from time to time at Temperance. The woman had been good to her, she had to admit, but she had a deep-seated mistrust of adults.

Finally she turned to watch Brennan sitting on his horse, his hands folded over the horn. His head was tilted forward and his hat pushed down over his eyes. "Why, he's asleep. No wonder. He's been drinking all morning." She started over and when she got close, she said, "Brennan, why'd you put my brother on that ox?"

What happened then startled Rena. At the sound of Rena's voice, Judas, who evidently had just been waiting for an outrage, humped his back, put his hooves together, and going high in the air, came down hard. The jolt tore Brennan loose, and he was flung over the horse's head as if he had been shot out of a cannon. Rena watched with shock as he turned a complete flip and landed on his back, uttering a large "Wooosh!" as he landed.

Rena ran forward at once, noting that Judas made no attempt to run away. Indeed, if she had had any idea that horses could think, she would have said that he looked pleased with himself. Brennan was lying with his hat off and his eyes wide open, staring at the sky.

"Are—are you okay?" Rena asked somewhat tentatively. She thought he might have broken his neck; he was so still. But he moved his arms and legs and managed to sit up.

"What's the matter with you?"

"Can't . . . breathe."

Rena had fallen once on her back and had her breath knocked out, so she realized that Brennan's breathing apparatus was out of order. She watched, keeping well out of range as he struggled for breath, and finally she saw color coming back into his face. He was heaving mightily, trying to suck air in, and finally he cussed her and said, "Stop sneaking up on me and scaring my horse, you crazy kid!"

"If you hadn't been drunk, he wouldn't have thrown you."

"I ain't drunk." Brennan's eyes were bloodshot, and his speech was slurred. He reached down and picked up his hat. Jamming it over his head, he stared at her. "I ought to take a switch to you and I ain't drunk."

"I reckon I know a drunk when I see one."

Brennan was embarrassed at being thrown. He was an excellent horseman and could ride the roughest of broncs, but the stallion had caught him completely off guard. He was furious with himself; he should have known better. "How do you know so much about drunks?"

"I grew up in a saloon, that's how, and my pa and ma were both drunks."

Brennan stared at her, unable to answer for a moment. "Well, you don't have to be a drunk just because they were."

"I know that!" Rena snapped. "Why are you a drunk, Brennan?"

Brennan searched for an answer. He pulled his hat down over his eyes, walked over, and, picking up the reins, threw them over Judas's neck. "I ought to shoot you, you stupid horse," he said. He stared into the distance. Finally he turned and said, "There's the fort." He stared at the girl for a moment and shook his head. "You look like a ragamuffin."

"What's a ragamuffin?"

"A beggar girl. Look at that dress. It's falling apart. Full of holes. And look at your shoes. Ain't nothing to them. While we're at the fort, you get you some good clothes and some shoes."

"I ain't got any money."

"Well, you tell the preacher woman. She's got money."

"No, I won't ask her for anything."

"Why not?"

"I don't like her, that's why not."

"You've got to have a reason for not liking somebody."

"No, I don't, but I'll tell you. I don't like her because she's so good. That's why I don't like her."

Brennan suddenly grinned. "Well, I'll tell you, kid, that's why I don't like her."

"Don't call me *kid*."

"Why not?"

"My name's Rena."

"OK, Rena. Well, anyway, we've got something in common. We don't like the boss lady, but I'll tell you what. I'm going to win some money at poker. I'll take some of it for some clothes and boots for you and your brother."

Rena shook her head in disgust. "You're drunk, Brennan. You got to be sharp to win at poker."

Rena was disgusted as Brennan began to boast about what a great poker player he was. She had heard it all before from her own father and from other drunks in the saloon.

"You won't win nothing," she said, "and if you did, you wouldn't buy me and Bent any clothes."

"Sure I will."

Rena glared at him. "I don't believe a word you say. You're just a drunk, and drunks never keep their word!"

❧

"WE'LL PULL UP HERE," Brennan said. "Better to stay outside the fort. Lots of meanness going on in there." He grinned suddenly at Temperance. "Don't reckon there's a church in this place, at least there wasn't the last time I was here."

"All right. You set up the tent."

Brennan, for once, was agreeable. He was efficient enough when he had a job he didn't dislike and was half-sober. It gave Temperance some hope that maybe a change would come in the man. She helped him with the tent although he had complained that she got in the way more than anything else. Finally, when the tent was up, he nodded, "Well, there it is. Now, preacher lady, I need some money. Give me an advance on that five hundred dollars you're going to pay me when we get back East."

"What for?"

"Why, I need some underwear. Maybe you haven't noticed, but I hadn't changed underwear since we left Walla Walla."

"I noticed," Temperance said wryly. "How much do you want?"

"Well, tell you what. I've got to find a blacksmith. We ain't got a spare wheel for this wagon. If one of them broke, we'd be out of luck. Might ought to get two. We're going into some mighty rough country. And I got to get Judas shod. You'd better give me fifty dollars."

"That seems like a lot."

"Blacksmiths come pretty dear around here. There ain't too many of them, but I know this one that's pretty good."

Temperance struggled with herself for a moment and then reluctantly agreed. Going to the wagon, she found her reticule where she had concealed it in a sack of dried beans. It seemed safe enough from Brennan there, for he never interfered with groceries unless they were in their finished state. Taking the bills out, she went to Brennan and handed it out. "Be sure you do what you say."

"Well, I might have a drink or two."

"You just be sure that you get the wheels and the horse shod and some clean clothes."

"Oh, I'll do that, Sister Peabody. You can be sure of it."

Temperance watched as Brennan mounted Judas and headed for town. Then she turned to the older children and said, "Come on. We're going into town."

℮

FORT BOISE WAS A terrible disappointment. It was a small place with a travesty of a fence around it that had fallen in places and could not have stopped one Indian much less a party of them.

Inside the fort, Indians were everywhere, for it was on the river and the Indians had brought their fish in. Many of them had been thrown away and left to rot. The ground inside the fort was flat and dry, pounded by feet and hooves, and Temperance didn't see one white woman nor any children. All seemed to be dirty mule skinners, half-breeds, and half-naked Indians. She passed by Indians cooking fresh salmon and cakes of pounded berries to trade for clothing, powder, knives, and fish hooks.

Rena said, "This place stinks."

"It sure does," Bent agreed. "I never saw such dirty people in my whole life."

The Indians for the most part seemed to be childlike—dirty and naked, except for a few lousy rabbit skins.

"Look at that!" Rose exclaimed. "That Indian is eating grasshoppers."

Sure enough, she saw one of the Indians, an older man with few teeth, munching on a grasshopper. He had a sackful of them and pulled them out and ate them like candy.

A shudder went through Temperance. "Let's go to the store," she said. "I hope it's better than anything I've seen here."

The store proved to be somewhat better than the rest of Fort Boise. It was run by a one-eyed man named Causey, who greeted her with some surprise. "Are you on your way to Oregon City?"

"No, we've just come from Walla Walla. We're on our way East."

"You tell me that?" Causey said. "Why, ma'am, that's a long trip you got. How many wagons in your train?"

"Just us."

Causey stared at her. "You ain't startin' this trip in just one wagon."

"Yes, we are."

Causey looked over the children. "These all your younguns, ma'am?"

"My name is Miss Peabody and they're not my children. Their parents died of cholera, and I'm taking them back to their relatives."

Causey reached up and rubbed his balding head. "Well, ma'am, I hope you know what you're doing. It's a long trip, and the Indians have been acting up some."

"The Pawnee or the Cheyenne?"

"Oh, the Cheyenne. The Pawnee, they're pretty peaceful right now. What can I do for you?"

Temperance found it difficult to get what she needed for the children, but she did the best she could. She did manage to buy a supply of dried food, including coffee beans, and finally she turned to Rena and said, "You and Bent need shoes."

Rena stared at her. "No, we don't. Thad's going to get me some."

"Brennan doesn't have any money."

"He's going to win at poker and buy us some stuff."

Instantly Temperance felt anger run through her entire body. She was an even-tempered woman, and this did not happen often. But she recalled Brennan's face, how innocent he had looked, and the list of things he was going to do with the fifty dollars she gave him. She suppressed her anger, thinking, *Why am I shocked? It's just the kind of thing he would do.* Turning to Causey, she said, "Is there a place where we can get something to eat, I mean already cooked?"

"At the boarding house, Miss Peabody. Right down the street. You can't miss it."

"Thank you, sir. My man will be back to buy trading goods."

"Be glad to serve him, Miss Peabody."

As Temperance led the small group out of the store, she was aware of Causey's voice, and his words followed her: "A woman that's taking a bunch of kids all the way back East will never make it, not over that trail with one wagon. Women ain't got no sense anyhow."

Temperance had to struggle with her anger. *He's out getting drunk somewhere right now. Wait until he gets back. He'll be drunk, but I'm going to tell him a thing or two!*

❧

BRENNAN ENTERED THE SALOON, and one look around told him little had changed. He had been here before, and he walked to the bar and said, "Hello, Clint."

Clint Clausen was a rotund man, tall and full-bodied. "I forget your name, but I remember your face."

"Thaddeus Brennan."

"Oh, I remember. You created quite a ruckus the last time you was here. Two or three years, ain't it?"

"About three, I guess. Thomas still own the place?"

"Nah, he sold out. Belongs to that fellow over there in the fancy vest. His name is Vince Blackmon."

Brennan glanced at the group playing poker. There were only three in the game—one with a fancy vest, a big, burly man across from him, and another nondescript man, apparently a mule skinner. "Not much action is there, Clint?"

"Not much. Watch out for Blackmon though. He can be a handful."

"I don't reckon I'd be too scared of a man who wears a vest like that."

"Don't let it fool you, Brennan. He's dangerous as a snake, and that big one across from him, that's Alec Carnes. He kicked a fellow to death in a fight here last month. He's tough."

"How about buying me a drink?"

Brennan turned to see one of the two saloon girls he had already noticed. She was a tall brunette with toughness in her face but still with traces of beauty.

"What's your name, honey?"

"Leona. What's yours?"

"Just call me Thaddeus."

Leona laughed. "Fancy name. Where'd it come from?"

"Why, it's out of the Bible."

Leona suddenly laughed harshly. "Probably the only thing you got out of the Bible."

"What are you talking about? I'm studying to become a preacher."

"I'll bet! Well, how about that drink?"

"Tell you what, Leona, you go ahead and have one. Fill 'er up, Clint. Let me go over and play a few hands of poker. Then maybe I'll own the whole saloon and you and me can celebrate."

"I've heard that before," Leona said. She downed her drink and Brennan drank with her. He winked at her, turned, and walked across the room. The floor was littered with cigar butts, shavings, and leftover bits of sandwiches. A lemon yellow dog lay by the wall, watching him narrowly.

"I got some money I need to lose if you fellows would let me sit in with you."

Carnes looked up and said, "We don't need no bums in here."

"Be sociable, Alec," Blackmon said. His soft look was belied by the glitter of his gray eyes. He was dealing the cards, and his hands looked strong but supple. "What's your name, partner?"

"Thaddeus Brennan."

"Well, sit down, Thaddeus. You just get in?"

"Yep."

"Headed for the post?"

"No, going the other way, all the way, back to Missouri."

"Is that right? Most folks are trying to get to that free land."

Brennan grinned at the gambler. "I hate to sit in here because I'm going to lose every dime I got."

The other poker players stared at Brennan, and he shrugged his shoulders expressively. "I'm the most unlucky card player in the world. I can't quit until I've lost every penny."

Carnes laughed. "Well, let's get started. I'd like to have some of that easy money."

"It's like taking candy from a baby," Brennan said. "I've only got fifty dollars, but I'll leave here with none of it, I suppose. Just my rotten luck."

"Why do you play," the smaller man said, "if you know you're going to lose?"

"Why, it's a sickness, partner. I just can't help it. I don't sleep good if I've got any money. Have to go out and find a game to lose it in."

Vince Blackmon found this amusing. He began to deal the cards, and five minutes later Brennan was staring down at the pot. He turned his hand over and said, "Well, I'll be dipped in gravy! Look at that. I got three of a kind. It beats you fellows."

Alec stared at him. "What about all this bad luck you're complaining about?"

"Oh, I always win a little at first, but it never lasts. I'll probably lose the whole thing on the next hand."

But on the next hand Brennan, to his apparent surprise, won again, and the cash in front of him was beginning to look like something. He stared at it with awe. "Why, I can't believe it! I never had no luck like this in all my life. But it can't last."

"I'll take your word for it," Vince said dryly. He looked at Alec Carnes and said, "I think you was right in the first place. We shouldn't have let this fellow in the game."

"Leave him in, Vince. I'll take him," Alec glowered. He had been drinking heavily and he had the air of a troublemaker. "Deal the cards."

An hour later, Brennan had won most of the money. The cash had come mostly from Alec Carnes, who had gotten angrier by the moment. Brennan had lost occasionally, but always small pots, and had won the big ones. Vince had pulled out, for the most part, making only token bets, and the other shorter man had dropped out entirely. The game had become a contest between Alec Carnes and Thaddeus Brennan.

"Well, I just can't believe it, Leona." The saloon woman had stationed herself beside Brennan and pushed against him from time to time to remind him of her presence. "All my life I've lost at cards, and I just wander into this here saloon and I win. Why, it's a miracle!"

"You're doing fine, honey," Leona said. She ran her hand through his coarse, black hair and said, "You better quit while you're ahead."

"No, I'm not quitting until I lose the whole thing. What do you say, Alec. One more hand. All we got."

"Deal the cards, Vince. I'm going to trim this sucker."

The cards went around, and the pot went up until finally everything Alec had was in the middle. It was his turn. "I'll call and raise. I ain't got the money for it, but I'll give you an IOU."

"My Uncle Seedy told me never to take IOUs from strangers, but I'll take that ring," Brennan said, waving toward the diamond on Alec's left hand.

Carnes cursed. "It's worth more than this whole stinkin' saloon." He turned to the saloon woman standing beside him, a short overstuffed blonde with tired eyes. "Give me that box I brought you."

"You can't gamble that. You gave it to me."

"You heard me. Give me the box. You'll have it back in about three minutes."

The woman glared at Carnes but moved across the room. She was soon back with a large box. "You better not lose these, Alec, they're mine."

"Shut up!"

"What's in your box, friend?"

"How about this?" Carnes pulled the top off the box and, reaching in, held up a lacy nightgown. "Pure as silk," he said. "All the way from Paris. Got all kinds of fancy underwear along with this gown. Cost me a bundle."

"Brennan doesn't look like a man who needs ladies' underwear," Vince said mildly.

"Well, you're wrong about that, Vince. This kind of thing always comes in handy, don't it, Leona?"

"The way to a woman's heart," Leona grinned.

The bet was made, and at once Carnes turned his hand over. "Full house," he said. He laughed raucously and reached out to draw in the winnings.

"Well, what do you know about this," Brennan said. "Never had this happen to me in my whole life. Look at it."

"A straight flush!" Leona breathed. "Don't see that too often."

"You cheated!" Carnes yelled. His hand went to his gun, but before it half cleared the holster, the .45 at Brennan's side had magically appeared in his hands and was pointed directly between the big man's eyes. "Now, don't be that way, Alec!" Brennan said sharply. "Here I've had bad luck all my life. You wouldn't regret me winning a few hands here."

Carnes was breathing heavily. Everyone in the room saw that the gun in Brennan's hand was rock steady. With a curse Carnes got to his feet, driving his chair backward with a crash. He lurched out of the saloon, cursing, and Brennan looked at Vince. "You don't think Alec's going to be my friend?"

"I don't think so, Brennan."

"Well, that's sad. I purely hate to lose friends." Brennan gathered the money, crammed it into his pockets, and picked up the box of lingerie. He picked up the drink on the table, downed it, and then said, "Leona, I've got to go meet my boss, but I'll be back later."

"I'll be waiting for you, big man."

As soon as Brennan was gone, Leona turned to face Vince. "What do you think of him, Vince?"

"He could have put Alec's lights out. I never saw a man unlimber a gun faster. I think Alec better hide while this fellow's in town."

❧

TEMPERANCE HAD BEEN WAITING impatiently for Brennan. Rena was watching her carefully. Moving closer, she said, "Don't ever believe a word a drunk says."

Temperance started to answer, but at that instant Brennan came riding in on Judas. He was carrying a big box under one arm, and his eyes were lively as he stepped out of the saddle. He also had a tow sackful of bottles. "Well, Rena, let's go and get you and Bent some new boots."

Temperance glared at Brennan. "Where's the money I gave you? What'd you spend it on?"

"Why, here it is. I got the wheel paid for and I got Judas shod. I got me some new underwear, too, but I ain't had time to put it on."

"What's in the box, Brennan?" Rose piped up.

"Why, it's a present for the preacher lady. Merry Christmas."

"It's not Christmas, and you don't give me presents."

"Well, shucks, you hurt my feelings, Peabody. I thought you're supposed to be full of graciousness or something like that."

"See what it is, Temperance," Rena said, moving closer.

"I don't want to."

"Well, here. You open it, Rena. What I bought, when the lady sees it, she'll want it sure enough."

Rena eagerly took the box and pulled the top off. She reached down and pulled out a sheer nightgown made of black silk. "Why, you can see right through it," she said.

"Oh, that's the way it is with ladies' underwear. The thinner it is the more it costs. You want to try it on, Peabody?"

Temperance flushed crimson. She knew Brennan had done this just to aggravate her. Her voice was unsteady as she said, "You are an *awful* man!"

"You don't like these things? I thought you'd look real nice in this one. It'll look good on your *anatomy*." Brennan laughed at her and said, "Let's go shopping, Rena. And, boss lady, we've got to buy some trade goods. Maybe we'll do that in the morning."

❧

BRENNAN HAD DISAPPEARED AND returned early in the morning, smelling of liquor and cheap perfume. Temperance did not speak a word to him. She got up and fixed breakfast, and Brennan said, "I picked out most of the trade goods yesterday. The storekeeper said he'd have it all ready for us."

Temperance sat on the wagon seat, refusing to answer him. Rena sat beside her, holding Bess, and Rose and Billy also occupied the seat. Timmy was peacefully asleep in his pallet in the back. Brennan led Babe and the other oxen straight into town and stopped before the trading store. He helped Temperance down, something he had never done before. She glared at him but took his hand and stepped to the ground.

"Don't guess you slept in that pretty nightgown, did you?"

"No, I didn't and I never will!"

"Why, Peabody, you ought to appreciate the nice things of life."

Temperance ignored this, went inside, and bought a few more things while Brennan loaded the wagon with the trading supplies. Finally he came inside and said, "I reckon we're ready to go, Peabody."

Temperance followed him outside, and as soon as he stepped on the boardwalk, she was aware of three men standing there. She didn't know them. One was much larger than the others and had an ugly glint in his eye. "Well, this is your woman and kids, is it, Brennan?"

Brennan had stopped abruptly. "This is my boss," he said easily. "Miss Peabody, let me introduce you to Alec Carnes. He's financing our trip. His money bought all this nice stuff and all that pretty underwear. Them pretty things belonged to Alec's lady friend, but he had an unlucky night."

What happened next was so abrupt Temperance could not believe it. Carnes began to curse, and then with a move she had not anticipated, he reached forward and grabbed her by the arm. He pulled her close with his other arm and said the most vulgar, obscene thing she had ever heard from a man's lips.

She started to struggle, but before she could move, she saw Brennan make one of the fastest moves she had ever seen in a human being. In what seemed one motion, he pulled the heavy revolver from his holster, raised it high, and in one sweeping motion brought the barrel down on Carnes's head. The sound it made was like hitting a watermelon with a hammer! The big man simply dissolved, falling bonelessly to the board sidewalk.

Brennan, still with the gun in his hand, turned to say, "You fellows want a part of this?"

"Not us," one said nervously.

"Well, you better get him to a doctor. I don't think I kilt him, but you never can tell. Come along, Miss Peabody."

Shocked beyond measure, Temperance managed to climb into the wagon. She saw the children trembling, and finally they were all aboard. Brennan walked along beside Babe. He was singing a song she had never heard, and she was surprised at the good quality of his voice.

Rena was sitting beside her, and neither one of them spoke until they were outside the gates of Fort Boise. Rena turned and said, "Thad done good, didn't he?"

"No."

"Yes, he did. He bought me and Bent some clothes and some boots. The first time a drunk ever kept his word to us, and he gave you that pretty underwear too."

Temperance's face grew scarlet again. "I'll never wear a thread of it."

"I would if I was big enough," Rena said. She was quiet for awhile, and then she turned to look at Brennan and said softly, "Maybe Brennan's not as bad as I thought."

"He's terrible!" Temperance said.

Rena shook her head. "He ain't as bad as some I've seen."

Chapter Ten

FOR TEMPERANCE EACH DAY had become just like every other, like a series of severe illnesses. She'd had some vague but rather good memories of her trip from the East to Oregon Territory, but the harsh realities of the grinding struggles she faced now were an ever-present reality. Every day brought laborious work, unending fatigue, and bad weather. The constant care of the children added to all of this, and the antagonism of the two older Overmeyer children tested her patience to the limit. She had no idea how many miles they covered each day, but it seemed the trip had no end. The dry complainings of the wheels as the wagon lumbered over the broken earth ceased only when they stopped for the night. Whether they traveled five miles or twenty, it didn't seem to matter, for the endless waste was always before them.

The oxen were suffering, too, and Temperance grieved over them. They were hard to keep together overnight and had to be hobbled, a task that required more of Brennan's time and energy. Always the question of water loomed before them, and thirst was a never-ending torment. The country itself was ugly, at least to her, a land that seemed to have been left over from Creation, broken by yawning fractures and raw gullies. The mountains, some of them far ahead and others fading in the background, seemed to her more like walls of a great prison.

The great gorge that bordered the Snake River was cut so deeply that getting to it took every bit of strength and endurance a person could summon up.

Fatigue had dragged Temperance down, and she was dozing on the seat when suddenly the right front wheel of the wagon dropped off into a deep rut. The abrupt jolt caused the hard seat of the wagon to pound against Temperance almost with the force of a heavy blow. She was holding Gus in her lap, and with a yowl he jumped away from her and disappeared under the canvas.

"That's a crazy cat," Rena remarked. She was sitting beside Temperance on the wagon seat holding Billy, who seemingly could sleep through an earthquake. The jolting pace of the wagon never seemed to trouble him.

With a grimace, Temperance shifted on the hard seat, trying to find a more comfortable position. Up ahead she saw Brennan sitting astride Babe, rocking with the motion of the ox. *Only Thaddeus can ride an ox while he's drunk!* She swallowed her irritation with the man, and nodded at Rena. "I've had him since he was a kitten. He was so tiny I had to feed him with an eyedropper."

"I had a cat once. Her name was Queenie. She was black all over and had big green eyes. She used to sleep with me at night. But Ma made me get rid of her."

"Why did she do that?"

Rena gave Temperance a look that reflected the hard core of her personality. "Because she was mean."

"Your cat was mean?"

"No, Queenie was sweet. Ma was mean."

Temperance had known that both Rena and Bent had an ingrained bitterness against their parents. She was well aware of the effects of bitterness on an individual spirit, but this did not seem to be the time nor the place to reason with Rena. "I'm sorry," she said finally. She almost suggested that her relatives would let her have a pet, but Rena had already spoken in adamantine tones about her uncle and aunt. Finally Temperance said, "Gus has been a lot of company to me."

Rena said moodily, "Cats are funny. They don't come and make over you like a dog does."

"No, they're pretty independent, but I love Gus. He's been my companion."

"I guess if you don't have a man, a cat's a pretty good thing to have."

Instantly Temperance felt her face go warm. She glanced at Rena and saw that the girl was studying her in a curious fashion. The girl was a strange mixture of child and woman, and the remark could have been casual, but Temperance saw the slight glitter in Rena's eyes and knew it was a gibe aimed at her unmarried state. It was the sort of hardness—even cruelty—that Temperance had seen in Rena, but beneath that harsh surface Temperance sometimes caught a hint of another person who cried out for some of the gentler things of life. She could not think of a proper answer to make.

Rena stared at Temperance for a long moment, then asked, "Have you tried on any of that fancy underwear that Brennan won at the poker game?"

"No!"

"Why not? They're real soft. I bet they'd be comfortable."

"They're—they're not for a woman like me."

"They're just underwear is all they are. Why, you always try to make things mean something."

"They're for a different kind of woman."

"For a saloon woman, I reckon you mean. That's who they were meant for, Brennan said." Rena laughed suddenly. "I don't see what difference it makes. If I was you, I'd wear 'em." Rena waited for a response, and when she got none, she shifted Billy in her arms into a more comfortable position, then asked, "You ever had a man?"

The question seemed to be innocent enough, but still the color deepened on Temperance's cheeks. She could not think of a way to answer the question, and Rena pressed on. "I bet you ain't."

"It's not something I want to talk about, Rena."

"You're pretty old not to have a man. How old are you anyhow, Temperance?"

"I'm thirty-two."

"That's pretty old."

Suddenly Temperance had to laugh. "I suppose it is to you. When you're twelve, everybody over twenty seems ancient."

"How come you never got a man?"

"Oh, I don't know. It just never happened."

Rena fell silent, for which Temperance was thankful, and as the wagon lumbered on, Temperance began to scan the horizon. Brennan had told them there was no problem with Indians in this stage in their journey, but she could not believe it. She felt unsafe, uncertain somehow, when he got out of sight and felt that this was a weakness she could not acknowledge.

"That was really something how Brennan knocked that feller down just with one lick, wasn't it?"

"He's a violent man."

"Reckon he is," Rena shrugged. "But I'm glad he's with us. He sure took care of that feller, though, and them other two that was with him, they was scared green."

"He's not a good man, Rena, but he's all I could get."

Rena pondered Temperance's reply and then said flatly, "He's good enough to get us over this desert. That's all I know."

$\mathcal{C}$

BRENNAN FOUND A SMALL spring late in the afternoon, and they made camp for the night. Their day had been longer than usual, and by the time Temperance washed the diapers and made a meal of sorts, the darkness seemed to be complete. The children were all asleep now, and Brennan disappeared without a word. He had that way about him, of simply walking off without a word of good-bye, exactly as he would return without a word of greeting. His manners were terrible—almost as bad as his appearance, in Temperance's judgment, and as she sat on an upturned box beside the fire, she felt a loneliness of the land. They had passed two wagon trains headed westward, but Brennan had steered clear of them.

Looking up at the black canopy of the sky, she was momentarily pleased by the stars that seemed to flash like diamonds. She wished she knew the names of them, but one of only the few she knew was Venus. She remembered once when she was very young, her mother had pointed that one out to her, saying, "That's the morning star." She also knew Polaris, the North Star, and the Big Dipper. As she sat there she thought about sailors to whom the skies were a map they could follow across the trackless waste of the ocean.

From far off came the sound of a wolf's plaintive cry, a mournful incantation that seemed to increase the loneliness. Brennan had told her that wolves were usually as shy as coyotes and would never attack them, but she wasn't sure.

The days had exhausted her, and she reached down and rubbed Gus's head. "It's been a hard day, hasn't it, Gus? I bet you'll be glad to get to the other end of the trip. I know I will be." She heard nothing but suddenly a shadow separated itself from the darkness of the night, and Brennan came in carrying his rifle loosely in the crook of his arm. He had not shaved in several days and made a rough figure as he leaned the rifle against the wagon, then moved to the fire. "Anything left to eat?" he asked.

"Yes, I'll get it for you." Temperance pulled a meal together—antelope steak again and two baked potatoes with three biscuits grown hard. "I'll make biscuits tomorrow or the next time we stop early," she said.

He took the plate, sat down, and ate hungrily. As he washed the meal down with swallows of black coffee, Temperance studied him. He was a man roughly put together, like a machine made to perform hard labor. The flickering firelight cast shadows on his face, and she noted that his heavy nose swelled somewhat at the base to accommodate wide nostrils. His hair was black and coarse, almost like an Indian's, and his eyes were deep-set, a smoky gray with just the faintest suggestion of blue, a color she had never seen before in a man or woman. He was, she knew, a trifle over six feet tall, long of arms. She noted, not for the first time, a scar shaped like a fish hook at the left corner of his mouth and she wondered what sort of violence had put it there. The edge of his jaw was sharp against the heavily tanned skin, and he sat there apparently unconscious of her presence. "We ought to be in Fort Hall tomorrow, maybe the day after."

The words broke the silence of the night, punctuated only by the cracking and popping of the fire, and a log shifted, sending a swarm of red and orange sparks swirling upward. Leaning over, Temperance put a large chunk of green wood on the fire, then asked, "What's it like?"

"Fort Hall? A little bit better than Fort Boise. We need to get a few more supplies. Some more trading goods for the Indians."

Curiosity about the man's background came to Temperance then. She had put her life in this man's hands, yet she knew nothing about his past. It was almost as if he had been created the day she met him, and it struck her afresh how she was willing to put her life and the lives of the children in the hands of a man about whom she knew nothing.

"Where did you grow up, Thaddeus?"

Her question caught the tall man by surprise. He sipped the coffee and shrugged his shoulders. "Tennessee."

The answer told her nothing except that he was a Southerner, which she already knew from the cadences of his speech. "What about your family?"

"Why do you want to know?"

"I'm just curious."

"Women usually are." He, for a moment, appeared to ignore her question and was silent. "My pa died when I was two. There was five of us kids. All I can remember is working on that rocky, mountain farm. Get up before daylight, work until dark, go home, eat a piece of cold cornbread, and go to sleep. Get up and do it the next day all over again."

"It sounds like a hard life."

"I don't like to think about it much. My ma had a hard time." He let the silence run on and finally picked up a stick and stuck it into the tiny, orange flame. He waited until it caught and then lifted it out and stared at it as if there were some sort of wisdom in the tiny tear-shaped flame that consumed the stick. "We were always hungry. Never had any clothes except what Ma could make or someone gave us. I had two brothers. I was the youngest of the three boys. My oldest brother was Mack. Next in line was Sims."

"What were they like?"

"Worked to death like me." He tossed the twig back into the flame and watched the fire turn it into a burning ember, then his voice took on a strange timbre. "When Mack was sixteen and we got back from plowing, Ma had Mack's things ready in a bundle. She gave them to him, and he stood there looking at them. She gave him a dollar then and said, 'I can't afford to keep you no more, Son. You have to make your own way.'"

Temperance could not understand such things. "And what happened to him?"

"He left and we never saw him again. The thing I remember is he started to go, and Ma ran to him and hugged him and kissed him, then he left."

"What a terrible thing!"

"Terrible times. Same thing happened to Sims a year later. Ma had his things wrapped up in a bundle. She gave him a dollar and kissed him and told him she couldn't afford to keep him."

"Did you ever see him again?"

"No. We heard he got killed in a sawmill accident in Louisiana. Of course, we never knew for sure."

Temperance said, "I feel sorry for your mother. That was just you who helped with the two girls?"

"Not for long. It wasn't but a few months after Sims left that I came in from plowing and Ma had my things together. I knew what she was going to say." He looked up at the stars, and then his gaze came to her. There was a harshness about him, and he

146

said, "She just gave me the bundle and didn't say a word, but I knew what it meant. I waited for her to give me a dollar and to kiss me, but she never did. I said good-bye to the girls and I left." He fell silent then, and finally in a voice so soft she barely heard it he said, "I could understand why she couldn't keep me, and I know she didn't have a dollar. But I never could figure out why she never kissed me like she did Mack and Sims." He suddenly turned and looked at Temperance and saw tears standing in her eyes. Gruffly he said, "Nothing to cry about. They were tough times."

Temperance dashed the tears from her eyes. Suddenly she felt that she knew the strange man in a way she hadn't before. She wanted to reach out somehow to him and let him know how his story had affected her, but there was no chance. Without another word he got up, walked over to the blankets he kept beyond the edge of the fire, rolled up, and was still.

Temperance knew there was a hurt in this big, rough man that no one knew about. She strongly suspected he had never mentioned his early life to anyone, and she knew that she could not feel the same toward him ever again. He was more than just a rough, untutored hooligan, and she knew she would never forget the story of how his mother had sent him away without even a kiss. She also knew why the mother could not kiss him; it was just too much for a woman to bear.

ℰ

FORT HALL WAS BETTER than Fort Boise, though not much. There were drunken Indians outside the fort and drunken soldiers inside. They pulled up outside the walls, and Temperance said, "I'm going to buy a few things."

"All right," Brennan said. "I've got to find a gunsmith to repair the rifle."

Temperance worked to get the kids clean. Rena, Rose, and Bent were all excited at what was happening. She had told them she would buy them a treat at the store.

The store wasn't much, but at least it had hard candy, and Temperance bought the children some, telling them they shouldn't eat it all at once but to keep it for the trail. She had purchased a few items and was enjoying simply looking around when suddenly Brennan came in. "Let's go," he said gruffly.

"But I'm not—"

"I said let's go."

Rena stared at Brennan. "What's the hurry?"

Brennan ignored her and herded them out. They went to the wagon, and he seemed nearly frenzied to get away. Quickly they pulled away from the fort.

Brennan walked beside the oxen, urging them on, but he made camp earlier than usual for the day. He was nervous about something, Temperance saw, and finally after supper, he went out to stand with his rifle, looking often back toward the fort.

Rena walked over and stood beside him. "Why'd you have to hurry us away from the store? We was having fun."

"You can go to the store at the next settlement."

Rena glared at him. "You and me are a lot alike."

"Why do you think that?"

"I heard you talking to Temperance about how your ma sent you away. I think that's why you act mean sometimes."

"Don't be makin' up stories. It ain't right to listen to other people's conversations."

Rena shook her head. "My ma and pa were mean to me. That's why I'm mean, I guess."

Brennan studied the girl. She was staring at him with a challenge in her eyes. He tried to think what kind of a woman she would be when she grew up. At twelve, she was already hardened in many ways, having grown up in saloons, with a criminal for a father and a prostitute for a mother. She could be little else, or so she thought. "You don't have to be mean. You can forget how they treated you."

Rena stared at him. "You ain't forgot how your ma treated you."

"That was different," Brennan said stiffly. "She didn't have a choice."

"Sure she did. She could have kept you. Better she had kept you and you all starved together than sending you off."

Brennan shook his head. "You don't know what you're talking about."

"Well, I know one thing. I'm going to be no good just like they were."

"That's crazy talk," Brennan muttered. "What about Bent and Bess?"

Rena suddenly bit on her lower lip. "I guess they got no chance either." She looked up at Brennan, and he saw the pain in her eyes. "I always watch other kids who had a ma and pa that took care of them. They got everything, Brennan."

"Maybe your uncle and aunt will be good to you."

"No, they won't," Rena said flatly. Without another word Rena turned and walked off, her back as straight as a ramrod. Brennan watched her, and in a few moments Temperance joined him. She said nothing, but he commented, "That girl's had a rough row to hoe, Peabody."

"I know she has. It may be worse. We don't know what kind of people her relatives are."

The two stood under the twinkling stars, and Brennan cast a half-embarrassed glance at her. "I know you wanted to stay longer at the store, but we had to leave."

"What was the rush about? I saw you were troubled."

"I heard a fellow say that a federal marshal was coming to pick up some prisoners. He probably knows Joe Meek. If he saw me"—he shrugged—"I'd be one of them."

"Well, of course we had to leave then. There was no other way."

Brennan seemed troubled, and finally he said, "What if the people we're taking the Overmeyer kids to are no good?"

Temperance said instantly, "God will get Rena and the others a good place."

The remark struck Thaddeus Brennan with a force that Temperance could see. She watched his face change and waited until finally he spoke.

"I wish I could believe like you do, Peabody, but I've been knocked down too many times."

She did not answer, and the two of them stood in the silence of the night until finally Brennan said, "Better get some sleep, Peabody. Be another hard day tomorrow."

Chapter Eleven

"WELL, WE MADE PRETTY good time," Brennan remarked. He was sitting before the fire with Rena and Bent across from him. Rose was feeding Billy mush that Temperance had cooked.

"How far we got to go?" Rena asked.

"We may be a third of the way there, maybe a little less." He glanced over at the wagon, and a puzzled look crossed his face. "It's strange that Peabody ain't up yet."

"She's sick," Rena said at once. "She was sick all night."

"Why didn't you tell me?" Brennan demanded.

"Because I knew you wouldn't care. You don't care who gets sick around here," Rena replied.

Casting a disgusted glance at Rena, Brennan shook his head. He walked to the wagon and looked inside. Temperance was lying under a blanket. He lifted it and saw that her face was flushed. "What's the matter with you?"

Temperance did not even open her eyes. "Don't know," she whispered. "Sick all night."

"Well, ain't this a pretty come-off! What am I supposed to do with all these kids?" Brennan demanded. He waited for a reply and then shook his head. Stepping back from the wagon, he stood uncertainly for a moment, and Bent asked, "Are we going on?"

"Can't go on until that woman gets better. We'll stay here for a spell."

"What if she dies?" Bent demanded.

"She ain't gonna die."

"How do you know?"

"I know everything, that's what. You come over here." Going back to the fire, he glanced at the two young girls, Rose and Rena. "We got to stay here for awhile, and you kids have got to help me."

Rose said, "I'm afraid for her, Brennan."

"She'll be OK."

"I wish there was a doctor here," Rena said, "but there ain't."

"You girls take care of them babies. Bent, me and you will go hunting after awhile, but we've got to have some breakfast first."

"I don't know how to cook," Rena said.

"Well, I do," Brennan said. "I'm the best cook you ever saw."

"Men can't cook," Bent replied stubbornly.

"You just watch my smoke." Brennan rummaged through the groceries and found what he was looking for. He held up a glass jar and said, "Remember these quail eggs I brought in? We're going to have them now for breakfast. After that I'm going to make some fresh bread."

At that instant Timmy began crying.

"What's the matter with him?" Brennan demanded.

"His diaper's dirty," Rose said. "We don't have any clean ones."

"Well, what are we going to do then?"

"We're going to have to wash diapers, that's what," Rena said. "You hadn't noticed that the diapers have to be washed every day?"

"Why, you kids start washing diapers. I'll cook breakfast, and after that I'm going to make enough bread to do us for a spell."

Rena sent Bent to milk the goat while she and Rose washed diapers at the small stream. By the time they had hung them to dry, Brennan said, "You got them kids all cleaned up; come and eat something."

Rena went closer and looked into the big pan Brennan was holding out.

"What's that?"

"That's corn pone. I grew up on it, and it won't hurt you. These quail eggs are just about right."

He had also fixed a bowl of mush, and they all sat down and began to eat.

"Corn pone is good," Bent said. "I never ate none before. What's in it?"

"Cornmeal, salt, water, and some onions. You think that's good, you wait until tonight. We're going to have Cherokee bean bread."

"What's that?" Rena demanded.

"You ask too many questions. Just eat up."

After breakfast, Brennan moved the oxen so they had plenty of fresh grass to graze on. Then he set up the Dutch oven, which they had not used since they started their trip. He had been against bringing it, but Temperance had insisted they had to have something to make biscuits in.

Finally Brennan heated some of the mush and walked over to the wagon. "Here," he said, "you've got to eat something."

"I don't think I can keep it down."

"Well, spit it up. We'll keep pouring it down you. You've got to eat."

Temperance said, "I want to get out."

"Come on then." He waited until she appeared, wearing a cotton nightgown. Ordinarily he knew she would not have worn such a thing before him, but now she was too sick to care. Coming out of the end of the wagon, she faltered. He quickly reached up and scooped her up as if she were a child. He carried her away from the wagon, set her beside it, and arranged a blanket. "Sit down there and eat."

Temperance thumped to the ground. She looked down and saw that her gown was wet with sweat and clinging to her, and it embarrassed her. "Get—get my robe. I can't sit here like this."

"It won't hurt you. Here, eat this."

Temperance took the bowl of mush and ate a few bites, and at his insistence she ate more. He squatted beside her and watched her. Finally, when she had eaten half of the bowl, he took it back and got water. "Drink all the water you can."

She drank thirstily and then said vaguely, "I don't know what's wrong with me. I never get sick."

"Well, it ain't cholera. Thank God for that."

"No, I know it's not that. What could it be?"

"Trail sickness."

"Trail sickness? What's that?"

"Don't know what it is, but after a time on the trail, some people get sick. As long as this is the worst it gets, we're all right. We'll stay here for a day or two until you perk up."

"What about the children?"

"I reckon they'll make out." With this cryptic remark he rose and left her. Rena came over at once and said, "How do you feel, Temperance?"

"Washed out. I never was so weak."

"You better just be still."

"What about the babies?"

"Me and Rose will take care of them." She smiled suddenly. "Maybe we'll make Brennan change their diapers a few times. He might learn something."

⌒

BY THE NEXT DAY Temperance was better, and on the second day after the sickness hit her, she said to Brennan, "I think I can go on now."

"All right," he said. "I'd just as soon be on our way."

Immediately he rose, and Temperance could hear his voice as he urged the kids to do the chores. Within an hour they were rolling along. Temperance stayed in the wagon, lying down. The swaying motion sometimes made her nauseous, but she steadfastly ignored it.

Early in the afternoon Brennan pulled up. He unyoked the oxen and came over to help Temperance out of the wagon. "I think there might be some squirrel or quail over yonder. I'll take Bent with me. Maybe we can get a mess."

Temperance was alarmed. She did not want to be left alone, but she did not say so. "All right," she said. "I'll get the fire started."

"No need to do that. I've been picking up wood all day, throwing it in the box." He turned and walked away abruptly. She heard him say, "Bent, come on."

Rena appeared, asking, "Where are you going?"

"Going hunting." He walked to his gear, pulled a small pistol out, and handed it to Rena. "If anybody messes with you, shoot 'em."

Rena suddenly laughed. "You mean it?"

"Aw, nobody will show up. Come on, Bent."

Bent was there at once. He watched as Brennan swung into the saddle and then kicked his foot out of the stirrup. "Come on. Get on behind me."

Bent scrambled on quickly. He seemed a long way from the ground. He noticed that Brennan had brought the two shotguns, and now he handed the smaller one back. "That's your gun. Try not to shoot me, will you? It's Monday. It'd be just my dumb luck!"

❧

BENT'S FACE WAS GLOWING. He felt the weight of the bag and said in awe, "We must have ten squirrels in here."

"And about that many quail too. You're a pretty good shot. You must have hunted a lot."

"No, I ain't never been hunting."

"Well," Brennan said, "I'll just have to turn all the hunting over to you. We'd better get on back now. We've got to cook these critters up."

By the time they got back to camp, Bent was bubbling over. He almost fell off Judas, holding up the bag of game. "Look, Rena, squirrels! I shot four of them myself and I got three quail."

Rena came over at once. "You shot them yourself, Bent?"

"I sure did. He let me use the little shotgun."

"That's enough talk. Anybody know how to clean squirrels?"

"Not me," Rena said.

"Well, shucks! I got to do everything myself. You and Bent get the fire going. I'll clean all these critters. After supper I'm going to give you a special treat."

Temperance offered to help, but Brennan shook his head. "You stay out of this. I'm the cook tonight. I got something that's going to make you feel a heap better."

Since she was allowed to do nothing, Temperance seated herself and watched Brennan and was soon filled with wonder at how quick he was. He had a way of cleaning the quail so they practically fell out of their feathers. With the squirrels it was the same way. He had a huge knife that was sharp as a razor; and with two or three motions and one quick cut, he put his hand on the squirrel's head and ripped the hide off. He gutted them, tossed them in a pile, and then cut them into small pieces. He didn't speak, but she was amazed, as always, at how handy he was. He rolled the quail in flour and cut up the squirrels into serving pieces. There was a piece of salt pork, and he put the pork in the skillet and cooked them until they were brown, adding water and simmering them until they were tender. He cooked the quail in a half inch of hot grease and made gravy by adding flour to it.

He opened the Dutch oven and said, "Everything's ready." He pulled out the pan of biscuits. "Let's eat."

They all gathered around, and Bent's eyes were glowing. "I like to hunt. I'm going to hunt all the time. Maybe I'll get me a deer one day."

"Maybe you might even get a buffalo."

"Really!" Bent's eyes grew wide as half-dollars.

"Really. Now eat."

They all ate hungrily. After they were through with the meal, Brennan said, "All right. I got a special treat going." He took a large pot and disappeared. He was back in less than four minutes. The pot was brimming. "Everybody get a cup," he commanded.

They all scrambled for cups, and he poured each a drink and said, "Here, add some of this to it."

"What is it?" Rena asked.

"I mixed up some honey and some vanilla flavoring. Put it in that water."

They obeyed his instructions and he said, "Drink up." Temperance cautiously tasted it, and then a shock ran through her. "Why, this is like soda pop!"

"That's where we are, Soda Springs. I don't know what there is, something about this water, that's all bubbly, like they say, champagne here."

"It's the best soda pop I ever had," Bent cried. "Can I have some more?"

"Drink until you pop for all I care."

Bent tried to do that, and Temperance asked Brennan, "How long have you known about this place?"

"Everybody that goes over the trail knows about Soda Springs. I always used to stop here to drink the stuff. Almost anything is good in it."

It was growing darker now, and the sun was dropping into the west. The kids had followed his instructions and left the two infants on the pallet. They had gone to get more of the carbonated water. "Timmy's crawling away."

"I'll get him," Brennan said. He picked the baby up awkwardly and looked at her. "What do I do with him?"

"He just wants to be held awhile."

He brought the baby and handed him to Temperance, upon which Bess started crying.

"What do I do with her?"

"Hold her for a little bit. She likes to be held."

"I ain't much with babies," Brennan said.

"She won't bite you. If she does, she doesn't have any teeth."

Brennan awkwardly picked up Bess and stood there looking helpless. It amused Temperance that this man, so handy at all things, could not handle a small child. "Sit down, Thaddeus. She just needs a little company."

Brennan looked at the baby as if she were a foreign object. He held her at arm's length and Temperance laughed. "Don't hold her like that. Cuddle her like this."

"I ain't cuddling no baby," Brennan muttered. Nevertheless, his arms grew tired and he sat the child on his lap and supported her with the back of his arm. She looked up at him suddenly and grinned.

"Why, she just grinned at me."

"She's quite a flirt."

Cautiously Brennan stuck his finger out, and the baby took it and immediately tried to put it in her mouth.

"My hands are dirty."

"It won't kill her. She likes something to chew on."

Brennan allowed the baby to gnaw on his fingers, and he studied her own tiny fingers. "Look at that. She's got fingers just like a real human being."

Temperance could not help but laugh. "She *is* a real human being, you idiot! What do you think she is?"

Brennan did not answer. He seemed to be fascinated by the child. Finally Temperance said, "What comes next?"

"The next thing is the Sublette Cutoff. Named after an old-time mountain man. We can save a couple of days, but it's mighty thirsty. We'll have to fill up everything we've got with water. Be hard on the stock, but I want to save time."

"And then what?"

"And then we go through the South Pass. All the trains come through there." Brennan lifted his head. He saw the kids come back and said, "One of you come here and get this here baby. I ain't got time for messing with no youngun."

Rena picked Bess up. "First baby you ever held, I bet."

"No, she's not. I held my baby sister right after she was born and lots of times after." Brennan got up abruptly. "I've got to see to the stock."

"I never thought I'd ever see him hold a baby," Rena said, watching him disappear into the darkness.

"Neither did I, Rena." She held Timmy close and said, "I think I'll be better tomorrow. We can make better time."

"I don't care," Rena said. "I ain't in no hurry to get nowhere."

THE SOUTH PASS WAS a disappointment to Temperance. They had passed through the Sublette Cutoff and it had, indeed, been a dry, arid time, but Brennan had found one spring in the middle, so it wasn't as bad as he had predicted. She had been walking alongside Babe when he had brought his horse up beside her. "There it is, the South Pass," he had said.

Looking up South Pass was nothing like the dramatic gorge that Temperance had imagined. It was simply a graceful arch coming down from the mountains. The oxen had no trouble pulling over the rise, and when they had passed through, it was high noon.

"Reckon we'll pull in here for the day. I'll go see if I can shoot a deer. Could use some venison, maybe even a buffalo."

"Can I go?" Bent asked.

"Not this time. Next time, Bent."

Temperance watched with apprehension, as always, when he proposed to leave them alone, but she said nothing. When he had ridden out of sight, she walked to where Rena was already pulling out the implements for cooking supper. "It bothers me to be left alone, Rena."

"We'll be all right. Maybe a wagon train will come along. We'll get to see somebody. I get lonesome."

"We haven't seen many."

"That's because Brennan won't let us. What's he afraid of? Is he wanted by the law?"

In that instance Temperance almost spoke the truth, but she managed to keep the heart of the matter to herself. "I'll fix supper tonight. You fix the fire."

❧

AS BRENNAN RODE ALONG the width of the trail leading out of the South Pass, he scanned the area closely. They were getting close to Cheyenne territory, and the one thing he didn't want to see was a Cheyenne party. He saw no deer, but he had not expected to. The wagon trains were getting thicker now, scaring the game away. There was not time enough to go deeper into the hills to find game, so he was almost ready to turn back when suddenly he saw something on the ground a few hundred yards away. He could not identify it, so he urged Judas forward at a lope. As soon as he was within a hundred yards, the grim knowledge came to him. It was a body. He pulled Judas up, stepped out of the saddle, and tied him to a sapling. He thought at first it was a dead body, but a groan came from the figure, and when he reached down, he saw it was a woman.

Squatting beside her, he rolled her over and saw that she had been beaten severely. Her eyes were both blackened, and blood trickled down her cheek.

"Are you all right, lady?" He started to pull her up, but she cried out sharply, and he began to look for a bullet entrance in her dress. There was no arrow; he saw that at once.

"Now what am I going to do with you out here in the middle of nowhere?" he said. "And who left you in this mess?"

A scheme ran through his head—one that would work. There was a stream a few hundred yards away, and mounting Judas, he rode quickly to it. With his big bowie knife he trimmed two long saplings. He always carried strips of rawhide in his saddlebag, and using the blanket, he rigged a travois and rode back. He tied Judas to the sapling and went to the woman. She groaned and opened her eyes for an instant. Her lips were swollen, but she tried to speak.

"You're all right, ma'am. Was it Indians?"

The woman, who seemed to be somewhere around twenty-five, shook her head. "No—not Indians."

"Got to pick you up. I know you're hurt." She did not answer, and picking her up, he put her in the travois. He lashed her in with more strips of rawhide, mounted the stallion, and started back toward the wagon, avoiding the potholes and ridges as best he could. From time to time the woman gave a groan, but there was no help for that.

❧

ROSE WAS FEEDING TIMMY his usual meal of mush and goat's milk, Bent was taking care of Bess, and Rena and Temperance were washing diapers. Suddenly Bent stood up and squinted toward the east. "There comes Brennan." He peered harder and said, "He's pulling something with Judas."

Temperance at once stood up and walked over to stand beside Bent. "What is that?" she asked.

Rena joined them so that all three were watching. As soon as Judas was close enough, it was Bent who said, "There's somebody in that thing he's pulling."

Brennan stopped Judas, stepped out of the saddle, and said, "Well, just my luck. You might know it's a Monday."

Temperance, Rena, and Bent went at once. "Why, it's a woman!" Bent exclaimed. "What's the matter with her?"

"Somebody beat her up. Don't expect she'll live," Brennan answered, holding onto Judas's bridle to keep him still. "Just what we needed—a dying woman to take care of."

"Don't be foolish. She'll be all right," Temperance said. "We'll fix a bed for her. Rena, you help."

Quickly the two of them pulled blankets out and had a bed made. "Bring her over here, Thaddeus," Temperance said. She watched as the tall man loosened the thongs and scooped the woman up. "She's hurt pretty bad." He put her down carefully, ignoring the groans.

"Can you speak?" Temperance said.

They all watched her eyes, nearly swollen shut and already turning glorious shades of green and purple. "I hurt. Can I have some water?" she whispered.

"I'll get it," Bent said. He got a glass, filled it with water, and brought it back.

"Hold her up so she can drink, Thaddeus," Temperance said.

The woman drank thirstily and cried out when she lay down.

"You got some ribs busted, lady. What's your name?"

"Belle—Belle Vernay."

"What happened to you?"

The woman called Belle squinted up at him. She whispered, "I got rid of a worthless man."

"Looks to me like he got rid of you. He just left you there?"

"He was . . . even more worthless than I thought."

"That's enough talk. We've got to clean her up," Temperance said. She bathed the woman's wounded face as well as she could but then looked down. "Where do you hurt?"

"My side," Belle whispered.

"Might have some ribs busted. We'll have to tie them up," Brennan said.

"You know how to do that, Thaddeus?"

"Well, I've done it for a man or two. Never a woman, but if the Book's right, a man's got one less rib than a woman."

"Never mind that," Temperance said. "Tell us what to do."

"Got to have lots of strips of cloth. Maybe tear up a sheet or old clothes or something. And dose her up good with laudanum. She's going to need it."

Temperance rose and got the laudanum. She gave the woman a strong dose. Brennan said, "You kids vamoose."

"Why?" Rena said. "I want to watch."

"Mind what I tell you. Git!"

As soon as the kids left, Temperance began tearing a sheet into strips at Brennan's direction. "That'll be enough," he said. "Here, you've got to sit up, Belle." Belle cried out as he helped her into a sitting position. "Got to take your dress off," Brennan said. "You want to do this, Peabody?"

"I wouldn't know how."

164

"Her dress has got to come down."

Temperance unbuttoned the woman's dress and pulled it down. She was shocked to see the woman wearing nothing underneath it. Brennan paid no attention to the woman's naked form. He began putting the strips around her, pulling them tight. He ignored her grunts, and finally he finished and tied them off. "Put her dress back on." Temperance obeyed, and then he said, "I don't think they're broke—just cracked. Ain't nothing hurts worse than a cracked rib. You stay with her. I'll fix up some eggs."

"I need . . . . to lay down," Belle whispered. Temperance helped her, and Belle's eyes went to Brennan, who was before the fire. "Is he your man?"

"No, he just works for me."

Belle Vernay's eyes were mere slits, and her face was puffy, but she managed a slight smile. "Pretty handy sort of man."

Brennan was not gone long when he brought back a plate of eggs. "Reckon you can eat these. Nothing better for you than fresh eggs." Belle took a bite, and it was obviously painful.

When she had eaten and drunk a great deal of water, she looked up and said, "What's your name?"

"Brennan."

"Well, Brennan, I reckon you saved my life. I guess I belong to you now."

"Don't be silly," Temperance said. "No one should belong to anybody, not that way."

"What were you doing out here, all beat-up?" Brennan asked.

"I been in California. There was a man there, a good-looking fellow. He was going to take me to New Orleans and set me up. You think I'd know better, but I believed him. Maybe I just wanted to get back home again."

"You from New Orleans?"

"Baton Rouge."

"Why'd he beat you up?"

"We had a disagreement." Belle Vernay's eyes closed. The pain was getting worse. She began drifting off, and within a few minutes her speech was slurred. Temperance leaned forward to catch her words. "He won this one, but he won't win the next one though. I'll plant a bullet right between his eyes!"

Brennan stared down at the woman. "Well, that's what we needed—a sick, beat-up woman to help us along."

"I'm glad you found her, Brennan. She would have died if you hadn't."

"Maybe we'll run into that fellow that left her," he said, and his eyes gleamed. "That would be downright interesting."

"Will you shoot him?"

"No, I reckon I'd let Belle do that. It sounds like she is looking forward to it. Get some sleep. I guess we'd better get this hospital rolling as early as we can in the morning. Might be some more sick, beat-up women or orphans to pick up along the way."

Temperance reached out. "You did good, Thaddeus," she said, and her eyes were warm. "You saved her life."

The words embarrassed Thaddeus Brennan. "About time I did something good," he said. He rose and walked away without a backward look.

Chapter Twelve

FOR THREE DAYS AFTER Brennan found Belle, there was little haste on the journey. Temperance had improved rapidly and was back to full strength, with a glow of health in her cheeks. She now sat beside Belle in the wagon, balancing herself automatically as the oxen pulled them along at a faster clip than usual. Turning, she studied Belle, who was holding Timmy on her lap facing her. Her ribs had improved rapidly, although she still winced at times when she made a sudden movement.

"I think Timmy likes you," Temperance smiled, studying the fat baby who was gurgling and reaching for Belle's face.

Belle ran her hand over the baby's silky hair. "He probably thinks I'm a clown with these purple eyes." All of her bruises had turned purple but were fading. "I expect that's why he likes me."

"Be careful you don't hurt your ribs. I'm glad they weren't broken."

"Thad said I would be laid up for a month or more. He said he got his ribs broken once, and it hurt worse than anything he ever had."

"How did he break them?"

"In a fight somewhere."

Gus, who had been asleep under the canvas, suddenly appeared. He leaped easily onto the seat and crawled into Temperance's lap. He looked up, studied her, and said, "Yow!"

"That cat sure loves you."

"He ought to. I found him when he was a starving kitten and I treated him like a baby. He's spoiled to pieces."

"Nice to have something that loves you."

The remark caught Temperance's attention. "Yes, it is," she said curiously. Then she asked the question that had been on her mind for three days. "Are you anxious to get back home?"

"Be good to get back to Baton Rouge. I've got friends there, but I'm going to New Orleans."

"You know anybody there?"

"No, but it's not hard to meet people in that place."

Rena, who had been riding in the back, suddenly appeared. She did not crowd in the front seat but knelt behind it, balanced between the two women. She was fascinated by Belle but studied the woman cautiously. "Were you a saloon woman?"

"I've been just about everything, honey. Some I wish I hadn't been."

"Why'd you do it then? My ma was a saloon woman," Rena said and studied Belle's face to see the reaction.

"So was mine," Belle said. "I ran away from her when I was fourteen years old."

"I'm twelve. I'm going to run away if my aunt and uncle are mean to me."

"What about Bent and Bess? You can't run away and take two kids with you."

"I'll find a way."

"Maybe they'll be just what you need," Temperance said quickly.

"That's not what Ma said."

Temperance opened her mouth to make a remark but discovered she had none to make. She was relieved of the responsibility when Brennan, who had been walking alongside the lead oxen, called out, "Whoa!" and the wagon lurched to a stop. "We'll stay here for the night," Brennan said. "Been hot today."

That was a signal for the work to begin, and everybody except Belle went to his or her chores. Brennan had picked up dry wood along the way as was his habit, so there was no need to collect firewood. As the sun began to enfold itself on the earth in the west, the fire dotted the prairie with its cheerful yellow blaze. Temperance milked the goat and then cooked a quick supper. Brennan had knocked down a few sage hens. She baked them on sticks. As she tended the meal, which included baked potatoes and the inevitable mush for the baby, she saw that Brennan was talking to Belle. She could hear their words clearly enough and found herself listening intently.

"Have you ever been in New Orleans, Thad?"

"Twice. Wound up in trouble both times. That's a sinful place." He grinned rashly, his teeth white against his tanned skin. "I think I had a good time, but I was too drunk to remember most of it. What'll you do when you get there, Belle?"

"Oh, I'll find something." Belle reached up and touched her face. "These bruises will be gone by that time."

"What was that fellow's name that put you out?"

"Benteen. Dirk Benteen."

"Dirk's a funny name."

"That's another name that sailors give to a knife. He always carries it with him." She shivered slightly and said, "I saw him cut a man all to pieces with it in San Francisco."

"Be interesting to meet up with him."

"What would you do if we did?" Belle said, turning to face Brennan.

"Why, I might ask him to explain why he would beat up a nice lady and put her afoot on the prairie."

"Don't have anything to do with him if we do catch him. He's mean."

Brennan smiled. "I'm mean myself, Belle."

"No, you're not. You're rough, but you're not mean." Belle took a deep breath. "How long do I have to wear these bandages?"

"Oh, you can take them off just about any time."

Temperance had been poking the sage hens and called out, "Supper's ready!"

Brennan rose to his feet, stretched lazily, and said, "You know what I fancy right now? A nice glass of ice water. Been hot today."

Belle laughed. She seemed always amused by Brennan. "Well, you won't find ice water around here."

"You want to bet?"

"I don't have anything to bet, but maybe I'll think of something."

"There's no ice around here," Bent said, staring at Brennan. "You're always saying things like that."

"I always tell the precise, exact truth, Bent. You don't think I can find ice in this place?"

"No," Bent said stubbornly.

"What about you, Rena? You think I can find ice?"

"No, not out here. It's hotter than blazes."

"Well, it does hurt my feelings that my folks I travel with have no confidence." He turned and studied Temperance. "What about you, Peabody? You think I can work a little miracle?"

"I think that's what it would take." Temperance had grown somewhat accustomed to Brennan's ways. "If you say you can do it, Thaddeus, I suppose you can, but I don't see how."

"Well, I'm glad I got one believer in this crowd. You folks just watch this." He went swiftly to the wagon, picked up a shovel, and began digging a few feet away from the campsite.

"You're going to dig up ice?" Rena laughed and said scornfully.

Brennan didn't answer, but a few seconds later they heard the shovel hit something hard. "You hit bedrock," Belle said. "I didn't know rock was that close to the surface."

Brennan took the pick he had brought also and began striking the hard surface. He leaned forward and filled both hands with what appeared to be rock. "How about this?" he said. He handed one chunk to Belle and another to Bent.

"Why—it *is* ice!" Bent said with astonishment.

"It sure is," Belle said, blinking with surprise. "What's it doing here?"

"I ought not to tell you since you doubted me, Belle. But maybe you'll believe me from now on." He waved his arms around and said, "This is what they call Ice Slough. There's a bed of ice about a foot down. It's there year-round."

"What's ice doing here?" Temperance asked with astonishment. She went over to the hole and picked up a fragment of ice.

"You don't realize how high we are. About seven thousand feet. What do you say I chunk some of this out and we wash it off and if we had some lemons, we could have some lemonade—if we had some sugar too."

"I'll make up something," Temperance said. "Maybe vanilla soda. That worked with that carbonated water."

Soon all of them were sipping the ice they had washed in the stream, and Brennan was laughing.

Afterward the camp grew quiet, but they noticed that Brennan carried his rifle around camp, which was unusual.

"You expecting trouble, Thaddeus?" Temperance asked.

"Just pays to be safe."

"No, it's more than that. I can tell you're expecting something."

"Could be Cheyenne around here. I don't think so though. Just pays to keep your eyes open."

Temperance would have asked more, for she was worried, but at that moment Belle came over and said, "Well, Thad, I'm ready to get rid of these bandages. You want to give me a hand?"

Thad grinned at her, and she was staring up at him with a provocative light in her eye. Even with her face marked by bruises, she was an attractive woman. "It'd be unseemly for me to do that. I'd shock your modesty."

"Not mine. Yours, I expect."

"You're right. I'm easily shocked. Peabody, help this woman take them bandages off. Reckon I'll take a little walk around. You won't see me, but I'll be out there."

Temperance and Belle watched as the tall man disappeared into the darkness.

"Well, that didn't work," Belle said.

"What didn't work?"

Belle suddenly laughed. "Why, I was trying to tempt our guide. I was too beat-up when he stripped me down and put those bandages on, but I'm feeling better now."

Temperance stared at her and could not think of a reply. Finally she said, "Do you really want to take the bandages off?"

"No, leave them on. They don't do much good now, but it'll give me an excuse to get Doctor Brennan to help me with them." She looked at Temperance and saw something in her face. "What's the matter? You afraid I'll steal your man?"

"He's *not* my man, Belle."

Belle studied Temperance carefully. "You've never been married, have you?"

"No, I haven't."

"Why not?"

"There wasn't much of an opportunity for courting."

"What held you back?"

"My parents were very strict when I was growing up. Then they got sick and they kept men away from me most of the time." She found herself telling Belle about her strange life, how the religious group her parents were with had placed very rigid restrictions on their women.

Belle listened and finally said, "But your parents are gone now, you say."

"Yes, they are, both of them."

"Well, you must want a man." This was a simple enough matter to Belle, but it troubled Temperance.

"Not every woman has to have a man."

"Well, *I* want one." She looked out into the darkness as if she might see Brennan, then said, "There are worse out there than Thad. I met some of them."

Belle turned away and Temperance watched her go. The conversation had disturbed her deeply, but Timmy began crying, and she went to change him. Afterward she sat in front of the fire, rocking him until he went to sleep. Everyone else was tired from the day's journey, and the camp fell silent. She could see Timmy's face by the flickering light of the fire and realized she had become very attached to him. *It'll be hard for me to give him up*, she thought, *but it'll be the best for him*. The thought troubled her and she rose. She took two steps, turning as she did, and then came to an abrupt halt. Her mind seemed to stop for a moment, for there stood an Indian staring at her with obsidian eyes. He held a bow in his left hand, and the very silence at which he had appeared seized her throat with fear.

Temperance thought of screaming or running, but it was obvious she was helpless. She swallowed hard and finally said, "Hello." It sounded like the most ridiculous, mundane thing she could say as soon as the word was uttered; but to her shock and amazement, the dark face of the Indian broke into a smile. He held his hand up in what was obviously a sign of peace, and even as he did, Brennan's voice broke the silence. "Little Bear, I told you not to scare my folks."

The Indian was short and rotund, an older man obviously, for gray was in his hair. He turned to face Brennan, who had appeared almost as silently as the Indian himself. Brennan said, "This is Little Bear, chief of the Pawnees—one of them at least."

Little Bear said something in his native language. It sounded as if he was trying to talk around a mouthful of hot mush, but Brennan obviously understood him well. "He says he's hungry."

"I—I'll fix something."

She at once moved to put Timmy down and quickly brought out what food she could. The quality didn't seem to matter, for Little Bear ate everything she put before him, and finally the two men sat in front of the fire, speaking in the Pawnee language. Belle had not been asleep. She came closer, but the Indian took one look at her and asked a question. Brennan answered, and Belle asked, "What did he want to know?"

Brennan grinned, his eyes glinting with humor. "He wanted to know if I needed another squaw. He says two squaws are not enough for a great hunter like me."

Belle laughed, but Temperance was shocked. "He offered you a squaw?"

"Well, it was the polite thing to do."

The two women listened as the men talked, and finally Little Bear got up, looked at the two women and made a remark, and then left silently.

"What did he say, Thad?"

"Oh, he tried to get me to take the squaw. I figure she's causing some trouble with his tribe, and he thought I could tame her."

"Is that all he said?"

"Not all," Brennan admitted. He saw that the women were waiting for him. "He said be careful. He saw a Cheyenne war party a few days ago. Nothing to worry about. They're not likely to get this close to the fort."

Belle was smiling at Brennan. "Don't you even want to know what the squaw looked like?"

"Maybe I passed up a good deal, but I reckon I got enough to take care of with two women and a wagonload of kids."

Belle stared at him, shook her head, and said, "I'm going to bed. Wake me if the Cheyenne get here."

Temperance was still shocked about the Indian. He had appeared almost like magic, and she admitted, to herself at least, that she was frightened. The Cheyenne could come as Little Bear had and kill them all.

Brennan was studying her. "You're not worried, are you?"

"I am a little."

"It'll be OK. The wagon trains are pretty thick around here, and the fort's not too far away. The Cheyenne aren't likely to make a raid this close to the soldiers."

He looked down at the fire. "I had a good time with Little Bear and his people, but it was a long time ago."

Temperance felt better merely by his presence there. He stood so close she could have reached out and touched him, and finally her curiosity caused her to say, "Would you have taken the squaw if we hadn't been along, all of us, I mean?"

"I don't think so."

Brennan's form was tall and angular, outlined by the flickering fire that cast shadows over his face. "Did you ever have a special feeling for one woman?"

Brennan turned to stare at her. "I did once, but she didn't feel anything for me."

For a moment Temperance tried to imagine what that situation had been like, but then, without thought, the question that had been at the back of her mind for some time came to her and she asked it. The words almost tumbled out of her mouth. "Do you—do you ever think of me as a woman, Thaddeus?"

The question obviously caught Brennan off guard. "Why, Peabody, we haven't done anything but argue since we met. We're too different. One of us would have to change before anything like that could happen."

"I can't change."

"No," Brennan said slowly, "I don't reckon you can."

For a moment the two stood there, and then something whirled rashly between them, something that neither of them could explain. Brennan reached out, brought her to him like a man reaching for something he was not sure of.

When he pulled her close, it seemed that a temptress howling like the winter wind went through Temperance. She had never felt such a thing before, and for that moment she understood what it meant to be a woman. It frightened her but gave her a feeling such as she had never known before. She waited, saying nothing, and Brennan was suddenly aware of the strength and honesty of this woman.

For that one instant Temperance did not move away from the pressure of his hands. He didn't move forward. He pulled her to him, looked down at her face and he saw her lips tremble, and then something came to him. He was a man who had known women, and she was a woman who had never known a man, but at that moment by the flickering fire, he realized she was there waiting for him, and it was her innocence, perhaps, that caused him to stop. He suddenly dropped his arms and said, "I guess I'd better go back on guard."

His words caught Temperance like a blow. She hugged herself and thought, *I wanted him to kiss me, to tell me that I was a woman to be desired.* A bleakness came to her then, and she shook her head. *I'll never have anything like that.* The darkness seemed to close about her, but it was a darkness inside her more than the darkness of the heavens above or the prairie. With a soft meaningless cry, she turned and walked blindly back toward the wagon.

PART THREE
Quaid

Chapter Thirteen

A GUSTY BREEZE STIRRED the air with sweet, musty, and pungent odors as Rena plodded along beside the wagon. Sunlight ran fresh and fine across the prairie and on the surface of the Sweetwater River bordered by the road. From far up ahead she could see a wagon train approaching, and a queer twinge rose in her—a stray current of something painful from her past. A sharp regret brought a furrow to her forehead, and her mouth twisted in a grimace. Rena often had these moments of remorse that amounted almost to a psychic pain as she thought back over the tangled skeins of her twelve years. Sometimes she would think of girls her age who had pleasant, fine, warm memories of a home with a loving mother, a faithful father, and a life of stability. None of that had been hers, and there was an inner longing she could never subdue, try however hard she might.

Far off to her right, four antelope appeared almost magically, so it seemed, created for that moment. They stood motionless in their private tableau, watching the passing of the wagon, and Rena wondered what sort of thoughts went through an antelope's mind. She knew they were intensely curious, for Thad had once put a flag on a bush and told them to watch. She and Bent had waited, and sure enough the antelope, attracted by the white flapping cloth, moved closer and closer. Thad could have shot one of them easily, but they already had food and he passed up the opportunity by saying, "We'll save them for another day."

A slight cadence of sound caught her ear, and, turning quickly, she glimpsed a small bird with white stripes on its back. It was perched in a shrub watching her, its eyes like living beads, and it made a small syncopated sort of song as she passed. Her mind made a sudden leap and she thought back to the time when she was only five years old or six, she could not remember which. Her parents had gotten a calf, and in the dead of winter, one freezing night, the cold laid its iron grasp on the earth—and on the calf. Rena had gone out the next morning and found it lying stiffly. She had wept over it, but then a sign of life appeared in a mere flickering of its eyelid. She had run and gotten her father, and they had pulled the animal into the house where it revived. They nursed it back to health, and it became a pet for Rena. She remembered as she walked along, her eyes fixed on the horizon, how she had cried for days when her father sold the calf and then he and her mother spent the money on whiskey.

Suddenly a movement caught her eye, and Bent, who had been riding on Babe, slipped to the ground and came running to her, stirring up small clumps of dust under his feet.

"Where's Thad?" he demanded.

"Out hunting, I guess."

"I wish he had let me go with him."

"Don't try to make a friend out of Thad," Rena said shortly and watched an expression she could not quite define wash across her brother's face. It was almost as if a curtain had been pulled aside, and she saw there some of the pain and disappointment she herself felt.

"Why not? I like to be friends with Thad."

"He'll be gone soon. There's no sense making friends with somebody you know you're going to lose."

Bent lengthened his steps to keep pace with Rena. He glanced up in the wagon where Temperance was making cooing noises to Bess, who lay in her lap. He did not speak for a time, but his silence was eloquent. Finally he said, "I don't care what you say. I want to have friends."

Rena shook her head. "Don't get too close to anyone." Bitterness rang in her tone. "You'll get hurt."

"I can't help it. I've got to have some friends, don't I?"

"You've got me and Bess, but we're going to lose everybody else." Suddenly she heard Bess crying and shook her head. "I'm going to ride in the wagon awhile." She looked at him and suddenly reached out in a rare gesture of affection and ruffled his hair. "Maybe we'll find friends when we get older." She left him then, not looking back, for she knew she had hurt him and it grieved her. He and Bess were all she had now. The future was tinged with darkness, and a sense of fear touched her as she crawled up in the wagon.

"I think she needs changing," Temperance smiled.

"I'll do it."

"What were you and Bent talking about?"

Rena expertly stripped the diaper from Bess, and her hands were nimble as she fastened another one on. "I was telling him not to make friends with Thad."

"You don't like Thad?"

"It doesn't matter whether I do or not."

"Why would you say that?"

"Because, after you dump us in Baton Rouge, we won't ever see you again."

Temperance tried to think of a response. She had none and finally said gently, "Maybe it will be better than you think."

"No, it won't."

Temperance shook her head, then stepped out of the wagon. She made her way to where Bent was walking along, his eyes on the ground in front of him. "What's the matter, Bent? You look like you bit into a sour pickle."

"Nothing."

"Oh, come on now. You can tell me."

Bent looked up at her, and she saw the pain in his green eyes. The summer's darkness was on his skin, and a line of freckles crossed his cheeks and dotted his nose. "She said I can't be friends with Thad."

"Well, she may be right about that."

Instantly he looked up at her. "Don't you like Thad?"

"He's—he's not a steady man." She tried to think of some way to put it without completely destroying the boy's faith in Thaddeus, and finally she shook her head and lifted her eyes to the far distance. "I can't understand a man like that. Unreliable. You can't count on him."

"He takes me hunting sometimes."

"That's no trouble to him. He looks out for nobody but himself."

"I don't care what you and Rena say. I'm going to be friends with Thad. But when I get to Louisiana, I'm going to run away when I get old enough. I'm not going to live with those people."

Temperance started to speak, but before she could, Bent suddenly broke into a dead run. He ran lightly as a young deer, and she watched as he separated himself from the wagon. Pain came to Temperance then. She had had an unhappy childhood herself, but nothing like the Overmeyer children were facing. *God, help them*, she prayed. *They need You.*

❧

NOON CAME, AND THADDEUS had not appeared. Temperance had walked beside Babe and stopped the big animal with a firm word. Belle came up and asked curiously, "I saw you talking to Bent. What was that all about?"

"Rena told him that he couldn't be friends with Thad, and I guess I agreed with her. He's not a steady man. I never could understand a man like that."

"I can," Belle said. She was wearing one of Temperance's dresses, and being a larger woman, she filled it out almost to the point of immodesty, which did not bother her in the least. "I guess Thad and I are a lot alike."

"He's not a man that Bent and Rena can depend on."

"He's steady enough for me." Belle grinned suddenly, and despite the remaining marks from the beating, a sensuous beauty was etched across her features. "He wouldn't do for you, Temperance. You and him just would never make a match."

"Of course we wouldn't. I'd have no man who wasn't reliable."

Belle did not answer for a moment. Her mouth twisted in a hint of a smile, and her eyes sparkled. "Preacher lady, you've got some funny ideas in your mind about a man. This man you think of is perfect. He doesn't have any faults. He always does what's right, he never makes mistakes, and he's a perfect gentleman at all times." She suddenly laughed aloud. "The trouble is, there's not any man like that, and you'd never be happy unless he was perfect. You better learn to take people as they are."

Temperance turned quickly and saw that Belle was laughing at her. She was so different from this woman. The two of them had followed different pathways, had different values. She knew that Belle was immoral, that she had sinned against God in every way a woman could, yet despite this, there was a liveliness in the woman Temperance knew was lacking in her own makeup. It bothered her, and she suddenly felt an impulse to talk to Belle about her soul.

"Don't you ever think about what it'll be like to face God on judgment day, Belle?" she asked urgently.

"I don't think about things like that. Just make it through the day. That's all I've got to do." She waited to see if Temperance would preach her a sermon, and when she got no reply, she nodded. "You've given up on me. Good!"

"I haven't given up on you, Belle. I just don't know how to talk to anybody like you." Temperance paused before returning to the business at hand. "We need to get busy. I'll cook the stew if you'll take care of the kids."

They fell into the routine of work. Rena milked the goat, and Temperance soon had a stew simmering in a black iron pot over a quickly built fire. Rose was playing with Billy when suddenly she called out, "There comes Thad!"

"I declare, honey," Belle said, "you've got sharp eyes. You can see farther than any of us." She stood up and waited until Thad came in, then smiled at him. "We thought you'd left us."

"Not likely." Thad dismounted, and when Judas tried to bite him, he struck him in the nose with his fist.

"You're hard on horses," Belle remarked.

"Women and horses need a firm hand." Thad grinned. He glanced over at Rena, who was watching him. "Kids too. When I get married I'm going to have six kids, and I'm going to keep

4

seven switches. One for my wife and a special switch for each youngun. I'm going to start out every day"—he pulled out the makings of a cigarette and started to roll it—"by whipping them just to get ahead of the game. That way if they do something I don't like, they've already had their beating."

Belle laughed. "I'm glad you told me about all that. You know, if you marry me and you whip me, I'll wait until you go to sleep. Then I'll pour boiling water right where it hurts."

Temperance had been listening. She was accustomed to Thad's mild teasing and wished at times she had a lightness about her that Belle had—without Belle's other qualities, of course, that bothered her. "The stew's ready."

Thad came over, squatted before the fire, and took the bowl of stew she handed him. He began to eat noisily, and Rena said in disgust, "You eat like a pig, Thad. Don't you have any manners?"

"I'm saving them until I need them. You've got manners enough for all of us. You ladies can give us the manners."

"Your hands are filthy!" Temperance snapped.

"If you think my hands are dirty, you ought to see my feet." Thad grinned, pleased that he had irritated her, then slurped the stew noisily. When Temperance asked if he wanted more, he shook his head. "No. Going to have something better than stew meat tonight." He waved his arm toward the horizon on his left. "Found a small herd of buffalo. Kind of surprising. Most of them have wandered off to get away from the trail and the wagon trains."

"Why didn't you bring one back?" Bent asked.

"They're too darn big. We'll go where they are. I'll shoot one, and tonight we'll eat high on the hog." He was in a good mood although he had been drinking. His cheeks were flushed, and he leaned back and made a smoke, and when he blew a puff in the air, he waved it around. "The best part of a buffalo is the tongue and the liver. I'm going to give the liver to you, Peabody. You need to eat it raw. It's a lot better that way."

"I'm not eating any raw liver," Temperance insisted.

"Well, you'll miss out on a blessing then."

"You really eat the liver raw?" Bent said. "What does it taste like?"

"Raw liver." He laughed and said, "Come on, Bent, you're a mite small for a buffalo gun, but I'll show you how it's done. When you get a little bigger, you can shoot your own buffalo."

Bent immediately got to his feet, his eyes shining. He watched as Thad swung into the saddle and whispered to Rena, "You see, Rena, he does like me."

"It don't cost him anything to take you with him," Rena said.

Bent ignored her, however, and when Thad kicked his foot out of the stirrup, he scrambled aboard the horse behind him. "Just head right over that way, Peabody. It's not too far. I'll keep an eye out for you so you won't get lost." He kicked his heels against Judas's side, and the big horse leaped into a dead run.

"I'm not eating any raw liver," Temperance said defiantly.

"You ought to try it, Temperance," Belle laughed, her eyes shining. "You need to try new things. Get out of the rut you're in."

⁓

BENT LOOKED AT THE six buffalo that had found a small spring. He saw two of them wallowing in it, and Thad shook his head. "Buffalo can sure mess up a spring. Just imagine driving to get to a spring and there's a thousand buffalo done messed in it and wallowed in it."

"A thousand! You ever see that many, Thad?"

"Oh yeah. More than that. Sometimes there's just too many to count. Not like that anymore. Buffalo don't stay around where the wagon trails are. Still, up north you can probably find some big herds."

"How close do we have to get for you to hit one?"

"We're close enough. Jump down."

Bent slipped off Judas's back, and Thad nodded. "Here, you hold on to the horse while I bring one down."

With some apprehension Bent looked at the big horse. He knew that Judas was known for biting Thad every chance he got or kicking him, whichever was easiest. "He might bite me."

"Nah, he won't do that. It's me he likes to chew on." Thad pulled out his big Henry, checked the load, then threw the gun up. The explosion came with no hesitation, and Bent watched, then said, "You missed him, Thad."

"No, I didn't. Just watch that big one over there to the left."

Bent watched as the big buffalo seemed to be ambling away. He took four or five steps and then suddenly started to collapse. He hunched up in the middle and went down in a heap, his feet kicking.

"The rest of them didn't even run away."

"Buffalo ain't very smart. Come on, we'll shoo them off. Keep the wolves and the coyotes and the vultures off until the wagon gets here."

The two of them wandered over, and Bent edged closer to the dead buffalo. "I got him right there, right behind his front leg. See where the bullet went in?"

"I wish I could shoot one."

"You're a might small for a big buffalo gun like this Henry. When you get a little older, though, you'll try it."

Bent suddenly turned, and the words seemed to spring out of his mouth. "Do you like me, Thad?"

Thad was reloading the Henry. He stopped and turned to half face the boy. "Why, I reckon I do. What makes you ask that?"

"I just wondered."

Thad was studying the boy hard, wondering what prompted the question. He was thinking, *I guess he's had a hard time just like I did. I hope things go better for him.*

"Well, let's take the hide off this fellow and cut up some steaks. We can gather some firewood too. I'm mighty hungry for buffalo."

Bent watched for a time as Thad butchered the buffalo. It was hard, heavy work, and Thad shook his head and looked at the big knife he carried at his side most of the time. "Nothing like a buffalo hide to dull a knife."

He continued working and sweating profusely. The sun was easing down in the west as the wagon came lumbering over the broken ground. When it pulled up, Belle came running forward. "You got one!" she said.

"Why, my mama didn't raise no bad shots. 'Course I got one." He winked at Belle then reached down and pulled something from the sack of meat he had stacked on the hide. "Here you go, Peabody, just for you."

Temperance stopped, turned quickly and saw he was holding a mass of raw meat. "Fresh liver," he grinned. "Just take a bite of that."

"I won't do it."

"Would you do it, Thad?" Belle challenged, her eyes dancing.

For an answer Thad took a healthy bite and shook his head as he chewed. "Good stuff. Help yourself, Belle."

"No thanks. I'll take mine cooked."

"Well, if you're going to be that way, then here's the tongue. Cook it if you want to. It's almost as good as the liver."

The two women began cooking the steaks, and soon the juices dripped into the fire, lacing the air with the smell of roasting meat. They ate the steaks hungrily, and Thad said, "Eat all you want to. Buffalo steaks don't set heavy on your stomach. You can eat until you can't hardly walk, and an hour later you're hungry again."

"It is good," Temperance said. "A little tough."

"This was an older fellow. There wasn't no young ones with it, or I would have got it. This meat won't keep in this heat long. Maybe a day or two. We'll sure eat good until it's gone though."

❧

AFTER EVERYONE HAD FINALLY gone to sleep, filled with buffalo steaks, Temperance was holding Timmy, who had a tummy-ache or else was getting a tooth although she could not find one. She was sitting beside the fire, satiated with the full meal, and Thad was sitting with his back to the left rear wagon wheel. He took a drink from the jug and set it down carefully, and she asked suddenly, "Why do you drink so much, Thaddeus?"

"Because I want to."

"It's not good for you."

"It tastes good though. It makes you feel good—"

"I've seen you on some mornings when you didn't feel all that good."

"That's the way it is with life, Peabody. You do something that feels good, you have to pay for it the next day."

Temperance rocked Timmy gently and then said, despite her apprehension, "Bent looks up to you. He wants to be your friend."

"He ought to know better."

"He's six years old, Thaddeus, and he's had no love from anyone—except Rena."

"Well, he better go look somewhere else for it."

Temperance did not answer, but the displeasure was obvious in her face.

"You knew what I was when you asked me to take you over the trail."

Temperance shifted Timmy to her other arm and looked across at Thaddeus. He was sitting in the semidarkness, but the light flickered over his lean features. He had not shaved for several days, and he was a rough sight. "Maybe I thought you'd change."

"Well, I won't."

"Why not?"

"It's too late for me to change."

"That's not so. It's never too late for anyone."

Somehow, the words irritated Brennan. He had thought about Bent's question asking if he liked him, and it disturbed him. He lashed out angrily. "What do you know, Peabody? Why, you can't even catch a man!"

There was no argument. Temperance had heard the same remark from people or seen it in their faces for a long time. She could not answer him, and Thad, in his drunken state, was pleased she was hurt. "Never make me into what I ain't. You can be a preacher if you want to, but just leave me alone."

The fire crackled and a log shifted, sending a myriad of flaming orange and red sparks. They rose in the air and almost seemed to mingle with the real stars overhead. The two of them looked at each other, and then Temperance shook her head, rose, and took Timmy away to put him down. She lay down beside him, and Thaddeus took another swig from the jug. He muttered rebelliously, "That woman better leave me alone, that's all I got to say!"

Chapter Fourteen

BY THE NINETEENTH OF June, Temperance was tired of gathering buffalo chips for fires. So was everyone else, and both Bent and Rena complained about having to pick up the chips that littered the ground. The buffalo were abundant there. Twice they encountered huge buffalo herds, and the great beasts made a roaring noise as they trampled the earth beneath their feet.

"Better be happy they didn't stampede," Brennan said. "That can be downright pesky."

They camped early, and Thad disappeared, claiming to be hunting, but Temperance suspected he was trying to avoid work. She organized a work party to collect the buffalo chips. She had, after a fashion, mastered the art of burning the unusual fuel. They could be brought to a blaze only in a fire pit that Brennan had showed her how to build. It had to be well drafted, and the day before she had had to knead her dough, nurse the fire, and hold an umbrella over it and her skillet for nearly two hours, but she had been determined to bake bread.

Brennan timed his return when the supper was cooked, and Temperance gave him an irritated look. "I might know you'd come in when there wasn't any work to be done."

"I learned that from the Indians," Brennan said, tying Judas to a wagon wheel. "They can't be bothered with women and kids. They've got important things to do like—"

"Like what?" Belle demanded, knowing that Brennan was deliberately aggravating Temperance.

"Why, they've got to smoke their pipes and sit around campfires and tell their lies. Sometimes they play games with a ball of some kind or other. Oh, they've got lots of important stuff to do. They can't be troubled with a bunch of kids and women."

"What's that big rock over there?" Rose interrupted, pointing at an enormous granite monolith that dominated the entire landscape.

"That there is Independence Rock. The most famous rock I know of, I guess," Brennan replied.

"I remember that," Temperance said. "I carved my name on it when we came out headed for Oregon."

"Most everybody does."

Instantly Belle said, "That's what I want to do. Take me up there, Brennan."

"Oh, I've got more important things to do."

"No, you don't," Belle said. She grabbed a handful of his thick, coarse hair and yanked it. "You've got to take me."

"I want to go too," Rena said. And, of course, as soon as she did, Bent chimed in.

In the end they all went except Temperance, who volunteered to keep the younger children. Brennan led Belle, Rena, and Bent out of camp, leaving Temperance alone at the wagon.

"Why didn't you go with them, Temperance?" Rose asked.

"Oh, I'd rather stay with you and Timmy and Bess."

Rose smiled shyly. She had blossomed on the trip and had grown very fond of Temperance. She was watching Timmy, who was crawling industriously around in a circle, to be sure he didn't put anything bad in his mouth. She obviously had something on her mind and finally she said, "I'm afraid of

what's going to happen when we get to where my grandparents live."

"Why, what could happen?"

"They might not like me and Billy."

"Don't be foolish! They'll love you."

"They might not."

Instantly Temperance came over, sat down beside the girl,
and put her arm around her. She hugged her tightly and said
enthusiastically, "There's a foolish girl, you are. You're going to
love it there. You'll go to a nice school, and you and Billy will
have good people to take care of you. I read some of the letters
that your people wrote to your parents. They were always asking about you and saying how they would love to see you, but
it was just too far." For a long time she sat there encouraging
Rose, wondering what kind of people Luther and Rachel Norris
were. She felt more secure about them than she did about the
Overmeyers' people, and finally she challenged Rose by saying,
"Let's you and me cook something fancy tonight."

"Like what?"

"Well," Temperance smiled, "let's make my specialty. I call
it Mary Magdalene's never-fail potato rolls. We've got enough
potatoes left to make it, and it's fun. I'll teach you how."

"Why do they call it Mary Magdalene's?" Rose said.

"I don't know. That's what my mother called it. It's good
though."

For the next half hour the two were busy mixing the goat's
milk, potatoes, and plover eggs they had found on the trail.
Temperance let Rose do as much as possible. Finally they added
enough flour to make a soft dough and rolled it out half an inch
thick and cut it, using an empty can for a biscuit cutter.

"There we go," Temperance said as she shoved the potato

rolls into the Dutch oven and heaped the fire around it. "We let it cook there until they get all done. We may eat them all up, not leave any for the others."

"I like to cook with you, Temperance. I want you to teach me how to make other things."

"I sure will, honey. You'll be an expert cook by the time you get to Fort Smith."

⁓

BY THE TIME THE four had got halfway up Independence Rock, most of them were well winded.

Rena said, "Look at all the names that have been carved."

Indeed, the face of the rock was carved with literally hundreds of names. They all moved around, examining them. Some were marked with dates and others had messages, some of them misspelled.

"I want to carve my name, but I don't have anything to do it with," said Bent.

"Sure you do." Thad reached into his hip pocket and brought out a coal chisel and a hammer hanging from his belt. "Carve away, boy," he grinned. "I'll just sit here and watch."

Bent, after a great deal of rather inept work with the chisel, did manage to put his initials in. Thad took the chisel and said, "Here, it's your turn, Rena."

"No, I don't want to."

"Oh, shoot. Go on and carve your name."

"I won't do it."

"You're as stubborn as a blue-nosed mule! One of these days you can bring your kids back here to this rock, and you'll remember the good-looking guide you had."

Rena glared at him. "You don't care whether I carve my name or not. You don't care about anything."

"Why, sure I do."

"No, you don't. All you care about is yourself." She grabbed Bent by the hand and pulled him back down the trail. "We're going back."

"Wait a minute. Don't run off."

"You're just like my ma and pa," Rena said, glaring back at him. "All you want to do is get drunk."

"Well, ain't that a pretty come-off!" Thad exclaimed, watching the two as they left.

"Will they be all right going back?"

"Why, sure. You can see the wagon right down there. Don't see no Indians about." He was watching the girl with a puzzled expression. He rubbed his jaw thoughtfully. "I wonder what brought that on?"

"Well, she's pretty good at reading people," Belle said. "I was like that when I was her age."

"Why shucks, I drink a little, but I'd never hurt her. I'm getting them to their people just like I said I would."

Belle shook her head. "She's scared, Thad. Don't expect too much from her."

"Well, I ain't scared," he said.

The remark intrigued Belle. "What are you afraid of?"

"Lots of things—Cheyenne Indians cooking me over a fire, rattlesnakes, bossy women."

Belle laughed and sat beside him. He was cross-legged, and she moved close enough so that her body was pressed against his. She took his hand and studied it intently. He had strong hands with blunt fingertips scarred by a lifetime of hard work.

"We know life is hard, you and me. Rena knows it too. She's afraid of those people she's going to."

"Well, maybe they'll be better than she thinks."

A bitterness came then to Belle's generous mouth. "How many things have turned out better than you thought they would, Thad?"

"Well, not too many to be honest. Reckon you're right."

"We're alone up here. I thought there'd be lots of people."

"Sometimes there is. I came through here once when a hundred wagons pulled up down below by the river. You couldn't stir people with a stick. I'm glad they're not here now though."

Brennan turned suddenly and looked at her. He focused his eyes on her lips. They were closed but without pressure, full at the center. She lifted her eyes to his, and suddenly her eyes were heavy and the veiled expression she wore at times broke. Brennan was totally conscious of the touch of her body against him and the feel of her hand holding his. She was watching him in a peculiar way. She made a round, full figure in the daylight, and she was still waiting, her breathing soft, her bosom rising and falling to her breathing.

The urges of a lone man often move like the needle of a compass to a woman, and Brennan was no different. Belle had led a rough life, but she was still attractive. She was a long, round, contoured woman, and even in the relaxed attitude there was a rhythm and a vitality about her. The fragrance of her clothes came powerfully to Brennan, and her soft fragrance slid through the armor of his self-sufficiency. She was watching him in a way he did not quite understand, watching his face in a close and private way, and suddenly she was a shape and a substance before him and a fragrance, and the wall that he held up against most people seemed to drop away. They were alone, she was before him, and without really being aware, he reached out and pulled her close. She lay soft in his arms, her warmth a part of him, and her nearness bringing up his constant, never-lessening want. His urges made a turbulent eddy around them both, and he knew he could not hide what he was feeling from her.

But suddenly he stopped, and Belle stared at him. "What's the matter?"

"Nothing."

"You're not afraid of what that holy woman would say about us, are you?"

"No!" The answer was sharp and short.

"What's wrong with you then?"

"I don't know, Belle. I get mad when things don't work out."

"What's not working out?"

"Those kids. We don't know that their people will have anything to do with them."

She felt rebuffed and was angry, for she had meant to love him, and he had drawn back. "Things are working out. We'll get these kids to their people. You and me will go to New Orleans, and we'll have a good time."

She watched his face. She saw change turn his long lips, a faint impatience seemed to stir in his eyes, and his jaw showed determination shoving squarely at the chin. There was little discipline, she could see, in his face, but then she herself had little of that quality. She sensed a rash and reckless will and a latent storminess of subdued capacity for enormous gusts of feeling that he kept well under control.

Suddenly she pulled herself up and gave him a look of disgust. "We might as well go back."

"All right."

Sudden thoughts came to her and her eyes narrowed. "Temperance Peabody has got some crazy ideas of how things turn out good, but she's wrong." She turned and started down the incline, and Brennan followed her, his face fixed in a puzzled expression.

❧

BY THE TIME THE two got back to camp, the others had already started to eat. They ate the last of the buffalo steaks, but Thad only picked at his. He kept casting his eyes at Rena, who ignored him, and when he finally ventured, "That's a pretty big rock over there, isn't it?" she didn't say a word.

After the meal was over, darkness fell quickly. Belle and Rena helped Temperance clean up, and then Rose said, "Read something to me, Temperance."

"What would you like?"

"Read me a story out of the Bible."

"All right, I will." Temperance went to the wagon, fished her Bible out from under the seat, and returned. She turned a box upside down and sat on it, and Rose sat at her feet, looking up. Belle studied her for a moment, then fell silent, and Thad, who was accustomed to this, also had nothing to say.

"I'm going to read you the story of Daniel." She read the story of the man of God who stood up against the world, and when she had finished, Rose said, "I like that story, Temperance! Daniel was a good man, wasn't he?"

"Yes, he was. He's one of the few men in the Bible who was always faithful. There's not one time in the Scripture that he ever displeased God."

"I wish I could be like that," Rose said.

"Why, you can be, honey."

Rena had been listening to the story. She was disgusted with all that had to do with religion. Now she spoke suddenly, her voice catching Temperance by surprise. "Did you ever hear God speak?"

For a moment Temperance could not answer, and then she turned to look at Rena. The girl was sitting back from the fire, her legs drawn up. Her eyes were hidden in the shadows, but she was looking intently at Temperance.

"Not in words, Rena. But when I was eleven years old, I did something terribly wrong and I felt terrible."

"What was it?" Bent demanded, leaning forward to see her face.

"My mother had a set of beautiful ceramic figurines. They came from Holland. She kept them on the mantel. She never let me handle them. One day I took them out when I wasn't supposed to. I dropped one and I broke it. My mother asked me if I broke it and I lied. I said the cat did it. I felt absolutely rotten."

"Why, shoot, that wasn't much!" Bent exclaimed. "I've lied worse than that."

"Well, it bothered me. I couldn't get away from it. Finally I felt so bad I went out in the field all by myself. I just sat down there and cried. Finally I stopped crying and the strangest feeling came over me." Temperance paused and a softness touched her face. The firelight was kind, softening and tinting her cheeks. Her shoulders made a pleasant shape, and a remote smile turned the corners of her lips upward.

Suddenly Brennan's eyes opened wider, for he saw Temperance in a way he never had before. In the half light, she had a woman's mystery with a woman's softness and a fullness that shaped her. He noted with a sense of astonishment that her lips were full—the lips of a giving woman but certainly not a pliant one. "What happened?"

"I asked God to come into my heart. I had heard the gospel preached many times, and I knew that Jesus had died for me. But that was the first time that I ever asked God to forgive me in the name of Jesus. I still remember that peace that came into my heart when I was so young." She smiled suddenly. "It's still there," she whispered.

"Did you tell your mama what you'd done?" Bent demanded.

"Yes."

"Did she whip you?"

"Oh yes, she punished me, but I deserved it."

Belle had remained silent, but now she said abruptly, "I went to a brush arbor meeting once when I was about sixteen. People started confessing their sins. Some of them told about things they did that was a lot worse than lying about a broken figure."

Temperance lifted her head, and her eyes met Belle's. "I don't think it matters. We all need forgiveness, Belle, no matter what we've done, large or small. We all need God's forgiveness."

The fire crackled, and the cry of a night bird sailing overhead broke the silence. None of them spoke until finally Brennan said, "I'm going to take a look around." He disappeared into the darkness, and soon afterward the others all went to bed. Temperance remained where she was for a long time, thinking how strange it was that she had been able to share the gospel with a saloon woman like Belle here on this trail.

Chapter Fifteen

"THAT'S FORT LARAMIE?"

Thad had been plodding alongside Babe, and Temperance had joined him. He had kept to himself for the most part since they had hit the North Platte River. "Yep, that's it," he grunted. He took off his hat and wiped his forehead with his sleeve. "It ain't much, is it?"

"Looks like the United States government could build something better than that!"

It was nearly dusk, and Temperance saw that Indians were camped outside the fort. "Are they friendly?" she said.

"They are right now, with the soldiers so close by, but if they catch you out, they'll scalp you for that ring you're wearing."

As they approached the fort, Temperance studied the Indians carefully. She had somehow gotten the idea that they were a noble race, perhaps from the few novels she had read, but there was nothing noble about these Indians. Most of them seemed drunk. The smoke from their campfires rose, and the stench was almost unbearable.

"Reckon we'll go on inside. You notice all the wagons?" Thad asked.

"Yes, is that unusual?"

"It looks like about three or four trains got here about the same time. Nearly all of the trains going toward Oregon stop at Fort Laramie to stock up again."

Temperance hesitated. "Maybe we'd better not go in here."

"Why not?"

"Why, somebody could pass the word to Joe Meek."

"Don't matter. He couldn't catch up with me here, and as soon as the job's over, he'll have a chore catching me anyway. I plan to disappear. Come on."

The oxen pulled the wagon through the big gates, and looking around, Temperance saw that the fort was basically a broad quadrangle. It seemed strange to her. "It's funny," she said.

"What's funny?"

"We're inside something. We've been outside so long with nothing but the sky and the horizon, I feel—"

"Feel all cooped up and fenced in? Same with me. Pretty big stockade here. Room for hundreds of men and plenty of animals. The Indians outside are drunk and the soldiers inside are drunk, but maybe I'll find somebody I know here that can tell us how the trail is on down the way. Come on. Let's go to the store. We need to stock up."

"How much farther is it, Thad?" Belle had joined them and was looking around the fort calmly. "Are we halfway there?"

"More than that, I reckon. Ought to be easy going from here on."

The store was not much. It was large enough but stacked with supplies of all kinds and apparently without order. Temperance had made a list and proceeded to fill it.

The clerk, a tall cadaverous-looking man with the air of an undertaker, nodded to her, saying, "Evening, ma'am. Just get in?"

"Yes, we did."

"How big is your train?"

"Just us, and we're going east not west."

"Is that right? My name's Hoskins. You be staying all night?"

"Oh yes, I think so."

"You might like to go to the big meeting."

"What kind of a meeting is that, Mr. Hoskins?"

"It's a camp meeting. There's a preacher here that's some pumpkins! He don't put up with much foolishness. His name's Peter Cartwright, a Methodist sort of fellow. I'm Baptist myself, but I'm enjoying the meetings." He had reached the total and said, "That'll be fourteen dollars and twenty-six cents, ma'am."

"You say you like his preaching?"

"Well, he preaches pretty hard. He's a stout fellow, too, for a preacher. Kind of deceiving. The Ratlin brothers decided to bust up the meeting." The store owner grinned suddenly and his eyes sparkled with a mischievous look that belied the rest of his cadaverous appearance. "Rev. Cartwright, he grabbed them by the neck, banged their heads together, and escorted them out. Ain't had no trouble since. He preaches the gospel. I'll have to say that for him—for a Methodist, that is."

"Thank you, Mr. Hoskins. I would like to attend services."

As soon as she left the store and went back to the wagon, she said, "Rose, we're going to go to a meeting tonight." Turning around, she said, "I'd like for you to go, too, Rena and Bent. I think all of us ought to go."

"I'm not going to no preaching." Belle flatly refused.

Thad spoke up at once. "Rena, you and Bent ought to go."

Rena glared at him. "I'll go if you will," she said, a challenge flashing from her eyes.

Thad looked around, searching for an excuse, and Rena

laughed harshly. "You won't go though. You'll go to a saloon and get drunk."

"You got no respect for your elders, Rena," Thad said. He looked at Temperance and said, "That's a good idea you got there. Come on, Belle, let's go have some fun."

As they walked off, Rena said, "I knew he wouldn't go."

"I wish you'd go with me."

Rena started to refuse, but Bent said, "Let's go. It'll be something different anyhow."

"All right, I'll go, but I won't listen."

"That's all right. Just be company for me," Temperance smiled. "You shouldn't talk like that to Thaddeus."

"Why not?"

"It's not polite."

Rena tossed her head and walked off. "I'll go to your old meeting, but I don't want to hear your preaching."

உ

THAD AND BELLE HAD arrived at the Blue Moon Saloon and found it like most other saloons—dirty and smelling of alcohol, cigarette smoke, urine, and unwashed bodies. Thad immediately ordered drinks, and for awhile Belle stayed with him. Finally she shook her head. "I can't hold liquor. It gives me a headache the next day."

Thad grinned at her. "Then I'll have to drink for both of us. You just tell me when you think I've had enough."

For the next hour Belle told him almost steadily that he had had enough, but he merely laughed at her.

Finally a drunk sitting at the bar made a crude remark about the preacher Cartwright who was holding the meeting.

Thad turned around and said, "Shut your mouth or I'll shut it for you."

"You and who else, drunk?"

"I don't allow rude talk about preachers."

"When did you start doing that?" Belle said.

"Just now." He glared at the man who'd made the remark. "You gonna shut up, or am I going to have to shut you up?"

"I guess you'll have to shut me up, partner."

Thad took a swing but was so drunk he missed by a foot. He took a blow in the mouth and then threw himself forward. The two wrestled and fell into a table. Then the bouncer, a huge man, grabbed Thad and said, "We don't need you here. I'll escort you to the door."

Thad struggled, but he was helpless in the bouncer's grip, which was somewhat like that of a gorilla. When they got to the door, the drunk he had fought with said, "No hard feelings, fella. You better go to that meeting. You're no good at saloon brawls."

"I'll clean your clock—" But Thad was interrupted as the bouncer shoved him through the door. Thad went cartwheeling out on the boardwalk, turned a flip, and sat down in the dust. Several people looked and one laughed. Thad got up, ready to fight him.

"Let's go find another saloon," Belle said. "You're not drunk enough yet. You won't be drunk enough as long as you can stand up."

"No, I ain't going to a saloon," Thad said, pronouncing each word carefully as drunks do. "I'm goin' to that meeting. I bet I can whip that preacher even if I am drunk!"

Thad was weaving as he made his way to the meeting. It was easy to find because they could hear the singing. "You hear that, Belle. They're singing hymns. Maybe they'll let us join the choir."

"This ain't a good idea, Thad. Let's go back to the wagon. I'll fix you something to eat."

"No, I'm going to whip that preacher."

Belle pleaded with him, but he was at that stage when reason and logic meant nothing. Belle followed, and they found the crowd at one end of the rectangle. A mixed crowd of soldiers, Indians, and travelers made up the congregation. There was no rostrum, but a stocky man in a frock coat with a round, fleshy face and a pair of steady gray eyes was smiling out over the congregation. Someone had provided a few benches, and Thad made his way to the front. He almost fell once, but Belle caught him. On the way he saw Temperance. He stopped, took off his hat, and bellowed, "Hello, Sister Peabody, I've come to hit the glory trail. I'm going to sit right in the front row and be sure the preacher tells it like he ought to."

Belle saw Temperance turn pale and waved for her to come forward. Temperance was holding Timmy and shook her head.

Thad waved and said loudly, "I hope you confessed all your sins while we're having our meeting here, Sister Peabody. Come on, Belle, let's get these five-dollar seats down in front."

When he got to the front, there was a bench. He reached down and grabbed a skinny little fellow wearing a string tie and said, "Get out of the way, sinner. You're sitting in my seat." He shoved another man away and said, "Sit down, Belle. I want you to behave yourself. I won't tolerate no disruptions in my meeting."

The minister, Peter Cartwright, had watched all this without comment. He was thickset with a big chest, tall as well as broad. He was clean-shaven and for a moment studied Thad, then he tugged the front of his coat into position and came to stand before him.

"Are you the preacher?" Thad demanded, looking up at the minister.

"Yes, I am. My name's Peter Cartwright."

Thad leered at the preacher. "Well, Pete, turn your wolf loose." He looked around and said positively, "I see lots of sinners here tonight. I'm here to help you if you bog down in your sermon."

Cartwright looked down and said quietly but firmly, "You are intoxicated, sir. You may stay, but you will remain absolutely quiet and make no disturbance."

Thad stood up and grinned. "I done told you, Pete. I'm going to help you with this sermon."

"I think you'll leave now."

Thad instantly took a swing at the preacher. He found his arm suddenly seized, and then the world seemed to turn upside down. He found himself floating in the air for a moment, his mind confused and his brain spinning, and then he hit the ground flat on his back so hard that the breath was driven out of his body. He tried to speak but discovered he couldn't even breathe. Strong hands gripped him. He found himself being picked up like a body and set down on the bench. Peter Cartwright was smiling. "You sit right there, friend. You need the gospel about as bad as any sinner I ever saw."

Thad got his breath slowly enough to gasp, "You—can't keep me here."

"I could, but I won't. You're afraid to stay, friend."

"I ain't afraid of you."

"No, you're afraid of God. I see it in your eyes." Cartwright, his eyes magnetic and piercing, studied Brennan. "You'll run just like you always do." He turned around then and went back to the platform.

"You gonna run, Thad?" Thad looked down to see Rena, who had suddenly appeared. "You gonna run like you always do?"

"Not me! No sir! I ain't afraid of that preacher—nor of God neither! Now sit down and listen to what he says. Belle, you sit down too. You need a good dose of religion." He sat down hard and stared up at Cartwright. The world still seemed to be reeling, but he glared around defiantly. His eyes met those of Temperance Peabody, and he said defiantly, "I ain't running, Peabody. You just hide and watch me!"

❧

TEMPERANCE DID NOT HEAR much Peter Cartwright said in his sermon. She knew he was preaching about the death of Jesus, and he described the Crucifixion in a terrible, graphic fashion. He quoted Scripture from the Old Testament and New, and his voice rose in volume. Time and time again he would call out in a stentorian, trumpetlike voice, "Jesus died for your sins. He died for you!"

The sermon was directed at sinners, and Cartwright's voice was like a flail as he pulled no punches. Temperance stared closely at Thad and saw that the accusations of sin did not move him, but every time Cartwright said, "Jesus died for your sins," Thad flinched as if touched with a hot iron.

Finally Temperance caught her breath, for Thad stood to his feet. He stumbled toward the aisle and then pushed his way through those who were standing.

Peter Cartwright's voice rang out, "We will pray that God will catch up with that poor sinner!"

Temperance felt herself trembling, and she heard nothing that Cartwright said during the rest of the sermon. As soon as it was over, individuals began moving forward to be prayed for. She turned and met Rena and Bent. "What's wrong with Thad?" Bent asked. "He run out."

"He's fighting with God, Bent, and I hope he loses!"

At that moment a tall man, well dressed, with a low-crowned black hat and a snowy white shirt stepped forward. "Excuse me, ma'am. My name's Quaid Mitchell. I saw these children and this lady talking with the fellow who took off. He looked like an old friend of mine named Thad Brennan."

"That was him," Belle said. "You know him?"

"Oh yes. Are you . . . Mrs. Brennan?"

"No, I'm not," Belle said politely.

"Well, are you Mrs. Brennan?" Mitchell asked Temperance.

"No, he's our guide, Mr. Mitchell."

"Guide to where? I hate to be nosy, but Thad and me were partners once in the mountains, tracking. A fellow gets real close. I didn't know it was him at first, you know, he looked so bad. What's wrong with him?"

"He's drinking all the time."

"And where is he guiding you to, if I might ask?" Mitchell listened as Temperance explained the situation. Finally he said, "That's a mighty noble thing for you to do, Miss Peabody. I admire you for it."

Temperance studied the man carefully. He seemed to be in his midthirties and was tall and lean but strong. His face was tapered, his eyes deep-set, a blue gray, and there was somehow a daring look about him. He was dressed more like a gambler than anything else, or as she imagined a gambler might dress.

She was curious about his relationship with Thaddeus, and she asked, "Did Thaddeus drink a lot?"

"No more than the rest of us. You need a clear head when you're tracking beavers in Sioux territory. Are you pulling out soon?"

"I expect we'll be leaving tomorrow."

"Well, if it'd be all right, I'll come by and say howdy to Thad. Sure think a lot of that fellow. Good to meet you ladies. You, too, bub," he grinned at Bent.

As he turned and left, Belle said at once, "Watch out for that one."

"What's wrong with him?" Rena said. "He looks all right to me."

"He's too good-looking, that's what's wrong with him. Women must line up to get at him. He's rich too. You see that ring on his finger? That wasn't glass."

"He looks a lot better than Thad," Rena said.

Temperance shook her head. She was thinking of how Thad had run off. It occurred to her that he might be gone for good. He had had a look of abject fear on his face, and she knew that the Spirit of God had spoken to him. "I'm afraid for Thaddeus," she said. "When a man runs from God, he runs hard. He may have gotten on Judas and ridden out."

"Aw, he wouldn't go off and leave us," Bent said.

"I hope not," Temperance said. "I surely hope not."

Chapter Sixteen

THE SUN HAD STARTED climbing high into the sky, shedding its crimson beams on Fort Laramie, when Rena cried out, "Look, there comes Thad! He looks like he's been beat with a boat paddle."

Temperance, who had been feeding Timmy mush mixed with goat's milk and sugar, looked up and saw at once that Rena was exactly right. She said nothing but kept her eyes fixed on Thad as he came walking somewhat unsteadily toward the wagon. When he stood before her, she shook her head and said reprovingly, "You look terrible."

Indeed, Thaddeus Brennan did look as if he had been pulled through a knothole. His clothes were filthy, his eyes were inflamed, and his left ear was red. As usual, when he had a hangover, he moved carefully as if to move his head too suddenly would set off a dynamite charge inside. "Let's get out of here," he muttered.

Rena came to him and stared up in his face. She smiled maliciously, and her eyes were dancing. "Well, did God catch up with you?"

"Leave him alone, Rena," Temperance said. "You want some breakfast?"

"No."

Thad turned and went at once to begin putting the oxbows

on the oxen and hitching them to the wagon. Temperance glanced at Belle, who said merely, "That's just Thad, I guess. I don't think he'll ever change."

"He could if he wanted to."

"But he doesn't want to." Belle shrugged and something crossed her face; a wave of regret showed in her eyes. "Some of us never will change."

Temperance finished feeding Timmy and put him in his box in the wagon. She was gathering up the dishes when she looked up to see Quaid Mitchell riding up on a fine, bay horse with another horse looking almost as good and a loaded pack horse. He came out of the saddle with a smooth, easy movement, swept his hat off, and smiled. "Good morning to you, Miss Temperance."

"Good morning, Mr. Mitchell."

"Just Quaid will be fine, I think, or Mitch. I get called both." He turned then and without another word glanced to where Thad stood stock still, staring at him. "Well, my old partner," Quaid smiled. He punched Thad on the shoulder, reached down, and began to pump his hand. "I haven't seen you in a coon's age."

"Hello, Quaid. Where'd you drift in from?"

"Been out in California, getting rich."

"Glad to hear it."

Quaid started to speak but saw the sorry condition of his friend. "I was surprised to see you at that meeting last night."

"I didn't see you there."

"Well, in the old days neither one of us was broke out with church going much, but I got right with the Lord about a year ago. Still, I guess what you'd call a work in progress. God's not finished with me yet. You don't look too good."

"I never did look very good."

"You looked a lot better than you do now. What's this I hear about you taking Miss Temperance and these kids back East?"

Thad shifted his feet and shrugged his shoulders non-committally. "Something I had to do," he muttered.

"Well, I've got good news for you."

"I can stand some."

Quaid turned then and faced Temperance and Belle. They were both watching him carefully. Quaid looked fresh. His skin glowed with a recent shave, and his eyes were bright. "I'm headed back East myself. I thought I might join you if you wouldn't mind the company."

"Why, I think that would be nice, Quaid," Temperance said with a smile.

"That's right," Belle said. "When the Indians attack, you can help Thad fight them off."

Thad shifted his feet and put his eyes on Quaid critically. "We're going to be moving pretty slow, Quaid. You won't want to dawdle around with us."

"Oh, I got plenty of time," Quaid said cheerfully. "I can be of some help to you. Now, ladies, please introduce me to these fine young folks here."

Temperance said at once, "This is Timmy. This is Bent and Rena Overmeyer. That's their little sister, Bess. This is Rose Abbott, my right-hand helper, and her brother, Billy."

Quaid smiled at each of them and winked at Rena. "You better watch out, Miss Rena. A pretty girl like you, there'll be lots of no-good, worthless, trifling, young fellows lining up to get you to go to the dance with them."

Rena suddenly smiled. "They haven't been lined up so far."

"Why, Miss Rena, you're standing in the doorway of opportunity. There, right before you, a whole vista of wonderful times. But I'm going to take you in hand and warn you about all the tricks these young scoundrels use. Yes sir, I think the world has appointed me as a guardian for the morals of the young folks."

"I never noticed you broke out with many morals yourself," Thad said grumpily.

"Well, like I said, I changed."

"Did you really get rich in California, Quaid?" Belle asked.

"I'm ashamed to admit it, but I did. Nearly every venture I tried previously went bust." He winked at Thad, saying, "Me and Thad, though, went broke hunting beavers. We had enough to make us rich, and then the stinking Blackfeet came along and nearly got our scalps. They did get our furs, didn't they, Thad?"

"Yeah, they did. Look, I can't stand around here. We got to get on the road."

"Why sure. Miss Temperance, you just let me know anything that I can do."

"Could I ride that extra horse of yours?" Belle said boldly.

"You sure can. She's a real lady. Her name's Cherry."

"Named after an old girlfriend of yours?"

"Now, ma'am, it would be unseemly for me to talk about my past. That's all behind me now. I'm on the straight and narrow."

Thad gave a snort of disgust and said, "Well, if you got to go, it'll be all right, I guess."

"What's the matter with Thad?" Rena asked Belle. "He doesn't seem to like Quaid much."

"Well, in the first place he's got a bad hangover. Second place, it looks like his old partner has made it. Struck it big out

in California somehow, and Thad's a little bit jealous, I think."
She smiled and tapped her chin thoughtfully. "Be interesting to
have a good-looking man like that in camp, won't it?"

❧

THE FIRST DAY OUT was interesting for everyone except Thad.
Quaid Mitchell was in high spirits. He and Belle, who rode
astraddle the horse, letting her skirt divide as it would with her
calves showing, trotted ahead of the others, and he took her
on side trips, showing her different sights. When they came
back for the noonday break, he sat down and ate the meal that
Temperance and Belle had prepared and entertained everyone
with stories of his past life. "How'd you get rich in California,
Mitchell?" Bent asked.

"Why, it was easy as falling off a log. Easiest thing I ever
done." He winked at Thad, who was eating his first real meal of
the day. "Why, you should have been there, Thad. I heard about
that gold rush, so I rushed. I got out there just in time to find
me a claim, and wouldn't you know it, after failing at ranching
and soldiering and fur trapping and half a dozen other things, I
hit pay dirt the second day I was there. I dug out enough to find
out for sure the claim was good. I let word get around so I sold
out. Made a killing too."

"Why'd you leave, Quaid?" Thad muttered. "I would have
stayed there and dug gold out until there wasn't no more."

"Life's too short, friend, to do a thing like that. No sir, I'm
headed back to civilization. Going to buy me a plantation,
marry a fine-looking woman, sit out on the front porch, drink
mint juleps, watch the hands raise cotton, and get even richer."

"Sounds like a good kind of life," Belle grinned.

"Just what I've always wanted. Always talked about that, didn't I, Thad?" He waited, but Thad, without a word, got up and stalked off, muttering something under his breath. "Thad don't seem happy," he said.

"He's not. You saw how he acted at the meeting. He's running from God," Temperance explained.

"He was a mighty good friend to me back in our trapping days. We got snowed in one winter. When you do that, you'd better like the fella you're snowed in with or you'll wind up cutting his throat, or he'll cut yours." Quaid smiled crookedly. There was a brash attractiveness about the man that charmed the rest of them.

"Tell us some more about the gold," Belle said. "I like to hear about money. I don't have any myself, but I like to be around people who do."

"Why, we've got all the way back to Independence to talk about anything you want to, Miss Belle," Quaid grinned. "You just name the subject."

Temperance noticed that Thad stayed away most of the day. She couldn't understand it. The two had been good friends, but she finally figured out that Thad was ashamed of his poor condition, and the sight of Quaid Mitchell dressed in his finery with bags full of money was more than he could take.

That night after supper Quaid entertained them with tales about the time he and Thad were partners. He kept them awake until late, telling stories, his eyes bright and his hands constantly in motion as he illustrated with wild gestures.

It was later that night, just before Temperance went to bed, that Thad, who had not spoken one word, approached her and said, "I've got to warn you about something, Peabody."

"What's that?"

"You better watch out for Quaid."

"Why would you say a thing like that?"

"Because he's a ladies' man. I hate to say it about a friend, but young ladies ain't safe around him."

Suddenly the situation amused Temperance. She looked up at Thad and saw his face set with displeasure. "Well, Thaddeus, you've already warned me that no man would want me, so I don't have to be careful around your friend, do I?"

Thad glared at her and tried to find an answer. Finally he nodded shortly and said, "You watch what I tell you now. He's a dangerous man where women are concerned."

Belle had been close enough to overhear the conversation. She came over and smiled. "Well, you've been warned. Quaid's a danger to women. Are you afraid?"

"No, he's a Christian now."

"Yeah, I've heard that before too," Belle said cynically. "You know what's wrong with Thad? He's just jealous, that's all."

"Jealous? Of who?"

"Of Quaid. Why, it might be because of you."

"Of me! Are you crazy, Belle? We haven't done anything but fight since we left Walla Walla."

"I know that, but he's got a funny way of looking at you when you're not watching. I think he likes you."

"He's already made it plain he doesn't, Belle. Now don't talk foolishness."

❧

AS THEY MADE THEIR way through the Platte Valley, Quaid gave a running commentary. "All the Pawnee are up to the north and the Cheyenne to the south, but they won't be attacking this close to Fort Kearny. At least I don't think so. Never can tell what an injun will do though."

They had stopped for noon, and Temperance had fried antelope steaks. They weren't very good, being tough, but at least they were fresh. She suddenly waved at furniture that had been piled to one side—a cherry chifforobe and a desk. "I'm surprised people leave things on the trail. We've passed more things like that. People just throw their things away."

"Well, they got big ideas when they leave Missouri. They pile everything on the wagons and the animals start playing out, and they have to set it aside."

"I'd like to ride your extra horse, Quaid."

"Why sure."

"But I don't have a riding skirt."

"Nobody to see out here except me and Thad, and, of course, we're both perfect gentlemen."

Temperance laughed. The man had an easy, light humor, although she also detected an underlying fiery temper. "I couldn't do that," she said.

"I'll tell you what. Just take one of your old skirts, split it up the middle, stitch it. Kind of like make two legs out of it. It'll look just like a riding skirt."

"You know, I think I will do that."

"You go put it together. You and me will take a ride."

Temperance made quick work of the dress. It was easy as Quaid had said, and in the shelter of the wagon she slipped it on. When she stepped out, she called, "Quaid, I'm ready."

"That's right fancy," Belle said, watching with envy. "If you got another old dress, I'll make me one."

"We'll find you one, Belle."

Thad had been plodding along beside Babe. He stopped and looked down at Temperance's costume. "That's a forked dress you got on," he accused.

"It's modest enough. That's all that counts," Temperance said. "I'm sorry you don't like it."

"I thought you were so persnickety about dresses and things like that."

"Well, as Quaid pointed out, there's only you and him, and you're both perfect gentlemen, so I'm sure it'll be all right," she said sweetly.

Quaid brought the mare and helped Temperance into the saddle. He got on the stallion and said, "Come on, let's let them out a little bit. Hang on now."

Thad called out, "You don't wander too far off. It could be dangerous."

Belle edged closer to him and was smiling slightly. "Looks like the holy woman's found herself a man."

"Don't be foolish, Belle. He ain't for her. Women like him. I don't know why."

"Why, I can't understand it either," Belle said mockingly. "All he's got is good looks, fine manners, and a ton of money. Can't understand why a woman would be interested in a man like that."

"She don't need to be going off alone with him."

"Don't be silly. He's a perfect gentleman."

"No, he ain't. He ain't respectful to women."

"Oh, not like you, Thad?"

Thad looked at Belle and frowned. He had not been drinking that day, for a change, and his eyes were clear. "I know he looks pretty good, and he's a good man to have at your side if we get trapped by a bunch of Cheyenne or Blackfeet, but

women ain't got no sense about him. They just seem to—
I don't know—kind of melt."

"I know what that's like," Belle said. "Some men can just
make you do that."

"Well, he's one of them."

"I heard you trying to warn Temperance. She didn't seem to
take it too well."

"She's too innocent. She needs to know that not all men are
as trustworthy as—" He broke off.

She laughed. "As trustworthy as you, Thad?"

Thad stared at her. "I'm going to keep an eye on them," he
said. "She's like a babe in the woods."

❧

QUAID AND TEMPERANCE HAD a good hard ride on the two
horses. When Quaid pulled up and Temperance brought the
mare to the halt, too, she said, "That was such fun." Her cheeks
were flushed and her eyes were bright. The wind had freed her
hair, and she had a vibrant look.

"You're a good rider."

"I used to ride a lot. Not so much lately. Mostly in wagons."

"How'd you wind up in Oregon?" Quaid asked, leaning
over to pat his stallion on the neck. "You're from back East,
aren't you?"

"Yes, from the coast in Maine. My parents went to Oregon
to start a colony."

Quaid listened intently and found himself more interested in this woman than he had been in others of late. She
had a wealth of light brown hair with tints of auburn, but
she had a blend of qualities that struck him. She had a pride

and an honesty and somehow a grace of heart and body that stirred him in a way he could not quite understand. The wind ruffled the edges of her hair, and her smile gently enhanced her appearance. He watched the slight changes of her face, the quickening and loosening of small expressions coming and going, and once, when a private and ridiculous thought seemed to amuse her, he saw the effect dancing in her eyes. When she finished telling her story, he studied her for a moment and then said, "You never married."

"No."

"Men in Walla Walla must be fools to let a woman like you get away."

Temperance did not know what to say. She was unaccustomed to handling compliments. "I'm not attractive, not like Belle. Men want that."

Quaid shook his head suddenly and abruptly. "You've got something I admire in women more than good looks, though you've got that too. That's character."

Suddenly Temperance smiled. "Thad tells me you're good with women."

"Used to be. Not anymore."

"I don't suppose you'd care to tell me about any of your romances."

Quaid smiled briefly and then a sadness touched his face. "Well, just one maybe. I loved a woman and she failed me."

Temperance perceived that the woman had brought tragedy to Quaid Mitchell. He was a cheerful man full of vigor and humor, but the woman had scarred him deeply. "I'm sorry," she said quietly.

"Well, it's all over. Funny thing. I found God after she left me. Since then I haven't been looking for a woman. I guess

I wanted to get rich. Now even that doesn't seem too important." He moved his horse closer and looked into her face. "It's a good thing you're doing, Temperance, taking these children back. I hope you don't mind my tagging along."

"I don't mind at all, Quaid," she said quietly. The exchange hinted at a brief moment of intimacy, and she felt something stir within her. "Come on. Let's try these horses again."

❦

LATE AFTERNOON WAS DRAWING its shadows across the trail, and Quaid and Temperance had returned from their ride. Quaid was trekking alongside Thad. They talked about the old days trapping, and finally Quaid said, "That time remembers pretty good. I don't know why. Too much to eat or not enough. Scared half the time that the hostiles would be over the next ridge. Still, it was a good time."

"It's about gone now, Quaid."

"I expect so."

The two were silent for awhile, and finally Thad said, "Something I got to say to you, partner."

"Say on, brother."

"You got to understand Temperance Peabody's not like other women."

Quaid shot a quick look at Thad and saw his face was dead earnest. "I guess I figured that out for myself. We used to say of good horses they had bottom. Not a fitting thing to say about a woman, but you know what I mean. She's a stayer. I admire her more than I can say."

"Well, take this right, or take it wrong, Quaid, but I want you to leave her alone."

Quaid was somewhat shocked. "What are you talking about?"

"I've seen you before with women. They fall for you. You've got a way that breaks down their defenses."

"You don't have a thing to worry about. I respect her just as much as you do, maybe more."

"I'd hate to have to make this stronger than just a warning, Quaid. I ain't forgotten that you pulled my bacon out of the fire more than once when we was in the mountains."

Quaid did not answer for a time. He was considering Thad and finally he said, "Couldn't be you care for her yourself, could it?"

"No, nothing like that. I promised to get her and these kids to where they're going, and I aim to do it."

"That's fine. I'll go along and give you a hand, Thad." Quaid's voice developed a sharp edge, and he said, "But let me tell you this. I see something in Temperance I've never seen in another woman. You're a fool if you don't see it yourself."

"You remember what I said, Quaid."

"I don't forget."

226

Chapter Seventeen

JULY HAD ARRIVED. THE hot breath of wind scoured bare earth and stirred up the dust in rising clouds that seemed to rise to meet those in the sky. The plains on each side of the Platte River were covered with short grass. Three miles away on both sides of the river, the land rose in sandstone cliffs, which became less and less broken as the trail moved east.

Temperance and Quaid had ridden every day, and the interlude had made the trip enjoyable for her. The long hours on the trail still offered plenty of time; except when they were stopped for nooning or camped for the night, there was really nothing to do. But buffalo chips still had to be gathered for the evening fires.

Temperance was amazed at the wildlife. Antelope and coyotes abounded, and once she even saw a grizzly with two cubs, which delighted her. Another day she saw black bears and, of course, the buffaloes came and went in small herds. The prairie dogs were a source of amazement as well. "I can't believe there are so many of them," she said to Quaid as they rode along.

"Some people like to eat them, but they're pretty small game and not too tasty."

"Their villages are just like big cities, aren't they?"

"I expect they have fewer problems than folks in New York."

"Is that where you're going, Quaid, to New York?"

"No, I don't think I'd like the East. I'm not even sure that I'll like it in the South. I grew up there, but I left when I was only eighteen. What about you? Will you be going back to Walla Walla?"

"I suppose I will. My home place is there."

"Reckon you're pretty well tied to it."

"I never even thought about it. It's the only home I've known since we left Maine. I suppose I know every foot of it."

"Sometimes a body needs a change. It might be good if you thought about staying somewhere in the South. Maybe Virginia. That's good-looking country. Blue Ridge Mountains. The prettiest part of the United States, I do believe."

"What would I do there?"

"Admire the mountains. The weather is good. Eat Virginia hams."

"I don't think that kind of life would suit me very well."

"Don't you have any people at all?"

"Just an uncle and an aunt. They live in Michigan. I don't even know them."

"You're like me," Quaid nodded. "Just rolling along. Nothing to tie to."

They had talked for some time until finally the mare Temperance was riding developed an obvious limp. "Pull up beside the river. The closest thing to trees as there is for a little shade. Give the horses a drink. Us, too, maybe."

The place was pleasant. The cottonwood trees that hugged the banks of the Platte were few, but here some had taken root somehow and had been spared the usual fate of being chopped down for firewood. Temperance got off the mare and watched as Quaid had her hold up her foot. He poked around, pulled out his sheaf knife, and dug something from the horse's hoof. "Sharp stone. This will make her feel better. Say, let's tie the horses up and stay out of that sun for awhile."

"All right."

He tied the horses, and she went down to the river. "It's not very deep, is it?"

"Six inches deep and a mile across the saying goes. Not much of a river after the Yellowstone. I wish you could see that, Temperance. The water's so clear there that if it's twenty feet deep, you could still see right to the bottom. I dropped a gold coin in once, and it was so clear I reached over to pick it up and found out it was twenty feet down. Don't see rivers like that every day in the week."

"You've had an adventurous life, Quaid."

"Yes, but I'm ready to settle down now. I'm thirty-four, and it's time to think about the real things."

"What do you mean the real things?"

"Well, a fellow gets to be my age, he begins to think it'd be nice to have a son or a little girl, and a wife, of course."

"They do come in handy, don't they, for things like that." Her smile crinkled at him, and he laughed aloud, saying, "Yes, they do."

"I can't tell you how much these rides have meant to me, Quaid."

"Been fun for me too. I think Brother Thad's a bit jealous."

"He's bothered by thoughts about God. I've seen it in him. The theologians, I think, call it conviction."

"I know what that's like. I wasn't at a revival. I just started thinking about God, and the more I thought about Him, the lower I got. It just struck me that here I'd found all this gold and had money and everything I ever wanted, but what if I died? It scared me more than the Cheyenne ever did."

"I'm so glad you found the Lord," she said.

After several seconds of silence, she decided to change the subject. "How much farther is it? What lies just ahead of us?"

"Why, we'll be in Fort Kearny in a couple of days. After that another few days to Alcove Springs and then an easy road past Fort Leavenworth right into Independence." He leaned toward her slightly and smiled. "I know you'll be glad to get this trip over, but I'm enjoying it."

"It's been easier the last few days."

"Is that a left-handed compliment to me?"

"I suppose it is. But you know, I'm really worried about handing the children over. Especially the Overmeyer children. Evidently their relatives aren't very good people, but there wasn't any other choice."

"Well, something will work out."

"But you won't be there to see it. You'll be on your way to Virginia."

"Or maybe New Orleans. Oh, I'll tag along. I'm in no hurry. I'd kind of like to see something work out. It's kind of like a storybook."

Quaid waited for her to speak, but she didn't, and finally he said, "I'm wondering something, Temperance."

"What's that, Quaid?"

"I'm wondering if you trust me. I mean, after what Thad told you about me being a woman chaser, and, of course, he was right. I did have a bad reputation."

She turned to face him and said quietly, "Yes, Quaid, I trust you, but I don't know much about men. I have no experience."

"You're an unusual woman, Temperance. I've never known another one like you."

She suddenly smiled. "You wouldn't have noticed. You were after beautiful women."

Suddenly he reached over and took her hand. The river made a sibilant whisper at their feet, and he turned her to face him. "Beauty's a funny thing," he said, his eyes thoughtful. "The most beautiful woman I ever knew was twisted and warped inside. A man's a fool to chase after that—which is what I was for a long time." His hand tightened on hers, and he saw her chin lift and a faint color stain her cheeks. "I've been reading the Bible lately," he said. "I read something not long ago that reminded me of you. I was thinking about what I was going to do with my life, if I would ever get married, and it was in the Song of Solomon. I don't understand that part of the Bible, but I understood this. It says, 'Many waters cannot quench love, neither can the floods drown it.'"

"I don't understand that book either, but I've always loved it. There's a sweetness in it."

"Some of the things are downright embarrassing. I was shocked to find out that the Bible spoke about love between a man and a woman in such blunt terms."

"I don't understand that either. One of my pastors said it was a book about Christ's love for the church."

"It may be that, but that fellow knew something about a man and a woman too."

At that moment Quaid Mitchell saw in the woman who stood before him a goodness and a richness that unsettled him. He had known other kinds of women, but hers was the first good spirit he had ever really known or remembered. He realized this was because he was always after the flesh instead of a woman's spiritual qualities. Now as she stood before him, her smile was soft and shining, and he knew that this woman's loyalty would be reserved for one man alone. This new awareness suddenly made him hungry to know more about her. He leaned closer to catch a better view of her face, and at that moment something seemed to cut a restraining cord. He put his arms around her waist and drew her closer, desperately wanting not to make a mistake with this woman. He felt no resistance, which surprised him, and then he lowered his head and kissed her.

Some kind of barrier had broken, and somehow Temperance knew they had stepped beyond a mere friendship. This was the feeling she had heard about from other women and had even read about. They were standing on the brink of the mystery that enters into a man and a woman when they face each other, not knowing whether good or bad would come of it. She stayed with him longer than he thought, and when she drew away, she whispered, "What did that mean, Quaid?"

"It means you're worth kissing."

"I—I don't know how to act with a man."

Quaid suddenly laughed. "That's what I like about you." For a moment they stood on the riverbank in an immense space stretching out in all directions around them, the sky overhead a bold blue. "We've got a long trip ahead of us. Time to get to know each other."

For a long time she was very quiet, and then she looked him in the eye and said in a voice that was gentle, yet firm as granite, "Don't play me false, Quaid. It would be easy for you."

He knew exactly what she meant. "I won't do that, Temperance. You can count on it."

LATER THAT NIGHT, AFTER supper, it was obvious Thad had been drinking. Quaid, as usual, kept everyone entertained with stories from his past, of which he had a limitless fund. He tried to get Thad into the conversation but without success. Finally, when they all began going to their blankets, Quaid said, "I'll take the guard tonight."

"No, I'll do it myself. You're too wore-out from riding around with the boss."

Quaid started to answer hotly but got a warning look from Temperance. "All right. You're the wagon boss. Maybe I'll spell you after awhile."

"No need for that."

Thad sat there, ignoring the others. They all went to bed, and still he sat, drinking from the jug. He knew he was drunker than usual and finally stirred himself. He picked up his rifle and took the jug with him. He knew, as he walked away from the wagon into the pale moonlight, his thoughts were a million miles away from Indians. In his judgment there was no danger. They were too close to Fort Kearny for roving bands of Cheyenne or Blackfeet to risk a raid.

Finally he sat beside a rock and despite himself began nodding. What kept him from going completely to sleep for a time were memories that crept into his drunken state—memories of Peter Cartwright and the meeting. He had been caught completely off guard, and although he'd been very drunk, the voice of the minister had penetrated to the deepest part of his being. Even now, he could still hear it: "Jesus died on the cross for your sins." Why this should trouble him he didn't know. He had heard it before more than once. He tried to blot it out by taking another drink, and after a time the world became dimmer. He dropped his rifle and knew he was drunk because the sound was vague and far away.

How long he sat there he didn't know, but suddenly he felt a sense of danger. He tried to get up, but before he did, he was struck in the head, and the world turned into a wheeling kaleidoscope of flashing red and yellow stars.

⁓

BRENNAN CAME AWAKE WITH a tremendous headache. Blood was trickling down his cheek, and when he tried to sit up, he discovered he was tied hand and foot. Fear grabbed him, for he knew the worst; and his fears were confirmed as he saw outlined against the full moon a small group of Indians, all wearing war paint. This was enough to stir up terror for he had seen what Indians could do to white men, torturing them in ways beyond imagination.

And then Thad's heart seemed to stop. He saw Bent and Rena both held by an Indian, rawhide gags over their mouths. He struggled to get up, but he was tied to a tree and a gag had been put in his mouth.

Before him he saw the figure of Black Eagle. Hope died within Thaddeus Brennan at that moment, for this was his deadliest enemy. Thad had killed this man's son, and now he prepared himself the best he could for a terrible death. He had no hope that Black Eagle would kill him quickly and cleanly. Why he was tied up he could not know.

Black Eagle's eyes were obsidian, and hate glittered in them. He spoke English roughly, but there was no doubt of the fierce bitterness that tinged his speech.

"You killed my son. You owe me a son, so I will take your son and your daughter too." Black Eagle came forward and pulled a knife from his belt. It glittered in the moonlight, and he pointed it at Brennan's chest. "You Christians—the black robes carried carvings of Jesus on a cross, but your Jesus will not save your son or your daughter. I will leave a plain trail. If you follow me, I will kill you slowly. I will still keep your son and your daughter. She will become a wife and the boy will become a Cheyenne. He is young enough we can make a Cheyenne of him."

The moon seemed to hang high in the sky, throwing its silver light on the face of Black Eagle, outlining the high cheekbones, the aquiline nose, and the sharp delineation of muscles. "You will not follow me," he said. "You are a slave to whiskey and you are a coward. You will not come, though I wish you would. Think of your son and your daughter, but you will not do that either, for you are a coward." He turned and spoke suddenly to three Indians. Thad watched helplessly as two other Indians brought horses. He saw Rena's eyes fixed on him in a soundless pleading with the rough gag cutting off her cries. Bent was the same. He had time only to receive that one look when Black Eagle, now mounted, stopped and aimed his lance at Brennan's heart. "I will not kill you. You are a coward and a slave to firewater." He turned then and led the band away. Brennan watched, and the most helpless and hopeless feeling he had ever known in his life settled on him as he sat in the light of the moon.

Chapter Eighteen

WHEN TEMPERANCE CAME OUT of a deep sleep, she noticed the sun had not yet created the faint line of light in the east she had grown to look for. Nevertheless, she woke with a vague sense of uneasiness she could not explain. Moving as quietly as she could, she dressed in the shelter of the wagon without waking the children. Rose was holding Billy in the crook of her arm, while Timothy and Bess slept soundly under a coverlet. Temperance stepped out of the wagon and looked first underneath where Bent and Rena customarily slept. Slight shock ran across her. Neither of them was there. She stepped back and called their names softly.

"What's the matter, Temperance?"

Temperance turned to find Belle had come out of the darkness to her left.

"Bent and Rena aren't here."

"Not here? Why, they've got to be!"

"Maybe they've gone to relieve themselves," Temperance said. She called out, "Bent—Rena, where are you?"

Only silence echoed back to her, but suddenly Quaid's voice came, "What's wrong?" He had been sleeping close to the fire and evidently had slept fully dressed.

"Rena and Bent are gone."

The three of them stood for a moment motionless, and then Quaid said, "Where's Thad?"

"He's not here either."

"Well, you stay here. I'll start making a search of the camp."

"Belle, you stay here. I'll help Quaid."

Quaid said, "I'll go over to the left, and you take the right. Go in a short circle and call their names. Maybe Thad took them for a ride or something."

"No, his horse is still here," she said.

They started searching, and the morning began to assume a milky luminescence. Temperance found herself breathing harder than usual, and she could not say why. Ten minutes later, however, she was moving in a circle and listening to Quaid's voice when suddenly she stopped dead still. There at the foot of a small sapling she saw what looked like a bundle. She took a deep breath and then moved forward and saw that it was Thad with his hands bound behind his back and tied to a tree with a gag in his mouth.

"Thad!" she cried and rushed forward. He was awake, straining in his bonds, and quickly she untied the gag, which was a filthy piece of cloth. He spat and could not speak for a moment. "Untie—my hands."

She could not untie the rawhide. It had been wet and was as hard as iron.

"Knife in my pocket."

Awkwardly she reached into Thad's pocket and pulled out the large pocket knife he always carried. With trembling hands she opened it and managed to cut the rawhide. Thad nearly fell over but caught himself.

"What happened, Thad?"

Thad stared at her, unable to speak for a moment, then he shook his head and the depth of misery was revealed in the tone of his voice. "Indians," he rasped. "They took Rena and Bent."

"How could they?"

Instead of answering her question, Thad broke off and moved toward camp. He approached the wagon, and Belle was waiting. "What happened, Thad?"

"Indians. They raided us last night and took Bent and Rena."

Thad moved to his blanket and was pulling it to him and as he did, Temperance called out, "Quaid—Quaid, we found him!"

The two women were joined by Quaid, who came running from the darkness. "What's up, Thad?"

Thad was strapping on his gun belt, and the light was growing as he pulled out the Navy Colt and checked the load. "It was Black Eagle," he said slightly. "He took Bent and Rena."

"How'd you get away?" Quaid asked. "I never knew him to leave a prisoner alive. He could have killed all of us."

Thad slid the Colt back in the holster and filled his pockets with ammunition. "I think he came to get me, but he thought of a better revenge. He thought Bent and Rena were my kids. He took them and dared me to come after them."

"How many were with him?" Quaid demanded.

"Five. They got a good start." He moved toward his horse, and Quaid said, "Wait a minute. Let me get saddled up. We'll catch up with them."

"You're not going, Quaid."

"What are you talking about?" he demanded. "This is no one-man job."

"That's what it is."

GILBERT MORRIS

Quaid suddenly looked stubborn and shook his head. "You know better than that. I'm not going to let you tackle that bunch alone."

Temperance was trembling. "If you hadn't been drunk," she burst out suddenly, "this wouldn't have happened!"

"That's right." Thad's voice was flat and as hard as a knife blade. "It's my doing, so I'm the one that's going after them. I told you I was no good, and I guess you believe it now."

"No time to argue about that, Thad. Both of us need to go."

"Got a favor to ask of you, Quaid."

"What favor?"

"We can't leave these women and babies out here alone. I'm going after them, and you and I both know it's a good chance that I won't be able to get them back. I'm going to follow them until I do or die. I'd appreciate it if you'd stay with the women and see that they get these other kids back to their people."

"It goes against the grain, it purely does," Quaid protested.

"It's what you need to do. I'll come back if I can." He wheeled suddenly and moved to where Judas was tied. Quickly he saddled the animal, took the hobbles off, and then filled two large sacks with grain, for he knew he'd find little grass for Judas. He swung into the saddle, paused, and looked at Temperance. In the pale beginnings of the morning, he saw tears running down her cheeks. "I've got to go," he said. He struggled to find the obvious words, then shrugged his shoulders, and said, "Sorry." He turned Judas and kicked his side. The big horse moved at once, and Thad did not look back.

"How much chance does he have, Quaid?" Belle asked in a tremulous voice.

"It's a long shot," Quaid said. "I feel bad letting him go alone, but I guess he's right. Come on, I'll get the animals hitched, and we'll get out of here. We'll get to Fort Kearny, and the commanding officer will send out a company to find Black Eagle."

"Do you think they can?" Temperance asked.

"Most of them can't find their nose with both hands, but a few of them know Indians. Come on, let's go."

As Temperance turned, she found she could not control her tears. Noticing this, Quaid put one arm around her. He held her tightly and said, "I've seen Thaddeus do some things that looked impossible. Don't give up on him yet."

"But they'll be waiting for him to come."

"You and I'll have to pray for him, that's all. He's on his own this time."

"What about Rena and Bent?"

"Cheyenne like to take children captive. They'll make Cheyenne out of them if they can."

His words chilled Temperance, but she knew there was nothing she could do. "We'll ask God to guide him," she whispered, then turned to the work at hand.

&

"BLACK EAGLE WAS TELLING the truth."

Thad murmured the words aloud as he bent over the saddle. There was no need to look closely at the ground because the Indians had made no attempt to hide their marks of passage. The sun was climbing in the sky, and Thad moved at a slower pace than he would like. It was obvious the Indians were going at full speed; the tracks showed that. Besides, they had extra horses, and it was hard to cover the tracks of the band.

The land had broken up into hills that lifted themselves into the sky and soon gave way to washes and canyons, some of them large enough to conceal a war party. Thad had to follow the tracks, but he also had to sweep the horizon, constantly searching for a possible ambush. He knew Black Eagle was the best of war chiefs among the Cheyenne, and though the chief might have a low opinion of Brennan, he would take no chances.

All morning he followed the obvious trail left by the war party, and with part of his mind he tried to anticipate what might happen when he caught up with them. One man attacking six Cheyenne warriors was not the best odds in the world, but doggedly he forged forward.

At noon he stopped by a small spring and saw that the Indians had paused there too. He drank but had no hunger. After resting Judas for an hour, he mounted and continued his pursuit. All afternoon he deliberately built a wall around his thoughts. He attempted to block images of Bent and Rena that trooped through his mind vividly.

Brennan had thought he was past the point of feeling responsibility for anyone else. His life as a loner had made caring for others of no account. But now a renewed sense of duty was driving him.

The sun reached the meridian, then began its journey into the west, and it seemed that the Indian ponies were slowing down. Several times he dismounted and leaned down close, looking at the prints. They were not the prints any longer of horses traveling at full speed, and he was grateful for this. There was no letup in his pursuit.

Finally the sun dipped below the mountains in the west, and it was too dark for him to follow the trail clearly. An impulse came to him to rush ahead, hoping to come upon the band, but that, he knew, would be futile. He unsaddled Judas, staked him out, and fed him some of the grain. He was not hungry, but he knew that unless he was lucky, the pursuit might take several days and he would need his strength. He fried bacon and ate it morosely, then washed it down with water from his canteen. He sat before the fire, his mind blunted by the tragedy. He had been in tough spots before with Indians, but never when the lives of two children were at stake.

He fed the fire carefully, not needing the warmth of the blaze, but it made a cheerful crackling noise, and the orange dotting the darkness seemed to be a counterpart to his dark spirit. He could not sleep for a time, but finally he lay down on his blanket. Sleep did come but only in fitful snatches, and it was never deep, the kind that rested a man.

He came awake from a fearful dream he could not remember and then sat upright and found himself trembling. The dream had been unlike any he had ever had. The details were vague, but in the dream he felt he was falling into a hole that got blacker as he fell. He remembered crying out with fear and terror, something he had never done in his whole life.

He rekindled the fire and drew the blanket over his shoulders to ward off the chill. It was useless to make plans, so he gave up trying. But as he sat in the night's thick darkness, he still felt the fear from the dream. With a shock he realized what it meant. Falling down the deep hole was what his life was like, and at that instant he could almost hear Peter Cartwright crying out with a voice like a trumpet: "Jesus died for sinners."

That was the beginning of the worst night Thad had ever known. He sat there, and as he did, a portion of the Scripture came to his mind: *Prepare to meet thy God*. He had heard a sermon on that when he was just a boy, and he was surprised that it had lodged in his mind. He tried to shove it away, but it was almost like a physical force. *Prepare to meet thy God*.

"I reckon I need to prepare, but I'm too far gone for that."

His voice made an uneven sound, husky in the silence, but it brought no relief. The night was more than a physical darkness covering his eyes. It went down deep. There was something even deeper in his soul. And as Thaddeus Brennan sat there, he knew that God had found him at last!

He never remembered afterward exactly how it happened, but he could remember vividly that he had struggled against God, crying out finally, "I can't do it, God! I'm just no good!" And he remembered Temperance reading the story of the prodigal son one night. Twice he got up and walked stiffly around the small camp, once lifting his hands up and crying out, "God, I don't know what You want. I just don't know!"

Sometime before morning he had begun to weep. It was something he had not done since he was a small child, but weep he did. And then finally, as he was weeping, something came to his mind, to his heart, or to his spirit, he could never know which, that said, "Just call upon Me and I will take the darkness away."

Brennan remembered later that he called on God, claiming the blood of Jesus. His memory was never very clear, but the peace that came on him was clear. It came at dawn when the sun had broken over the horizon in the east, and it seemed that the brightness that warmed and gave life to the earth entered into his own spirit.

He finally rose, wiped his eyes, and muttered in a husky whisper, "Well, Lord, I'm a mighty poor specimen, but no matter what else happens, I'm going to do whatever You tell me. Right now, Lord, I know You love these children, and I'm the only one that can help them. And You're the only one that can help me. So, You tell me what to do and I'll do it." He saddled his horse and broke camp. As he rode off, his face was pale and he felt weak after the struggle. But new strength came to him, and he knew, somehow, that life would never be the same for him again.

*

RENA AND BENT WERE huddled together, watching the Indians. From time to time one of them would come over and look down at them. A tall thin Indian poked Rena with his finger and said something to the chief, whose name they found out was Black Eagle. Black Eagle had answered shortly, but the tall Indian called No Horses was insistent.

Finally Black Eagle shook his head and spoke sharply.

"What's he saying about me?" Rena asked.

Black Eagle looked at her, his eyes dark. They had traveled hard on the second day, but he showed no sign of fatigue. "He says he wants you for his squaw."

Rena was frozen and could not break her gaze away from Black Eagle's. She tried to think of some way to protest, but his gaze had the hardness of stone.

"I will not give you to him," Black Eagle said. "Maybe not now anyway. He has no horses to pay for you."

"What are you going to do with us?" Bent said in an unsteady voice.

Black Eagle rose and came to stand in front of the two. "You will be Cheyenne."

"I won't be no Indian," Bent cried out.

Black Eagle stared at the boy. He liked his spirit and said, "You will become Cheyenne or you will die." He gestured toward Rena. "And you will be a squaw to one of my warriors."

Black Eagle waited for them to reply, but neither of them did. He left and walked past the fire where the others were feasting on buffalo meat. They had killed a buffalo, which had slowed them. Rena watched as Black Eagle paced around the camp, always alert as a cat.

"I ain't gonna be no Cheyenne," Bent said. "Thad will come and get us."

"No, he won't," Rena said, her voice dead. "He won't do it."

"Sure he will. He likes me."

"He doesn't like anybody but himself. Well, I'll kill myself before I let any of these Indians touch me."

Bent stared at her, fear showing in his face, but he held on to his one hope. "Thad will come! I know he will!"

"No, he won't. He's nothing but a drunk, and he don't care about nobody but himself!"

❧

THAD MOVED CAREFULLY THE second day of the pursuit. He seemed to be two men. One was the relentless hunter on the trail of his enemies, and the other was the man he did not know, for in his mind was the strong memory of calling on God and promising he would be a servant, that he would follow God. Several times that day he paused and tried to pray, but his prayers seemed a failure. *God, I don't see You or feel You, but I'm just believing You're there and what happened last night was real. I'm asking You to help me get these kids back. That's the only kind of prayer I can pray right now.*

He followed the trail relentlessly and finally in midafternoon he became wary. A warning seemed to sound, and it was a familiar feeling. He had often had it when he and Quaid were fighting the Indians in their trapping days. He could never explain it, but immediately before trouble started, somehow, he felt a tingling along his spine. The sensation was mental as well as physical, and he was aware of it as the sun began to drift below the horizon.

"They can't be far ahead," he muttered. "I'd better take it easy." Dismounting, he led Judas forward for the next hour. The horses of the hostiles, he saw, were moving even slower.

"They'll be camping for the night," he said. "Black Eagle won't be looking for me to be coming this soon, so he might be careless."

He kept moving forward until finally it was dusk. There was still enough light to see by, but the tingling that warned him of enemies close by was stronger. He tied Judas securely to a tree, fed him, watered him from his canteen, then moved ahead. He could not go as quietly as the Indians, but he had no choice.

After he had walked no more than twenty minutes, suddenly he stopped. A sound had reached his ears. It was not the sound of a wolf or a coyote or a night bird, and as he stood there, straining every nerve, he recognized voices.

"Got 'em," he said exultantly. He looked up. *Thank You, Lord. You found them for me. Now help me to get those kids.*

He moved stealthily until the voices became plainer and he saw the orange dot of the fire. His nerves were alive, for he knew that Black Eagle would usually station a sentry, but he saw no one. The voices became louder and the fire larger. Finally he began crawling through the brush. He got within a hundred yards of the band, and with a shock he saw Bent and Rena sitting alone, unbound, and the Indians gathered around the fire. They had been drinking, he realized instantly.

He had to think what to do. He studied the situation and counted all six Indians. Black Eagle was sitting by himself. The others were laughing, and their voices were loud and slurred.

"They're all drunk. Good." He pulled his Colt from the holster and checked the loads. "Six shots," he muttered. "Six of them. If I miss, they'll get me." He considered returning to his horse for his rifle, but if he fired from a long-distance rifle range, they would know he was coming. He knew it had to be a sudden surprise attack and that he could not miss.

Give me a steady hand, Lord, he asked. Then he rose into a crouch. He advanced until finally he was only twenty yards from the Indians. He could see their eyes clearly and, with a wash of relief, noticed that Black Eagle had joined the others. Slowly he raised the revolver and steadied it on the Indian farthest from him. There was no turning back now. He put his left hand under his wrist and pulled the trigger. The Indian fell backward, driven by the shot, and instantly Brennan fired at the Indian who had turned to face him, stunned by the sound and the death of his companion.

The air was full of the Colt's roaring, and Thad shot three of them before they could regroup. Black Eagle jumped to his feet and scrambled for a weapon. He grabbed his knife and he must have seen the flashes for he ran straight at Brennan. Brennan then missed a shot but got the last two Indians. However, he had no time to face Black Eagle's charge.

Black Eagle crashed into Thad with a wild cry, and Brennan caught his wrist holding the knife. He pulled his own knife out, and the two rolled around the ground, slashing at each other. Brennan felt the keen blade of Black Eagle, slashing into his chest, and knew that he had to finish it quickly. He stabbed at Black Eagle and felt the knife enter. He pushed it farther, and

Black Eagle uttered a guttural cry and made one final cut that caught Brennan on the side and raked his ribs. Brennan pushed the knife still farther and held on. He felt the body of Black Eagle begin to tremble and then grow still.

Brennan rolled over and called, "Rena—Bent! You OK?"

Then the two were there and Bent was holding on to him. "I knew you'd come, Thad! I knew you would!"

Rena's eyes were big. She could not say a word for a time, then she said, "I didn't think you'd come, Thad."

"You didn't think I'd let that devil have my kids, did you?"

"Thad, you're cut-up bad," Rena cried.

"I guess you're right about that. We've got a long way to go. We've got to stop this bleeding."

By using some of their clothing, they managed to stop the bleeding, and Thad got to his feet. "Let's get out of here." The horses were tied out, and he put Bent and Rena on the two that seemed the most broken. He got on behind Bent and said, "Let's go get Judas. And then let's go home."

❧

"WELL, I'LL BE—" QUAID said. "Will you look at that?"

"What is it, Quaid?"

"Look who's come home."

Shocked, Temperance saw three horses. The two children were riding on each side of Thad, and her heart gave a lurch when she saw that the big man was hardly able to keep his saddle.

"He's been hurt pretty bad," Quaid said. "Come on."

"Well, you done it, partner. You beat the whole Cheyenne nation," Quaid said. "It looks like they got their licks in too."

Brennan was pale and sallow, but he managed a grin. "You wasn't there to mess it up."

Rena and Bent reached Temperance. Bent's eyes were shining as he gasped, "You should have seen him, Temperance! He came charging in and he killed them all, and he beat Black Eagle in a knife fight all by himself! Just him!"

Bent was holding Thad's limp hand. "I knew he'd come. I prayed he would. Rena didn't think so."

Rena's eyes were shining too. "I was wrong. He came for us."

"Always nice to have a hero around," Quaid said. "Now, let me get you off of that hoss. We have to get you patched up right."

Thad turned and said, "Hello, Temperance."

"I'm glad you're back. I've been praying for you."

"I've got something to tell you." Thad swayed in the saddle and licked his lips. "Out there on the prairie, God finally caught up with me."

A glad cry came to Temperance's lips. "Thaddeus!"

"Yep, I hit the glory trail," he said, a faint smile turning the corners of his broad lips upward. "Preach all you want at me now. I reckon I'm ready."

Temperance took his hand and laid it against her cheek. "I'm so glad, Thaddeus," she whispered and saw that, indeed, he was a changed man, and her cry went out in a prayer of thanksgiving to God.

PART FOUR
Rena and Bent

Chapter Nineteen

TEMPERANCE PULLED OUT THE wooden box marked "Ajax Soap Company" and placed it on the ground. Turning to Thaddeus, who was sitting with his back against the wagon wheel and watching her with bleary eyes, she said firmly, "Here, Thaddeus, sit on this box."

"What for?" Thad's tone was surly and his voice slurred, for Temperance had dosed him liberally with laudanum thirty minutes earlier. "I don't wanna sit on no dumb box!"

Temperance did not answer but took him by the arm. "I don't care what you want," she said. "I've got to clean that wound of yours." Thaddeus shot a baleful look at her, then struggled to his feet, pain shooting through his chest. Moving painfully, he made his way to the box and sat down. "Well, that shirt's ruined," she said and began unbuttoning it. Thad protested, "What are you doing?"

"Why, I can't see your wound with your shirt on, can I?"

"I didn't know you was supposed to be a doctor."

Ignoring his protests, Temperance carefully removed the shirt, which was caked with blood and slashed to ribbons. She tossed it to the ground, and Thad protested, "Hey, that's my good shirt!"

"It's filthy! It hasn't been washed since we left Walla Walla. Besides that, it's cut all to pieces."

Sitting there before her, Brennan felt naked and exposed. He watched her as she moved to the wagon, and when she returned with another small wooden box, he was aware a crowd had collected. Belle had appeared, and beside her were Bent and Rena, who was holding Bess. Rose stood next to her, and Billy was sitting on the ground, playing with a block of wood, his favorite toy. Timothy was on a blanket, sound asleep. Brennan looked around at the children staring at him and said, "Get out of here! Go somewhere else and play."

No one moved a muscle, and at that moment Gus walked slowly over to Brennan, reared up, and put his big paws on Brennan's leg. The two stared at each other, and Brennan snapped, "Well, what do *you* want?"

Gus said, "Wow!" and, dropping to all fours, walked away, his head in the air.

"You kids go somewhere! This ain't no sideshow," Thad snapped. Not a one of them answered him, but he could see Belle was grinning. By that time Temperance had found a pair of scissors and was cutting the rough bandages that covered his chest. "This is going to hurt," she said. "Maybe I ought to soak it off."

Thad shook his head. "Go on and pull it off."

"No, I'm going to soak it."

The soaking took considerable time. She took fresh water and slowly poured it over his chest. The blood had dried to a thick, brown crust, and it took the better part of twenty minutes until finally she had removed the last.

"Gosh, look at that!" Bent whispered. "That injun really chopped you, didn't he?"

Thad looked down at his chest. There were two major cuts, one down his side and another across his chest. Both of them were seeping blood, and he muttered, "Well, ain't that a pretty come-off! That's worse than I thought."

"It'll have to be sewed up," Temperance said firmly. "I'll get my needle and thread."

Thad stared at her with apprehension. "Did you ever sew anybody up before?"

Temperance's mouth pursed. "Just Suzy."

"Who was she, a relative?"

"No, she was our pig. Cut herself pretty bad on barbed wire, and I had to sew her up."

"Well, I ain't no pig! I don't want no amateur practicing on me."

Belle suddenly laughed. "That's what doctors do, Thad. They study awhile at school, then they *practice* on their patients until they learn something. Some of them never do, of course."

Temperance had walked to the wagon. She returned with a jug of whiskey, and Thad's eyes brightened. "That'll help deaden the pain."

"Laudanum's for that." She set the jug down, pulled the dark brown bottle of painkiller out, and said, "Here, take a couple more swigs of this."

"It tastes awful."

"You're going to need it," Temperance said grimly. "This is going to hurt."

Thad drank three healthy swallows of the laudanum and handed it back. He watched as she capped the bottle and then said, "What's that whiskey for?"

"To clean you up. I'm going to wash the wounds with it."

"That's a dadgummed waste of good whiskey!"

"Well, you don't drink anymore," Temperance said, her eyes suddenly showing humor. "Christians don't drink whiskey."

"Some of them do," Belle said. "They just don't let people find out about it."

Ignoring Belle, Temperance poured whiskey into a cup. She took a rag and began applying the alcohol to Thad's wound. His eyes widened, and he said, "Woman, that hurts!"

"I know it hurts, but it has to be done. Now be still."

The next half hour was about as painful as anything Thaddeus Brennan could remember. The laudanum helped, but still he was well aware of the needle poking his flesh. He tried not to look, but it was fascinating the way Temperance could stitch the skin together.

"Why, you sew better than anybody I ever saw, Temperance," Rena said. "You want me to try it?"

"You keep your grubby hands off me, Rena," Thad snapped. "Peabody's doing fine."

Belle watched for a time and moved closer. "You're going to have some scars there. You can tell your grandchildren about how you fought the whole Cheyenne nation."

"I don't have no grandchildren."

"Well, you're a young man. You'll have some sooner or later." She smiled and added, "You know, there's lots of things you're going to have to give up now, Brennan. Drinking, wild women like me, and gambling. Just about anything that's fun."

Temperance looked up and said, "Stop teasing him, Belle. I'm happy that he's found the Lord, and he should be too."

Finally the task was done, and she said, "I'm going to have to tear up a sheet to make bandages. Then we'll have to wash them out before we change them."

"Why don't you use some of that fancy underwear?" Rena grinned.

"That's a good idea, but it's too thin for that."

"What underwear is that?" Belle asked curiously.

"Thad won a bunch of fancy underwear, playing poker, but Temperance won't wear it. Says it's unseemly."

"I like unseemly things," Belle said at once. "Let me see them."

"No!" Temperance snapped. "Now, here. You have to have another shirt."

"I bet Quaid's got one," Bent said. "He's got lots of pretty clothes."

"That's probably true. You can just sit there until he gets back."

QUAID RODE IN THIRTY minutes later, and Temperance met him at once. "Quaid, do you have a shirt that Thad can wear? His is too far gone."

"Sure, but I'm bigger than he is."

"Are not!" Thad snapped.

"Am too," Quaid grinned.

"You ain't either, and I don't need your old shirt!"

"Get a shirt, Quaid," Temperance said.

"All right. After that, I'll tell you how to fix breakfast the way I like it."

Quaid brought a fancy shirt and said, "Here, the best shirt you've ever had on, Thaddeus."

Thad moved so abruptly he hurt his wounds, but he put the shirt on and buttoned it up. "There's something wrong with a man that wears fancy shirts like this. Like that man in the Bible."

"What man?" Quaid demanded.

"The one named Lazarus that went to hell. He had fancy shirts, I'll bet."

"Nothing wrong with a believer having nice clothes. Now, I'm going over and help Miss Temperance Peabody cook breakfast."

Brennan watched Quaid as he joined Temperance. Rena sat down beside him and pestered him with questions. Bent moved to his other side so that Thad was framed like a book with living bookends. Brennan watched as Quaid carried on a running conversation with Temperance, and more than once she laughed aloud at his words.

"I don't like the way Peabody's acting."

"Why not?" Rena said.

"You wouldn't understand."

Rena reached over and pulled the back of his hair. "You need a haircut," she said. "I'll cut it for you. And I understand, all right."

"You keep your hands off of me. What is it you understand?"

Rena was grinning mischievously. "I understand you're jealous of Mr. Quaid."

"You're—you're crazy! Why would I be jealous of him?"

"Because Temperance likes him."

"I don't see why."

"Well, I don't either. Maybe it's because he's rich and the best-looking man I ever saw and he's got good manners."

"I've got good manners."

"You don't have *any* manners at all."

"Well, when you get older, Rena, you'll find out that men with lots of manners shouldn't be trusted by women and especially dudes who wear foppish attire like Quaid Mitchell."

"Oh, I see. You think men who are dirty and need a shave and have bad manners are better for women."

"I told you you wouldn't understand."

Rena was quiet only for a few seconds, then she said, as if she had been preparing a speech, "I got to tell you something, Thad. When the Indians had us, I never thought you'd come after us."

"I did," Bent said eagerly.

"Yes, he did," Rena nodded, "but I didn't believe it."

A wonder had come into her face as she sat cross-legged. She looked at Thad and her voice was soft. "Nobody ever done nothing like that for me. I won't never forget it. It was noble, Thad." She got up and walked away quickly before Brennan could answer.

"What's the matter with her?"

"Aw, it's just that nobody was ever good to her before, or to me either. I think she's stuck on you."

"She's twelve years old!"

Bent ignored this. "When you get to feeling better, will you take me hunting again?"

"Sure I will, partner."

Brennan's reply warmed Bent. He said, "I ain't never had a friend like you." His countenance darkened. "What'll I do when you leave us?"

"Your people will be good to you."

"No, they won't."

At that moment Belle brought a plate of food and a brimming cup of coffee. She sat down and held his coffee as he balanced the plate on his knees. "Here," she said. "They're having so much fun over there that Temperance burned the bacon. I guess she's not used to a good-looking man fawning over her."

Brennan was ravenous. He quickly ate the bacon, freshly made biscuits, and the grits.

Belle watched him, then tapped her chin thoughtfully. "You know, I had pretty big plans for us, Brennan."

"What kind of plans?"

"Doesn't matter. They'll never happen now."

Brennan turned to watch her. She was still an attractive woman although hard living marked her features. "Why not?"

"I'm a pretty earthy type, Thad. You were just what I wanted. You and I could have had some good times. But you got a thing with God now." She studied him for a moment and asked abruptly, "You wouldn't sleep with me now, would you?"

Brennan stared at her, unable to answer, somewhat shocked although he was accustomed to her ribald teasing. "I don't know about that."

Belle laughed and squeezed his arm. "No, you wouldn't. Well, it's just as well. Rena would shoot me. You made a conquest there."

"Don't be foolish."

"She never takes her eyes off of you. She can't stop talking about how you came charging in and wiped out a whole set of Indians."

"She's just a kid."

"She's older than her years. She never had a father, and she sees that in you. If you let her down, Thad, it'll break her heart. You're the only man she ever knew that she can trust. I'm glad she found one. I never did."

Brennan was unhappy with her words. "She ought not to be that trusting with a stranger."

"By the time I was twelve years old, I'd fallen in love a dozen times."

"That's just the way with kids."

"I know it is. That's what I'm telling you." She suddenly met his eyes, and there was pain in her expression. "I wish somebody had been good to me when I was her age. Don't you hurt that child."

"Why, I wouldn't think of it."

Belle watched him and noted that he was thinking deeply. "You know, I was worried about you and that preacher woman. I think Temperance had as bad a case on you as Rena, but I'm not worried now."

"Why not?"

"Why, she's got an admirer. A gentleman friend. Look at them, Thaddeus."

Thad involuntarily put his eyes on the pair. They had finished the meal and were sitting together. He noticed that Quaid was wearing fine clothes, even on the trail, and he was close-shaven. His face glowed with health, and his eyes were bright as he spoke with enthusiasm.

He saw also that Temperance was looking at Quaid in a way he could not quite define. It had something of admiration in it, but it was more than that.

"They just look kind of like husband and wife," Belle said.

"You talk foolishness, woman! Get me some more coffee."

ᴄ⁓

FOR TWO DAYS THAD endured the jolting of the wagon. He was too weak to walk and knew he was unable to contend with Judas, so he had suffered the indignity of riding in the wagon. Most of the time Rena and Bent were obviously idolizing him. He was unaccustomed to children and found himself amazed at Bent's imagination. The young boy could make up stories one right after the other, and finally Thad asked, "Bent, how do you think of all those things?"

The boy stared at him with amazement. "Don't you think of stuff like that?"

"Nobody does," Rena said. She was sitting on the wagon seat next to Thad and said, "I think he's going to write stories for a living."

"I could do that," Bent said eagerly.

Rose was also in the wagon holding Billy. "It won't be too long before we get to Fort Smith," she said. "That's when I'll get to meet my grandma and grandpa."

"Well, I'll bet they'll like you and Billy," Thad said.

"What are you going to do after you get us all delivered?" Rena asked.

Rena's question brought only a silence from Thaddeus Brennan. Ever since his experience with God, he had been quieter than usual, and as he sat there with the children, he realized his only immediate destiny was to get them delivered. He had no plans after that. He finally shrugged his shoulders, which brought a twinge to his wounds, and said, "I don't know. Just have to wait and see."

✎

THE TEMPERATURE WAS CHANGING as they moved farther southeast. The flat plains of the Platte Basin had given way to hillier country. There were sections now of trees worthy of the name, and it was beneath a grove of these that Quaid pulled the wagon that night. As soon as the oxen stopped, Thad climbed painfully down. He started toward the oxen, but he was intercepted by Temperance. "Where are you going, Thaddeus?"

"Going to help unyoke the oxen."

"No, you'll pull those stitches out. You go sit down."

"A man can't sit the rest of his life, woman, for crying out loud!"

Temperance took him by the arm and led him to one side. "You sit right there. I'm going to dress those wounds of yours after supper."

"I don't need it."

Temperance shook her head. "You are just like a child," she said with exasperation. "Quaid will take care of the oxen."

Brennan glared at her resentfully, but she ignored him. "You're getting to be downright bossy," he muttered.

He sat there, all the time noticing again how Quaid never missed a chance to move closer to Temperance and say a word to her. He was an efficient sort of fellow and had the oxen unyoked and staked out for the night in plenty of time to chat with Temperance and Belle as they fixed the evening meal.

The supper was good, for Quaid had shot a fat doe, and the meat was almost as tender as home-grown beef. As they sat around the fire, eating the evening meal, Quaid, as usual, was lively. He tried to draw Brennan into the conversation by asking him, "You remember that time we run into that bunch of Kiowas? Tell them about how you saved our scalps that time."

"I disremember."

"Did he really save your life, Quaid?" Temperance asked.

"Oh, we took turns saving each other's lives. I forget which one of us is up on the other one. But old Thaddeus there, he's a good man to have on your side."

Finally the children went to bed, and Belle sat beside Quaid, listening as he told more of his story. Temperance came to Brennan and said, "I'm going to change that dressing now."

"It don't need it, woman!"

"Yes, you do." Without further argument, she unbuttoned his shirt and helped him take it off. "I'll have to wash this shirt," she said. She removed the bandages, which still showed blood-stains, and said, "I'll wash these in the creek. I've got some fresh ones." She once again applied whiskey to the wounds and saw that he didn't flinch. "That doesn't hurt anymore?"

"Not much." Reluctantly he said, "You're a good doctor, Temperance."

Temperance had been dabbing at his wounds, but she stared at him, open-eyed. It was one of the few times he had ever called her anything except Peabody. She looked up quickly and saw that he was watching her. She could not understand his expression. She didn't comment on the use of her name, but she hoped he would use it again. "I wish you'd tell me how you feel, Thaddeus."

"Feel about what?"

"Well, your life's going to be different now that you're a believer."

Thad glanced at the fire thoughtfully. "I've been thinking about that some. I don't know how to start."

"You mind if we talk about it?"

"I guess it's all right."

"Well, every new believer needs to be baptized."

"There's nobody here to do that."

"There will be in Independence. We'll look up a church and a preacher. I'll be so proud to see you baptized."

"Why is that so important?"

"Because Jesus commanded us to be baptized. It's kind of a sign."

"What do you mean 'a sign'?"

"Well, when a person begins a new business, they put a sign out in front of it: 'Mary Smith—Dressmaker.' People know what she does, what she stands for. When a man or a woman or a child is baptized, it's like they're hanging out a sign. Yours would say, 'Thaddeus Brennan—a Christian.'"

"Never thought of it like that."

"The next thing you need to do is read your Bible. Have you read the Bible much, Thaddeus?"

"No, I tried it a few times, but I didn't get much sense out of it."

"Well, it's God's letter to you. If you got a letter from me, you'd read it, wouldn't you?"

"I reckon so."

"Well, this letter's from God. You need to read the Bible and seek God's way."

"It's hard to understand."

Temperance had finished dabbing the wounds with alcohol, and now she took the sheet she had washed the day before. She placed the end of it under his left arm and leaning forward she passed the rest of it around him. In order to do this, she had to press herself close against him. Brennan looked down at her but made no comment.

When she had finally fastened the bandage, she said, "It's not all hard. For instance there are verses that say this: 'The steps of a good man are ordered by the LORD: and he delighteth in his way. Though he fall, he shall not be utterly cast down: for the LORD upholdeth him with his hand.' Now, that's not hard, is it?"

"Well, I guess I'd better memorize that one. I'm pretty sure to fall."

"Maybe not. Daniel is the man I admire most in the Bible. Most of the men in the Bible failed God, even David. He was a man after God's own heart, but he committed adultery and murder. But he had God's promise that He wouldn't abandon him. So, if you do fall, you have to get up and ask God's forgiveness."

Brennan watched her face as the flickering of the fire cast highs and lows on her features. He had discovered long ago, although he had kept it carefully hidden, that this woman had a power to stir his hungers and deepen his sense of loneliness. Watching her now, he saw something soft and gentle and appealing, qualities he had not sought in a woman before. It seemed to cling to his mind, disturbing him somehow. It was as if a warmth rose from her and touched him. Earlier he'd resented it. But now, somehow, her softness, gentleness, and goodness drew him like a magnet.

He put his shirt on carefully and then asked abruptly, "What are you going to do after we deliver these kids?"

"I don't know." She seemed to be hesitant, as if she were concealing something from him.

"Will you go back to Walla Walla?"

"I guess so. It's a good farm."

She seemed unhappy, and Thad spoke up without intending to. "I'd like to go back and help you at that place if it wasn't for Marshal Meek."

"Why, Thaddeus, you hated that place!"

"Oh, I didn't hate it that bad. I reckon it was good for me in a way, but I guess I'm pretty confused right now. You know, Temperance, sometimes a fellow bends over to pick something up, and when he straightens up, the whole danged world has changed. That's kind of the way it is with me right now."

She reached over and put her hand over his. "It's all right. It'll clear up. You're on the Lord's side now. He's not going to let you fall, Thaddeus."

FORT KEARNY WAS NO better than any of the other forts Temperance had seen. It was a busy place teeming with soldiers and Indians, many of them the worse for drink. They had pulled in late in the afternoon, and she had said at once, "Thaddeus, we need to get you to a doctor."

"No sense in that. I'm all healed up."

"You'd argue with a stump!"

"Well, you got his measurement at last. Stubbornest fellow I've ever seen," Quaid grinned. "Tell you what. I'm going to take you all to the restaurant for a meal. It's all on me. Eat until you pop."

All of them were excited about this. Belle had to squeeze herself into one of Temperance's dresses. She seemed to be bursting out of it, but that didn't bother her.

Quaid led the way to the restaurant and ordered the best in the house for everyone. Temperance enjoyed the meal, but she saw that Thaddeus said nearly nothing.

"What do you think is wrong with him, Belle?" she whispered.

"He feels left out. Quaid's got the money and buying all the things for us and taking care of us. Thad was the big man until Quaid came along."

"He's in a new world, Belle," Temperance said. "He doesn't know how to handle the one he's in now."

Thad suddenly got up and said, "Thanks for the meal, Quaid. I'm going to go look around a little bit."

Quaid watched him go and shook his head. "Thaddeus isn't happy. I thought he would be once he found the Lord."

"It's hard to move out of an old life into a new one," Temperance murmured. "We think we want to, but suddenly we have to learn a whole new set of rules."

"I'd like to live in a world where there weren't any rules," Belle grinned. "That'd be my kind of world."

"Well, you're going to New Orleans. That's about as close to a place without rules I know of," Quaid grinned.

"I hope he's not going to get drunk," Rena whispered to Bent.

"He won't," Bent said. "Don't you go to doubting him now, Rena."

☙

THEY HAD REACHED THE wagon, all except Thad, and all of them had the same question in mind. Belle gave words to what the rest were thinking. "I hope he's not drinking. Hard for a man to quit cold turkey like that, but he wouldn't be the first man to fall."

"He won't drink," Bent spoke up confidently. "I know he won't."

Ten minutes after this proclamation Thad walked into camp. He said nothing, but he had a small brown paper bag in his hand. "Pretty busy town," he said. It was obvious he had not been drinking.

Rena said, "I wonder if he's got a bottle of whiskey in that sack."

"No, he don't," Bent whispered. "You got to start trusting him, Rena."

"I want to, but . . ." She did not finish her words but watched Thaddeus carefully. He put the brown sack away with the rest of his things beside his blanket. She was determined to find out what he was hiding. It took a long time after everyone else was asleep. Rena was still awake, watching Thaddeus. He had not moved, but suddenly she saw the blue spurt of a lighted match and then a candle was lit, throwing its faint glow over Thad's face. Getting out of her blanket, she moved stealthily toward where Thad was. He had pulled himself upright and was leaning against one of the wagon wheels. He pulled the sack out and started when Rena said, "What's in the sack?"

"Rena!" he whispered, "don't creep up on a fellow that way!"

"What you got in there, Thad?"

"You're nosy as a coon."

"It's not whiskey, is it?"

"Here, look at it."

Rena took the sack he handed her and knew at once it was not a whiskey bottle. It was something flat and rectangular. She pulled it out and held it up to the dim light of the candle. "Why, it's a book." She looked at the spine and read the title: "Holy Bible. This is what you got?"

"Yes."

"Everyone thought you had whiskey in this sack. Why are you hiding it?"

"Don't ask questions, and you don't have to blab about this to anyone."

Rena felt a sudden glow of happiness. "I'm glad it wasn't whiskey and I'm sorry for doubting you, Thad, but I don't know why you're so ashamed of it. It's only a Bible." She flipped through the pages, and then a thought struck her. She had a vulnerable look, this young girl, despite the hard things life had dealt her. "What'll you give me if I don't tell what you're reading?"

Thad reached over and took the Bible. "Well, when you grow up, I'll sort through all the young fellows who come courting you. I'll throw all of them away but one, the best one."

Rena giggled. "That'll be fun. Now read me some of the Bible, Thad."

"Why do you call Quaid 'mister,' but you never call me by that?"

"'Cause he didn't save me from no Indians. Now, read."

Thad opened the Bible, holding it reverently, and then began to read: "'In the beginning God created the heaven and the earth....'"

Chapter Twenty

QUAID WAS LIFTING THE yoke to put on two of the oxen when a voice behind him said, "I'll help do that."

Turning quickly, Quaid saw that Thad had dressed and was walking toward him. They were a week out of Fort Kearny now and had left the Platte. The country changed more as they turned south, and wagon trains were fairly common.

"It's OK. I can do it."

"I'm sick of doing nothing."

Quaid started to argue, but he saw the set look of determination on Thad's face. "I think I know how you feel," he said. "When I broke my leg that winter up on the upper Missouri and couldn't do anything, I was ready to blow my brains out by the time spring came and I could get around. It goes against the grain doing nothing."

Thad picked up one end of the oxbow and Quaid the other. They laid it over the necks of two oxen and fastened it. They soon had the animals ready to go, and Thad gave Quaid a look of determination. "I'm going to ride Judas this morning."

"That's a pretty lively animal, Thad."

"I can handle him. If you'd saddle him for me, I'd appreciate it."

Reluctantly Quaid went to where the animal was staked out. He carefully approached the big stallion, for Judas was moody. Fortunately, on this particular morning, he seemed to be agreeable. Still, that meant nothing with the big horse.

After Quaid had saddled the animal and put the bridle on with nearly no struggle, he turned to find a small audience watching him.

"Why are you saddling Judas?" Temperance asked.

"Thaddeus aims to ride him."

Thad had come up and now settled his hat down over his head. He still looked raunchy and rather strange. He wore his dirt-encrusted pants but Quaid's fancy silk shirt.

"That's too dangerous, Thad. You're not ready yet," Temperance said.

"I reckon I can do what I want to," Thad said. He advanced toward the horse, took the lines from Quaid, and moving cautiously, put his foot in the stirrup. As he mounted, he felt pain across his wounds but nothing as it had been. He had healed well and knew it, and now as he sat there, he said, "Sorry to disappoint you. I've got this horse's number."

"I think that horse has got religion like you, Thad," Belle grinned.

Thad was hurting but wouldn't let on. He said, "I'm going to go on ahead."

"That's right. You wipe out all the hostiles waiting for us up around Fort Leavenworth," Quaid grinned.

Temperance watched as he rode off, sitting loosely in the saddle. "I wish he wouldn't do that."

"He'll be all right. He healed up well."

Temperance shook her head. She said, "I'm going to go after him. Can I ride your mare, Quaid?"

"Sure you can. I'll saddle her for you."

Fifteen minutes later Thad looked around to see Temperance ride up beside him on Quaid's mare. "I been worried about you," she said.

"A man can't be a baby forever."

She said nothing but rode alongside him. They passed a wagon train headed West—only ten wagons—and the people in the wagons waved as they moved by.

"They seem so fresh, and they don't know what they're looking for. They don't know how much trouble they're headed into," Temperance said.

"I guess that's the way with all of us. If we did, I don't guess we'd ever go anywhere."

The two rode past the last of the wagons, looked back, and saw the oxen plodding along.

"We'll be in Independence in less than a week, Quaid tells me."

"Reckon that's so."

"It'll be the end of something when we get there, won't it?"

"Well, it means we got there with our hair in place." He turned and smiled at her. His beard had grown and had a scraggly look, and his hair hung down over his collar.

She wondered what he would look like all barbered, for she had never seen him when he wasn't rough-looking. "I know you've been reading the Bible," she said.

"Rena tell on me?"

"Yes, she did."

Indeed, Rena had come every night to Thad as he read the Bible, and after a few nights she seemed to find intense pleasure in it. "She thinks it's wonderful."

"Well, it's got me buffaloed, and I can't understand much of it."

"What part are you reading now?"

"I started out to go right through it, and I made it pretty good through Genesis and Exodus, but that Leviticus has got me plumb bogged-down. I can't make any sense out of it."

"I know how you feel. Leviticus is hard for anyone. All those Jewish laws and rules."

"It tells about animals you can't eat. You know it says we can't eat a catfish? I can't understand that. I don't see what's wrong with a catfish."

"To be truthful, neither do I. Why don't you try the Gospels. I think that's what you need."

"Maybe I will."

As they rode, Temperance marveled at how the big man had changed. It was not so much in what he said as in his whole attitude. Since she had known him, there had been an explosive quality to Thaddeus Brennan. He had seemed to be filled with anger, but that was gone now, and he was quiet most of the time. She asked him suddenly, "How do you feel about killing all those Indians, Thaddeus?"

"Wish it hadn't happened."

Temperance was startled. "But you didn't have any choice."

"No, I didn't. Still, I can understand the Indian's point of view. I killed that chief's son. For an Indian that's the worst insult a man can give them. I would have done exactly what he did, I guess, if I'd been born in a teepee instead of a house. You reckon God will forgive me for that?"

"If you do ask for forgiveness, don't keep digging it up."

He suddenly turned to look at her. "What do you mean digging it up?"

"I mean there are times when we do a wrong thing and we know it." Her voice was even and her eyes thoughtful. "We ask God to forgive us, but the next day we ask Him again because we still feel bad."

"You think that's wrong?"

"How would you feel if you did something wrong to me and you asked me to forgive you and I did, and then the next day you came again and asked me again? What would that be like?"

"I guess it'd be tiresome."

"That's right. So God says He's buried our sins as far from us in the sea as the East is from the West. So, if we're serious and really ask God, once we ask Him to forgive us, it's all over with."

The two rode on for a time, and Thad started once to warn Temperance about Quaid. He could not think of a way to say it. Finally he said, "Quaid's quite a fellow."

"Yes, he is."

"Good-looking, got money. He always was good-looking, but, of course, he didn't have any money when we was together. I guess he's enough to turn a woman's head."

Temperance turned and smiled at him. "I like him a lot. I can see why you'd want him as a friend."

"Yeah, he's been that all right." It was on the tip of Thad's tongue to warn her that Quaid was a ladies' man, but he knew that would be useless. He finally fell silent, and Temperance wondered why. It was not an angry silence but simply something that seemed to trouble him. *He's got a long way to go*, she thought, *and I'll have to help him all I can.*

FOR FIVE DAYS THEY made good time, and finally when it was late afternoon, Thad pulled Judas up beside Temperance, who was in the wagon beside Rena. "There it is," he said, "the Missouri River."

"We're there?" Temperance cried with excitement.

"We cross the river tomorrow on the ferry. We'll camp out here tonight."

That night everyone was excited, and it was hard for Temperance to get the children to bed. She herself had trouble sleeping, and the next morning she woke a little groggy for lack of sleep. When she got up, she saw that the men had already fixed the oxen and Belle had cooked breakfast.

"You're getting to be quite a sleepyhead, Temperance," Belle said.

"I'm sorry, Belle. I don't know what happened to me."

"Guess we can go get on that ferry now," Quaid said. "We'll pull into Independence pretty soon."

"What's the date?" Temperance asked.

"July twenty-fourth."

"We made a pretty good trip, considering everything," Thad said. "And all of us made it. That's a good record for a trip."

"It is. We couldn't have done it without you, Thad."

Thad gave her a quick glance and seemed pleased. "Let's get going," he said brusquely. "I'm anxious to get to town."

❧

THEY HAD TO WAIT for a place on the ferry, so by the time they rode into Independence, it was growing late. They drove down the main street of the town. Independence, in essence, had grown up around its dignified, steepled, brick courthouse.

The town had all the businesses vital for a growing population. It housed, for the most part in two-story wooden buildings with steep roofs, a general store, hardware store, bank, hotel, livery stable, laundry, blacksmith shop, post office, sheriff's office, city hall, church, dentist's office, doctor's office, and several saloons.

Temperance exclaimed, "There sure are a lot of people in a town that doesn't seem that big!"

"Most of them don't live here," Quaid remarked. "They gather here from all over the country to start for Oregon."

"Well, where do they stay? They all can't stay in that hotel."

"Oh, they live in the wagons just like we did."

Temperance waited until they had pulled up in front of the general store, then Quaid and Belle took all the children inside to buy them soda pop. She went at once to the box she kept under the seat of the wagon, opened it, and pulled out some money. "Thaddeus, here's the money I promised you for getting us here."

"The job's not done yet, not until the kids are with their people."

Temperance hesitated, then said something that had been on her mind. "Quaid said he'd take us. If you want to leave, you can."

For a moment Thad looked startled, then he thought of how he would have given anything for an offer like this early in the trip. But now he felt completely different. "You want me to do that?" he asked.

"No."

"Then give me a hundred dollars. I've got some things to buy." Temperance counted out the bills, and he looked at the money as if it were a foreign substance. A smile tugged at the corners of his lips, and he said, "Well, Temperance, I've got things to do. I'll see you later."

Temperance watched him go, and then a moment's worry came to her. A hundred dollars was a lot of money for a man, enough to do anything he wanted. She put the thought out of her head. *I've got to trust him. He's not the same man he was.*

She went inside the store and found the children sucking on hard candy that Quaid had bought for them, and Quaid said, "Find you something pretty, a new dress or something."

"I couldn't do that."

"Well, I could," Belle said, smiling up at Quaid.

"Well, find yourself something nice then," he said.

It took awhile for Belle to pick out a new outfit. She had to try on practically all the man had in stock. Finally she found one she liked along with a pair of new shoes.

"Well, I don't have any diamonds, but I'm ready for New Orleans," she said. "How do I look?"

"You look fine," Temperance said.

"Let's go look the town over," Belle smiled.

They exited from the general store and walked down one side of the street. They had gotten only halfway to the end when suddenly Rena said, "Look, it's Thad."

It was Thad but a different Thad. He had been to a barber and had had a shave and a haircut. He was wearing a pair of new trousers, a new shirt, new boots, and a rolled-crown, wide-brimmed hat.

"Well," Quaid grinned as Thad came up to them. "If you drop dead, Thaddeus, we won't have to do a thing to you except put a lily in your hand."

Rena was walking around Thad, staring at him. "I didn't know you was so good-looking under all that dirt and hair."

"Well, thank you—I guess."

Temperance was somewhat shocked. Like Rena, this was a different Thaddeus. He stood before her loosely, a slight smile on his tanned face. He was several inches over six feet and didn't show the bulkiness of his two hundred pounds. The shirt revealed the broad flats of his shoulders and the muscles of his chest and upper arms, and she noted that his fingers were long and tapering. He made a big idle shape as he stood there with a half smile on his lips. She stammered as she said, "You—you look fine, Thaddeus."

"Well, that's enough about my manly beauty. Come on. I'm taking you to eat this time."

He led them to the café and seemed to take great pleasure in ordering a meal for all of them. Temperance was sitting next to Belle, and Belle said, "It's his way of showing that he's as good a man as Quaid."

After the meal was over, he said, "I got a surprise for you. There's a troop of actors in town. We're all going to see the performance."

"What is it?"

"I don't know. I do know they got a juggler, an acrobat, and they do some Shakespeare."

"Oh, I've never been to a theatrical," Rena said. "Can we sit up front, Thad?"

"You can sit up on the stage if you want to, honey. Anybody fools with you, I'll shoot their leg off."

Thad was in a mood Temperance had never seen before. His eyes were bright, and he seemed so different that she kept stealing glances at him.

Finally they reached the building rented by the acting troupe. A poster was pasted on the side of the wall, and they stopped in front of it. Quaid read it aloud: "Minstrelsy, burlesque, extravaganzas, Ethiopian eccentricities. Nothing to offend the most sensitive taste. Admission fifty cents. Private boxes three dollars."

"What's an Ethiopian eccentricity?" Temperance asked.

"I don't know, but I'd sure like to. Come on now, I'll buy the tickets."

They lined up, led by Thad with Temperance beside him, holding Timmy in her arms. Behind them Rose was holding Billy, while Rena with Bent beside her was holding Bess. They were grouped together with Belle and Quaid standing to one side, waiting.

The man stared at them and said, "Nice family you got, mister."

Temperance flushed, feeling the blood warm her cheeks, but Thad said loudly, "Thank you."

"These are all your kids, are they?"

"Of course they are," Thad said indignantly. "We got another six at home. We have to take them out half a dozen at a time."

The man, who was short and stubby and had a cigar stuck in the side of his mouth, looked at Temperance. "You don't look old enough to have a dozen children."

"She's fifty-six years old. Is that old enough?"

Suddenly Temperance giggled. When he had the tickets and moved away, Rena reached up and pulled at his arm. "Why'd you tell that man that lie?"

"He was rude. I can't abide rudeness. Just keep that in mind, miss."

The show was very poor, indeed, but it was the only show Rena, Bent, and Rose had ever seen. They were late getting back to the wagon, and as the children were getting ready for bed, Thad pulled Quaid to one side. "You don't have to make the trip to St. Joe and Fort Smith, Quaid. I got this thing covered."

Quaid grinned slightly. "You're always worried about me, aren't you, my comfort and all?"

"I know you got things to do."

"Why, I'm enjoying watching you, Thaddeus. A man never knows what you'll do next. I reckon I'll go the rest of the way just for the spectacle of it all. Why"—he grinned broadly—"you'll be more interesting than an Ethiopian eccentricity!"

Chapter Twenty-one

THE SMELL OF WOOD smoke and coffee laced the air as Temperance made the morning breakfast. A breeze stirred the musky and pungent odors of the pine trees that lined the banks of the Missouri River, and the smell of the river itself was strong. The sun was barely up, and as she put bacon in the frying pan, a fish broke the river's surface, the sound resonating through the still air. From somewhere to her left, a deer made a racket in the brush on its way to the water. As the bacon sizzled in the pan, a series of thoughts spread through her mind, and for one moment she stood still and motionless in a tableau beside the fire. They had been on the road from Independence headed for St. Joe for two days. During all that time Temperance had been more silent than usual, and the others had noticed. Quaid, who had been putting the oxbow on the oxen, came and stood beside her. "Breakfast smells good," he said.

Temperance did not answer. She removed the bacon and began to break eggs into the skillet. "I'm going to scramble the eggs. It's too much trouble to do them any other way."

"Scrambled is fine."

Moving to one side where he could see Temperance's face, Quaid studied her carefully. "You're not happy, Temperance," he said. "You hardly said a word since we left Independence. What's the matter?"

Temperance cast a look at Timmy lying on his stomach on a blanket. He was kicking and squirming, and she smiled but only briefly. "I've always wanted children, Quaid," she said finally, and her voice was muted. "I've gotten so attached to Timmy, and now I'm going to have to give him up."

Quaid had suspected this was the problem, and he said gently, "You'll have children of your own."

"No, I never will." She pushed the eggs around with a fork and added with a trace of bitterness, "No man has ever wanted me."

Quaid knelt beside her and put his arm around her. "You're wrong about that."

"No, I'm not."

"You're woman enough for any man." He suddenly pulled her around and kissed her. It came as a shock to her, and when he lifted his lips, she whispered, "Don't treat me like this, Quaid."

"Like what?" he said. "It was just a kiss."

"You've got a way with women. That's plain enough."

Quaid was troubled by her words and stood before her, his handsome face still but his eyes half-hooded as he thought over her words. "I've done my share of chasing," he said finally. "But it means nothing." He struggled to find the words and finally said, "You know, when a fellow passes a certain age, Temperance, he wants to make some kind of a mark that will live after he's gone."

"We all want that, I guess."

"On the trail outside of Fort Kearny," he said, "one day I was out and I found the traces of a grave. I think it was a child. It was very small. Someone had put a sign up made out of wood and it was weathered. All I could read was the name Alice. But the grave was hard to see. I almost stepped on it. Know what I did?" Quaid said. "I began clearing the grave away. I got some rocks and I outlined the grave, put the marker back on it. It was fading away and no one would know who Alice was. I wanted to do something to make her live a little bit longer."

"That was thoughtful of you. Not many men would think of a thing like that."

Quaid was thinking deeply, and finally he said, "The only thing a man can leave that will outlast him is some kind of a monument. Some men do it by their deeds. Nobody will ever forget George Washington. But most of us don't have that kind of life. The only other thing that we can leave that will be part of us walking around after we're gone is children."

This was another side of Quaid that Temperance had not seen. She lifted the eggs off the fire, put them into a large bowl next to the bacon on a plate, then still holding the skillet, she turned to him. "I didn't know you thought about things like that."

"I didn't when I was younger, but as we get older, we have some long thoughts. Most of us wish we could go back and live our lives over again. You can't do that though," he said and gave her a rueful grin. "We just have to start where we are now."

From across the camp Thad had been watching the two as they spoke. He could not hear their words, but he was studying their faces. Belle, who had been speaking to him of what lay on the trail ahead, fell silent for a moment and was watching him. He turned to face her and said, "He's quite a spellbinder. I wish he'd leave her alone."

"Why? What's wrong? They're not doing anything wrong."

Thad had no answer for that. He shook his shoulders in a restless motion and kept his eyes on the pair.

"Don't begrudge her this moment. She's never had a man."

"You don't know Quaid like I do. He can charm the birds out of the trees. I've seen women's eyes follow him when we went into restaurants. Whatever it is that women like, he's got it, but he never stays with a woman. He'll romance her and then get tired of her and go off and leave her."

Belle's face grew still and her mouth showed her displeasure. "Well, at least she'll have the memory of a man showing her some attention. That's more than she's got now."

"It's not enough."

"It's all some women get. Now leave them alone, Thad!"

⌒

A STEADY DOWNPOUR TURNED the road into a quagmire of mud that slowed their progress, but they arrived at Saint Joseph, Missouri, on the last day of July. They came into the town at three o'clock in the afternoon, and Thad, who was riding Judas, came up to say to Temperance, "I'll see if I can find out where the Blanchards live." Without waiting for an answer, he turned and moved the big stallion to where a man was sitting in front of a hardware store. He was tilted back in a chair, his eyes fixed on the newcomers. He was a small man with bright eyes and a bushy, black mustache. His clothes were rough, and he didn't move as Thad pulled Judas up in front of him. "We're looking for Tom Blanchard. You know him?"

"Of course I know him. Why wouldn't I?"

"I don't know." Thad grinned briefly. "Where can I find him?"

"He owns the hardware store, but he's closed for the day."

"Can you tell me how to find his house?"

"Why wouldn't I be able to tell you how to find his house? You think I don't know anything?"

"Sorry. Give me some directions if you will, partner."

"You go down this street clear through town and turn left at the livery stable. Go a quarter of a mile and you'll see a big house with white pillars in front. There's a bag swing out in the front and the nicest pinto horse you ever saw out in the pasture. What are you looking for him for?"

"Just some private business."

"If you can't find it, come back and I'll take you myself."

Thad smiled and rode back until he was beside the wagon. "It's not too far. Shouldn't be too hard to find."

Temperance was holding Timmy, possessively. She said nothing, but he saw that her eyes were disturbed. "Look," he said, "they're probably fine people. He'll be all right."

"Let's go find the house, Thaddeus."

The house was not difficult to find. It was a fine structure, a two-story white frame with three gables and a well-kept yard. Temperance got down out of the wagon, and, without asking Thad, walked up on the steps. He said nothing, but when she did not move, he knocked on the door.

After a brief moment the door opened and a tall, well-dressed woman in her forties stood there. Her eyes flew open as she saw Timmy in Temperance's arms, and she cried out, "Tom! Tom! Come here! Timmy's here!"

A tall lean man wearing a suit appeared, and his eyes lit up at once. "You must be Miss Peabody," he said. "I'm Tom Blanchard. This is my wife, Kate."

But Kate Blanchard paid no attention. She came forward and looked down at the child, and tears came into her eyes. "He looks like Martha, Tom."

Tom Blanchard came forward and put his arm around his wife. He touched Timmy's chin. Timmy gurgled, reached out, and took Tom's finger.

"He's—he's the one we've been praying for for so long, Kate." His voice was unsteady, and he said, "Come in right now. We want to hear everything. Your letter was quite brief, Miss Peabody."

"Well, there's some more of us, Mr. Blanchard."

Blanchard looked at the wagon and said, "Get them all in here. Wife, we've got to have a big supper tonight to celebrate our new boy."

"Can I hold him?" Kate Blanchard asked, and when Temperance handed him over, she handled Timmy as if he were very fragile. He looked up at her and grinned toothlessly. "Just like having Martha back," she whispered.

"Bring him on in. Is this your husband, ma'am?"

Thad at once said, "No, I've been the guide from Walla Walla."

"Well, bring everybody on in. We're going to have a feast tonight."

"Yes," Kate said, not taking her eyes off Timothy. "We want to hear all about Martha and Clyde and about your trip here." She looked up at Quaid and the children standing beside the wagon. "Is that your husband and your children out there?"

"No, that's a friend of mine," Thad said quickly. "We're taking the children to their people."

"Isn't that fine! God will bless you for it," Blanchard said heartily. "Now, let me hold that boy while Kate cooks supper."

℮

THE SUPPER HAD BEEN delicious. Kate Blanchard had apologized that there was not more, but the meal consisted of steak pounded and floured, fried, and drenched in gravy, an enormous bowl of red beans laced with onions, and vegetables including baked potatoes bursting out of their jackets and peppers of several different varieties. There had been sliced cucumbers, fresh bread whose aroma filled the whole house, all sorts of corn relish, jams, and hot apple pie with flaky crust.

Timmy had not been allowed to touch the floor, for either Kate or her husband, Tom, had held him constantly.

"I can't wait for this boy to get old enough to go fishing, and I intend to teach him how to play ball too."

Kate's eyes were moist as she saw the two. Then she turned and said, "We want to know all about Martha and Clyde. We tried so hard to get them to stay here. Tom offered to build them a house and set him up in business, but Clyde had wandering on his mind. Tell us all about them."

Temperance gave them the history, and both the Blanchards understood at once that she had done her best for them. They thanked her profusely.

"I brought all their personal things, pictures of the family, and letters. I think some of them were from you."

"Well, that was so thoughtful of you, Miss Peabody."

It took some time after the supper, but finally Kate Blanchard got everyone settled down. The big house had five bedrooms, and there was plenty of room.

Tom Blanchard came to Temperance before she retired and was beaming. "I want to help you with the expenses of the trip, Miss Peabody."

"You don't have to do that, Mr. Blanchard."

"I insist. God has blessed Kate and me financially." He cleared his throat and said, "I haven't cried since I was twelve years old, as I can remember, but I can't seem to stop blubbering." He had a sheaf of bills in his hand and he took her hand and closed it on them. "You've done a wonderful thing, miss, and I want to show our gratitude. You just use this to do whatever needs doing. Now, you go on to bed and get a good night's sleep. I guess you'll be leaving soon."

"Yes, we've got to take two of the children to Fort Smith."

"Well, the Lord will take care of you," he said simply. She went to the bedroom she was sharing with Rena, and as soon as she could, she undressed and got into the bed. She lay there for awhile and then prayed: *Lord, I don't want to be selfish. Timmy will have a wonderful home here, and I thank You for bringing us here safely. Help us now with the other children.*

e⁓

THE BREAKFAST WAS BOUNTIFUL—PANCAKES, eggs fried and scrambled, pork chops, grits, fresh biscuits, and four different kinds of jams and jellies along with pots of coffee and fresh milk.

After the breakfast, Quaid and Thad had the oxen yoked, and the moment came that Temperance had been dreading. Kate Blanchard was holding Timmy, and she held him out. "I guess you want to say good-bye, Temperance."

Temperance took the baby and held him for a moment. She looked down in his face, and touched his fat cheek, which made him grin as it always did. She kissed him, smoothed his hair, and then handed him back. She could not keep the tears back, and Kate Blanchard said quickly, "When you get settled, you write to us. You've got my address. We'll have pictures made of Timmy and we'll send them to you as he grows up." Kate reached forward, put her arm around Temperance, and pulled her close. She was a big woman, and Temperance felt small and vulnerable. "We'll never let him forget Miss Temperance Peabody," she whispered. Temperance pulled away when the woman released her and walked outside.

"You OK, Temperance?" Thad asked.

"Yes," she said and got into the wagon. Thad spoke to Babe, and the wagon lurched as the animals leaned into their oxbows. They left the Blanchard house, and despite herself, Temperance looked back and saw the Blanchards with Kate holding Timmy. They were both waving, and she did not have enough spirit to wave back but turned and kept her eyes down until the house was out of sight.

Chapter Twenty-two

"WHAT'S THE MATTER WITH Temperance, Rena?"

Rena and Bent were sitting in the wagon seat. Rena was holding Bess in her lap, rocking her gently. She was silent for a moment and then she said, "She misses Timmy, that's all."

"Well, shucks, she knew she was going to have to leave him."

"That didn't make it any easier, Bent."

Bent was whittling on a piece of wood with a knife Thad had bought him. He watched the shavings curl up for a time and then he said, "That was a good place for Timmy. He's going to have it good, ain't he?"

"I guess so."

"Well, if he's going to have it so good, I can't see why Temperance is so miserable."

Impatiently Rena said, "She needs her own babies, you dope!"

"Well, you got to have a man for that. She ought to get one."

"That shows how much you know. A woman can't always do that. She always has to wait until a man wants her and then asks her. The man has to do the asking."

"Why, I reckon I knew that, but I know what I'm going to do." Bent clicked the pocket knife closed and stuck it in his pocket. "I'm going to tell Quaid to marry her."

"You keep your nose out of it! It's none of your business."

Bent gave her an angry look, then jumped down to the ground and hurried to walk beside Thad, ambling along beside Babe. He started once to tell him his plan for Temperance to marry Quaid but then decided, *Maybe Rena's right. Maybe it ain't none of my business.*

~

THE OVERMEYER CHILDREN WERE not the only ones who had taken note of the changes in Temperance and also in Thad. Belle had been highly skeptical of Thad's "conversion," for she had had some unfortunate experiences with so-called Christian men who were hypocrites. She had been walking beside the wagon, and after Bent left to look for something, she walked up beside Thad and said without preamble, "You notice how quiet Temperance is? She's downright miserable."

"Yes, of course I noticed."

"Not much for butting into other people's business, Thad, but I know what's really wrong with her."

"She misses Timmy. She was real attached to that youngun."

"Well, if she had her own babies, she wouldn't miss Timmy."

Thad suddenly turned and gave Belle a hard look. "What are you talking about?"

"She needs a man."

For some reason this angered Thad. "She's got money and a farm. That's more than a lot of women have."

"Have you even talked to her, Thad? You're dumber than a ball of hair!" Belle exclaimed. "That farm doesn't mean anything to her. She needs a man and babies."

"I can't do anything about that, Belle."

"Well, you're even dumber than you look. But don't worry,"

Belle said. "She's got a man to cheer her up. Quaid's got more than loving on his mind this time. You wait and see!"

❧

BELLE'S REMARKS HOUNDED THAD, and he waited for an opportunity. That evening after everyone had gone to bed, Temperance was sitting by the fire, as she often did at night. Usually she was holding Timmy, but tonight she was simply staring into the flames, her arms empty. Thad walked over, pulled up one of the boxes they used for seats, and sat beside her. "Guess we'll be in Fort Smith in a couple of days." When she did not answer, he said, "I'm grieved to see how sad you've been."

"I'm foolish," Temperance murmured. "I know that. Timmy's just where he needs to be with his people, but I can't help missing him."

"Well, it'll get easier, I reckon." He waited for her to respond, and when she did not, he reached a hand out tentatively and started to touch her shoulder but then drew it back. "I hate to see you grieving, Temperance."

Temperance turned to face him. He made a tall shape outlined by the flickering flames of the campfire. The planes of his face were strong, and his deep-set eyes were watching her in a way she could not quite understand. She said quietly, "My father used to say that we all had to eat our peck of dirt in this life, so I guess this is part of mine."

"I guess we do have to eat some dirt along the way, but there are some good things too. This trip has been good for me in a lot of ways."

"You didn't think so. I had to force you to come."

"Well, that was just ignorance, but things are different now." Desperately Thad tried to think of some way to ask her if she would consider him as a husband. It had been on his mind for some time, but the idea seemed so alien that he at first rejected it. The fact that he had nothing and that she had money and a farm seemed to put a huge wall between them. But as he sat beside her, watching her, he knew that this was the woman he wanted. He traced the sadness in her expression and said huskily, "I hate to see you hurt." He put his arm around her, and then to his surprise she turned to face him. He pulled her close against his chest, and when she looked up, her face was so close to his that he could see tears fill her eyes and then run down her cheeks. The thick shadows of the night surrounded the wagon, but the slivers of light from the moon above highlighted her face. He thought suddenly, *A woman asks her own questions and makes her own answer, and a man can't really do anything about that.*

She was watching him in a way he could not define, and he saw in her eyes something he could not name. But it was something that touched him powerfully. It shook the restless, vague wish that had been with him for a long time though he had not recognized it, and then he pulled her close and kissed her. He caught the fragrance of her hair, which somehow revived an old forgotten memory, and at that moment her sweetness and strong spirit touched him.

As for Temperance, she was held in a sort of strange bondage. The weight of his arms was around her, pulling her close, and she sensed his strength. He had his weaknesses, many of them; she knew all about them, but there was an inner strength, too, and a sureness and dependability she suspected she needed in her own life. When he lifted his lips, she looked up and whispered, "Why did you do that, Thaddeus?"

Thad wanted to say something to let her know how he felt. The pressures that had driven him to her and brought her to him were a magnetism he had never felt with a woman, but he wasn't sure that she felt it too. The words would not come, and finally he blurted out, "I—I reckon I'm sorry for you."

Temperance suddenly stiffened. Her lips drew together in a tight line, and her eyes flashed. She reached out and struck him with her fist on his shoulder. "Go feel sorry for somebody else!" she grated. "I don't need your pity!" She was furious, filled with disgust and anger, and mostly disappointment that a man would kiss her for no other reason.

Thad watched her leave and stood there helplessly. *Nice going, Brennan,* he thought. *You can really charm the birds out of the trees.* He was filled with self-disgust and loathing. Some men learned how to talk to women, but he had not been one of them. Now he regretted that fact with every bit of his strength. He stood there under the stars, listening to the crackling of the fire and the far-off cry of a coyote, and he resolved: *I don't know how, but I know she needs a man, and I'm thinking that I'm going to be that man somehow!*

༄

ALL THE NEXT DAY Thad tried to think of some way to reverse the scene with Temperance, but she was cold to him, and he saw what he thought was abhorrence in her expression. He kept to himself that day, riding Judas far ahead, ostensibly looking for game for the pot, but that night when everyone had gone to bed, he pulled his Bible out. *I heard people talk about how God gave them Scriptures when they was up a tree, so, God, I reckon that's what I've got to have.*

He began reading the Bible, but, as usual, he was confused by the different books. He knew they were written by different men over thousands of years, but at this time he desperately needed scriptural guidance.

The Bible was not new, and he had come across several notes and passages underlined. When he flipped it open near the middle, suddenly he saw a passage underlined and he pulled it closer so he could read it: "Whoso findeth a wife findeth a good thing, and obtaineth favour of the LORD."

He noted the location, the twenty-second verse of the eighteenth chapter of Proverbs, and kept his finger on it. Slowly he began to feel that this verse was what God wanted him to hang on to. *All right, Lord, I'm going to take this as a sign from You. You say a wife is a good thing, and so I'm asking You to show me favor. I don't know how You can do it, but I know I can't. So, Lord, turn Your wolf loose on Temperance and let her see as how I'm the man for her!*

He closed the Bible, crawled under his blanket, and lay there for a long time looking up at the stars, far glittering points of light. *If You made all them stars, I reckon You can change one woman's mind*, he murmured sleepily and then knew no more.

ᶜᵛ

THEY REACHED FORT SMITH and, as he had done in St. Joe, Thad set out to ask directions to the home of Luther and Rachel Norris, Virginia's parents and the grandparents of Rose and Billy. He saw a man leaning against a pillar that held up an awning and saw a star on his vest. "Reckon a sheriff ought to be safe enough," he muttered. Dismounting, he walked over and said, "Howdy. My name's Thad Brennan."

"Cyrus Little," the sheriff said. He was a compact man in his midforties with a set of steady, gray eyes. "Just pull in?" he said, glancing at the wagon.

"That's right. Need you to help me locate somebody. We brought two children to their grandparents."

"What's their name?"

"Luther and Rachel Norris are their names."

"Do you tell me that!" Sheriff Little exclaimed. "Why, Luther and me are deacons in the church. We've known each other all our lives. I knew his wife's people. You say you brought their grandchildren?"

Sheriff Little listened as Thad explained the situation, then shook his head. "Well, I'll be switched. I'm plum sorry to hear about Virginia and Vance. I knowed them both, but I can tell you, Luther and Rachel will be tickled to death to take the younguns. Why, they told me as how they intended to go all the way to Oregon before that lady wrote and said she was bringing them. Is that her in the wagon?"

"Yes, it is, Sheriff."

"Well, let me meet that little lady."

Thad accompanied Sheriff Little and introduced him to Temperance. Little swept off his hat and said, "I plum admire you, Miss Peabody. That's a noble thing. Now, you come right along. We're going down to Luther's smithy. He's going to jump over the moon when he sees these kids!"

Sheriff Little led them down the main street and to a blacksmith at the end of the road. He called out, "Luther, come out here," and a strongly built man with crisp brown hair and warm blue eyes walked out.

"I want you to meet your grandchildren, Luther," Sheriff Little grinned. "All the way from Oregon Territory."

Luther Norris's eyes flew open, and he threw a bit of iron bar away as he ran to Rose, who was holding Billy by the hand. He got down on his knees and looked at the small girl in the face. "So this is Rose. I'm your grandpa, Rose."

"I'm glad to meet you, Grandpa. This is Billy."

"Well, ain't he a fine one!" The big blacksmith picked up the boy, who was watching him intently.

"He likes you," Rose said. "He usually cries when strangers pick him up."

"Well, you come right along with me, missy," Luther Norris smiled. "We're going to take you right now to meet your grandma. She's going to have one hallelujah-shouting, Methodist fit when she sees you two!"

The sheriff accompanied them as Norris led the way, carrying Billy and holding Rose by the hand. She was looking up at him with a smile as he spoke, and when they got to a white-framed house on the edge of town, he called out, "Rachel, get out here! Rose and Billy have come."

A tall motherly woman burst out of the door and flew to her husband. She grabbed Billy, kissed him, and then leaned over and hugged Rose. She looked at Rose's face and cried out, "Look, she's just like Virginia."

"These folks brought them all the way from Oregon Territory, Mother," Norris said. "I think we ought to feed them."

"Why, of course we will."

"There's too many of us," Temperance tried to protest. But, as had been the case with Timmy's family, there was no argument.

"I guess Billy and Rose are going to be all right," Rena said to Belle.

"Looks like it," Belle answered. She put her hand on the

girl's shoulder and said, "I'm anxious to meet your family." She noticed that Rena said nothing and saw fear on the girl's face.

⌒

THE DINNER WAS EVERY bit as enormous as the one they had had with the Blanchards. The table seemed to be groaning under the weight of the meats, vegetables, and desserts.

But the big difference was the visitors kept coming in. The Norrises had four grown children. All of them were married and two of them had children. They were all strong, prosperous-looking people, Temperance noted, and each one of them made friends instantly with Rose and Billy. One daughter-in-law, a handsome and well-dressed woman, said, "Mama Norris, you're going to have to let Darryl and me keep these two."

"That's right." Darryl grinned then added. "Give us a start on a family."

"I'm keeping these children myself for awhile, and then"— Rachel smiled at Rose and winked—"we'll let her pick who she wants to be her mama and daddy."

During the meal Luther Norris tried to talk to Rena and Bent, but they were very quiet. Luther then began praising Temperance for what she had done. He was so fulsome with his praise that she finally grew nervous and said, "Well, if you must thank somebody, thank Mr. Brennan. He's the one that brought us all the way here safely—and Mr. Mitchell. The two of them are the ones that need to be thanked."

"That's not so, Mr. Norris," Thad spoke up. "As a matter of fact, I fought against having to come, but Miss Peabody there, she's the one that got all this together."

"And where's your next stop?" Mrs. Norris said.

"We're going to take these children to their relatives in Baton Rouge, Louisiana."

"Oh, that's a terrible long ride and bad roads. You can get there a lot easier by boat."

Temperance was surprised, for she knew little about river transportation. "Is that possible, Mr. Norris?"

"Why, it sure is. I've got a nephew that runs a boat—the *Mary Alice*. It goes from right here in Fort Smith, all the way down the Arkansas River to the Mississippi River. From there you can get on one of them big floating palaces that'll take you right into Baton Rouge."

Temperance was weary of the wagon and of the trail. She looked at Thad and asked with hesitation. "What do you think?"

"Well, the oxen have done good, but they're plum wore-out. I'd hate to put it on them. What I say is let's sell the wagon and oxen, and we'll use the money to pay the fares to Baton Rouge."

"There won't be no fares," Luther said and slapped the table. "If that nephew of mine charges you, I'll put him flat on his back. He wouldn't have been a river pilot if we hadn't helped him. Time for him to start paying back. Of course, you'll have to pay your fare on the Mississippi, but that won't be much."

There was much discussion then, and finally with a sigh of relief, Temperance said, "All right then. Thad, you sell the wagon and the oxen. I'm going to miss Babe." Then a thought came to her. "Where will we stay? When does the boat leave, Mr. Norris?"

"The day after tomorrow, but you're staying right here with us, missy. Anybody we can't crowd in, why, we got grown children that'll be glad to have you." He reached over and took Rose by the hand and smiled. "I'm not letting this one get away though. She's staying right here where she belongs."

❧

QUAID HAD SAID LITTLE during the supper. He liked the Norrises very much and said so to Temperance. He stayed in a hotel, though, and the next day when he came by, the children were outside playing. When he stepped inside the parlor, led by Belle who said that Temperance would be right in, he found that Thad had followed him. Thad's face was very serious, and he said, "Quaid, you've been a help on the way. I don't know what we would have done without you when I got cut up, but we don't need you from here on."

Quaid stood perfectly still, but there was anger in his eyes. "I'm going to New Orleans and I'm going to ask Temperance to marry me. I've already told you that."

"You can't marry her, Quaid."

"What do you mean I can't marry her? I guess I'm old enough to get married." He laughed, but suddenly Thad grabbed his arm. "Get out of here, Quaid! You can't marry her because God's told me she's going to marry me."

Quaid jerked his arm loose. "You lost your mind? God hasn't told you anything. You're just crazy!"

Thad lost his temper. He grabbed Quaid by the arm and started dragging him toward the door. Quaid jerked loose and hit Thad in the chest with his fist. "Take your hands off me!"

The blow triggered something in Thad, and he countered with a roundhouse right that caught Quaid high on the neck. It drove him back so that he overturned a small, fragile walnut table, knocking a lamp over, and then he crashed into the wall, knocking pictures down. He came up swinging, and the two men battered each other all around the room, breaking furniture. Belle cried, "Stop it you two! Stop it!" but they could not hear her.

As they were throwing wild punches, Temperance came in. "What are they doing, Belle?"

"Fighting over you. You better stop it before they kill each other."

Temperance ran forward. "You two stop it at—"

She didn't finish her sentence, for one of them—and afterward neither would own up to being the perpetrator—threw a blow with a hard fist that caught Temperance in the temple. It drove her down, and she fell loosely, unconscious.

Thad stopped, his eyes wild, and ran to her. "You see what you done, Quaid!"

"Me!" Quaid shouted. "I didn't do a thing. You was the one that busted her!"

Mrs. Norris came in, along with Luther. "What's going on here?" Luther said.

"These two idiots got in a fight over Temperance," Belle said, "and one of them hit her and knocked her out."

"It was him!" Thad said, pointing at Quaid.

"Was not! It was you."

"Both of you keep your mouths shut! The very idea!" Mrs. Norris snorted. "I'll get some cold water, Belle. Somebody put her on the couch."

"I'll do it," Quaid said and stepped forward.

Thad shoved him. "No, you're not picking her up. I'll do it."

"Neither one of you will do it," Luther Norris said sternly. "Get out of my way. I'll handle this." He was a burly man with the strength of a blacksmith's arms, and he picked her up easily. Belle sat down and held her, and when Rachel Norris returned with a bowl of cold water and a cloth, the two began washing her face.

"She's going to have a terrible black eye," Belle said.

"She's—she's all right, isn't she?" Thad said.

"Yes, no thanks to you!"

Eventually, Temperance's eyes fluttered. "She's coming out of it," Belle said. "Are you all right, Temperance?"

Her eyes opened, and she was totally confused. Belle helped her to sit up, and Temperance reached up and touched her head. "Who hit me?"

Both Quaid and Thad pointed at each other and said at the same time, "He did!"

Quaid at once stepped forward. "It was his fault. I just told him I was going to ask you to marry me, and he—"

"He can't marry you because God told me to marry you!" Thad said loudly.

Temperance was regaining her balance and her senses now, and she looked around at the room, which was wrecked. "You're both insane! Get out of here! Go marry squaws like you're always boasting about. I'll take the children by myself. Leave!"

"I reckon you fellows better go. Let the lady calm down. If you want to fight, maybe we can sell tickets," Luther said sarcastically, and they had no choice but to leave.

Belle hugged Temperance. "I thought I'd seen fools before but never two like these. Well, you've got your choice now. Two men want to marry you."

"No, Thad feels sorry for me, and Quaid just wants a woman to sit on his veranda and make him mint juleps. That's what he's got in mind for the rest of his life."

"Well, you may not take either one of them," Belle said, "but at least, honey, you've been asked."

Chapter Twenty-three

"I GOT A GOOD price at the auction for the wagon." Thad extended a fistful of bills toward Temperance. "This is a good place to sell stock and wagons. Everybody's heading to Oregon country."

Temperance had been aloof since the fight in the Norris house—at least toward Quaid and Thaddeus. She felt humiliated by the whole scene although Belle had told her she ought to be honored to have two men fighting over her. Belle's words did not ring true. She felt that both of the men were somehow playing a game for which she didn't know the rules. She had tossed and turned for two nights, waiting until the boat was ready to leave, and each night she had cried and thought, *They're making a fool of me. Quaid's a woman chaser, and Thaddeus doesn't know what he is.*

To Thaddeus, she now said stiffly, "Thank you," and took the money. She was surprised at how much it was and counted out four hundred dollars and handed it back to him. "Here's the rest of the money I promised you."

Thad took it reluctantly and shook his head. "You better keep it, Temperance. You don't know how much expense you'll run into getting the kids to Baton Rouge, and then I guess you'll be going back to Walla Walla."

"No, you've earned it."

Her tone was cool, and Thad tried to think of a way to express his feelings, but he could not. She turned and walked away, and as she did, Rena approached him. "Is she still mad at you, Thad?"

"Reckon so."

Rena reached out and took his hand. "She'll get over it. Don't you give up now."

"I need to be as stubborn as you are. To tell the truth, I don't know how to act around women."

"She got her feelings hurt, but she likes you. I know it."

At that moment Luther came to say, "I guess we're ready to go to the boat now, so you'll be on your way."

Rena and Bent found Rose, and both of them hugged her. Then Rose kissed Bess. "I'm going to miss you so much," Rose whispered, clinging to Rena. "I won't ever forget you!"

"We won't forget you either," Rena said huskily. She released the girl and walked away, her eyes filled with tears. When Bent caught up with her, she said, "We'll never see them again." Bent stared at her but could think of no answer.

Thad had bought a small canvas bag to carry his few clothes and shaving items. He got into the carriage along with Mr. Norris, and the Overmeyer children got in the back. Glancing over his shoulder, he saw that in the second carriage Quaid was sitting beside Temperance.

Luther spoke to the horses, and they broke into a trot. "You'll enjoy the trip on the Arkansas. My nephew's a good captain."

"Nice of you to put in a word for us, Mr. Norris."

"Not at all! Not at all! Not after what you folks done for us." He glanced over his shoulder and then turned his eyes on Thad. "A little problem with Miss Temperance, I see."

"She'll be all right."

"She's a mighty fine woman."

"Best I've ever known."

"Well, you did a good job getting her here. Miss Belle and the kids have been telling me how you got them through. Rena told me about how you saved her and her brother from the Indians." Admiration shaded his tone, and he shook his head. "You took out six Indians? That's some pumpkins, Thaddeus."

"I guess the good Lord was with me."

"I know you're a little bit downhearted now, but serving the Lord goes that way sometimes. I remember when I was courting Rachel. Sometimes I got so downright despondent I wanted to blow my brains out. There were two other fellows wanting her. I whipped one of them, and the other one whipped me. I thought she would take the winner, but she took me instead." He grinned slyly. "I asked her one time why she didn't take him. She told me his eyes were too close together. Who knows what a woman's thinking? I watch them sometimes at the market. You ever notice how they go around pinching the fruit? They'll pinch every tomato before they pick out the ones they want. I think they're that way with menfolk, looking for the right man. They just pinch a little here and a little there, but don't you give up, son. I think she's got something in her eye for you."

"I don't see how you can say that."

Luther chatted all the way to the wharf, and he led them up the gangplank. A man wearing a uniform and a captain's hat was there to greet them. "Morning, George. Here we are. This is Miss Temperance Peabody. Her and her friends brought our grandchildren back to us. We've got Billy and Rose now."

"I heard about it." Captain George Marsh was not tall, but he was a deep-chested, powerful-looking man. His skin was tanned a deep mahogany and there were lines around his eyes from the blistering sun. A life on the deck of his boat had hard-ened him, but there was an openness in his expression. When he shook hands with Thad, his grip was like a vise. "Glad to have you aboard, all of you." He nodded to the rest. "Of course, the *Mary Alice* isn't really a passenger ship. We've got a few empty cabins. You ladies can settle among yourselves, and we've got a good cook. Come along. Let me show you around."

Temperance followed him to the cabin, and Captain Marsh said, "I'll let you and your husband have this cabin."

"I don't have a husband. It's *Miss* Peabody."

"Oh, sorry. I thought that tall fellow standing by you was your man."

"No, he's guided us all the way from Walla Walla."

"Pardon me, Miss Peabody."

Temperance looked around the cabin, which was small, but at least it had a bed, then she turned and went out on the deck. She saw that Quaid had come aboard, and he quickly said, "Got to get to New Orleans, Temperance, and this boat's going that way."

Temperance started to speak, but she noticed Thaddeus coming up the gangplank. "You don't need to go all the way to Baton Rouge with us, Thad," she said.

Thad swallowed hard. Captain Marsh and the others were listening. "I'm going to do what I set out to do and that's to get these children to their people." He turned and gave Quaid a hard glance and then asked Marsh, "How much is the fare?"

"My uncle says he'll break my back if I charge any of you any money," Captain Marsh smiled.

There was some confusion getting everybody on board, and Captain Marsh moved over to speak to Belle. She had bought a new dress at one of the stores in Fort Smith and had her hair fixed. Marsh obviously admired her. "Good to have you aboard, Miss Belle," he said. "Maybe you and I can have dinner. I want you to come to the captain's table."

"Will your wife like that?" Belle asked.

"I haven't been fortunate enough to find a bride yet." He smiled, and Belle found him roughly attractive. "Those two men, Mitchell and Brennan, I don't quite understand. Seems like there's some problem with Miss Peabody. Is one of them engaged to her?"

Belle shook her head. "No, Captain, but they both claim they want to marry her."

Marsh was amused, but his mouth was set in a stubborn line. "They better not cause any trouble, or I'll put them ashore. What about you, Miss Belle? You're headed for Baton Rouge?"

"Going to New Orleans. It's my old home."

"Well, I'll make life as pleasant as I can. Doesn't hurt to have the captain for a friend."

Belle smiled as the captain flirted with her. She knew he had spotted her for what she was, and it didn't trouble him. "We'll have a good time, Captain," she said. She slipped her hand in his arm. "Now, show me around the *Mary Alice*."

The days seemed to flow by as evenly as the Arkansas flowed to the south. The trip was pleasant and restful. Thad spent most of his time with Rena and Bent, which pleased them a great deal. Belle was romancing Captain Marsh, and Quaid and Thad each took every opportunity to speak to Temperance, but her comments to them were so short they were both kept at a distance.

On a Thursday evening after supper, a knock came at Temperance's door. She had been sitting on the single chair in her room, reading from her Bible. She laid it down, and when she opened the door, she found Quaid standing there.

"Can I come in? I need to talk to you."

With a sigh Temperance stepped back. "Come in, but we don't have anything much to talk about."

"I think we do." Quaid stepped inside and looked down at her. He was accustomed to having his own way. He had found out, however, that this woman could not be pressured, and his voice was conciliatory as he said, "I don't know why you're acting like I was some kind of a monster, Temperance."

"I just want to be let alone."

Quaid shook his head. "I have to tell you how much I admire you. I want to marry you."

Temperance gave a short laugh. "You admire the president of the United States, but you don't want to marry him."

Quaid's judgment failed him at that moment. He had known women who needed persuading, and usually a full-scale assault was his method. He reached out, grabbed her, pulled her to him, and tried to kiss her, but she turned her face away so that he could not and avoided his caress. "Let me go, Quaid!"

Quaid released her reluctantly and said, "Do you think I'm not an honorable man? I'm asking you to marry me. That's about as honorable as you can get."

Temperance had spent most of the trip avoiding both Quaid and Thaddeus. She was confused and could not understand it. Had this been what she wanted, a man to make a life with? Why was she then running from the two men both professing to care for her? Something was wrong with the whole situation, and she desperately wished to find a way out, an answer, but she had not been able to. Now she said as evenly as she could, "I want you to go now, Quaid."

"But we need to talk."

"There's nothing to talk about." She opened the door and shook her head. Her lips were set in a stubborn frame. "I'm not the kind of woman you want."

Quaid Mitchell looked at her, and at that moment he understood that for once in his life he had failed with a woman. He could not understand it, for it was the first time he had ever asked a woman to marry him. All of his other women had been merely for ornament or convenience, but this woman, who was not nearly as beautiful as some of the others, had a spirit he knew he could never overcome.

"All right, Temperance," he said flatly, "I won't bother you anymore."

As soon as the door closed, Temperance sat on the bunk and found she was trembling. *What's wrong with me? He's handsome and has money and he's a Christian. What do I want? Have I lost my mind?*

She heard the engines of the *Mary Alice* churning and the paddle wheels slapping the water, and had the sense of motion as the ship plowed downriver. She dreaded making the trip to Baton Rouge, for she had apprehensions about the Overmeyer children's family. She finally muttered, "As soon as I get the children settled, I'm going back to the farm in Walla Walla and stay there the rest of my life!"

❧

THAT NIGHT AT SUPPER at Captain Marsh's table, Temperance noticed he was favoring Belle. She was well aware that Belle was carrying on a romance with the captain, but she said nothing. Belle was Belle.

"I know a lot of the captains of the boats, big pleasure palaces, are going down to the gulf," Marsh said to Temperance. "I'll get you a good deal on passage."

"Thank you, Captain. That's nice of you."

After the meal Temperance went to her cabin, and Rena said, "I'm going out on deck and sit with Thad."

"All right, Rena."

"We like to sit up in the front of the boat and talk."

"What do you talk about?" Temperance asked curiously.

"Just about everything. I didn't like him at first, but I guess now I've told him everything that's ever happened to me, and he's told me a lot of stuff too. He was a soldier and a trapper. He's done all kinds of things."

"You're going to miss him, aren't you, Rena?"

"Yes, I am and Bent is too. He—he's been nice to both of us and to Bess. He even likes her. Most men don't pay any attention to babies unless it's their baby." Rena asked suddenly, "Why don't you want to get married, Temperance? I thought you wanted a man and children."

"Oh, I don't know, Rena."

"You never had a man. Now you got two of them ready to cut each other's throats for you. Why are you running away from them?"

Temperance began to speak, and as she tried to explain to Rena her hesitancy, it all seemed to come together in her mind. "Marriage is forever, Rena," she said carefully. "At least for as long as a person's on this earth. If a woman marries the wrong man, she's tied to him for all her life."

"But people do get married. Maybe you just have to take a chance."

"I can't do that, Rena. I can't gamble my life like that. God will have to tell me what to do."

Rena stared at her unblinkingly, then turned and went out on deck without another word.

As soon as she was gone, Temperance sat down. Her hands were trembling, and she was not far from tears. She thought about her life, what a desert it had been for so many years and how she had feared the loneliness of never having anyone beside her. The very thought of going back to the farm in Walla Walla suddenly turned into a bitterness that seemed to sour in her throat. Yet, what else was she to do?

A knock sounded and she started. Quickly she got up and paused for a moment to be sure that her mind was clear. When she opened the door, she found Thad standing there.

"What are you doing—taking turns with Quaid?"

"No, just have something I want to say to you."

"Do you want to come in?"

He shook his head. "No, I know you don't want to be around me, but there's something I got to say." Taking a deep breath, he looked down at her, and for a moment the silence was broken by only the slapping of the paddle wheels on the water and the cry of a night bird that haunted the edge of the river.

"I didn't say it right when you asked me how I felt about you, Temperance. I do feel sorry for you, but then I feel sorry for myself. I made a wreck out of my life." His lips grew hard, and his eyes had an unusual sadness. "But you made me do one good thing. Helping get these children to someone who will care for them has been the only decent thing I've ever done."

Temperance suddenly realized that this man looking down at her was as lonely as she was. She saw him struggle for words, and when he finally spoke, she discovered something about him that he kept covered up. "Quaid—he's good with words and I'm not, but I've changed in the last months. I've watched you, Temperance. You're the only woman I've ever wanted to spend the rest of my life with."

Temperance stood very still and felt her throat tightening. Something about the simplicity of this big man touched her.

"I—I want you to be happy. That's all I want. I was wrong to fight with Quaid. He's a better man than I am, Temperance, and if you love him, why, I'll understand." He suddenly whirled and walked away, leaving her standing there feeling incomplete. She wanted to call out after him, but then she realized she didn't know what she would say to him. Slowly she closed the door and looked out the small window. The thick woods were passing by as the *Mary Alice* forged steadily downriver, and she knew they were headed for the Mississippi and then for Baton Rouge. A sudden thought came to her: *I wish I knew where the rest of my life was going as well as I know where this boat is going.*

Chapter Twenty-four

TEMPERANCE STOOD BESIDE THE railing of the *Memphis Queen*, an enormous side-wheeler, and watched the banks of the Mississippi flow by. It was the middle of August, and three days had passed since they had transferred from the *Mary Alice*. Temperance had kept mostly to herself in her cabin. Quaid had spent much time in the saloon, and Belle had accompanied him for most of the time.

Thad had spent the days on deck with the Overmeyer children, his nights alone. He had come to the stern of the ship accompanied by Rena, and the two had been quiet. Suddenly Thad turned to the young girl, examining her face. He had become very close to her and to Bent, and a sudden gust of compassion for her came to him.

"What's wrong, Rena," he asked.

"I'm afraid."

"Afraid of what?"

"You know. I'm afraid of losing you. So is Bent." She turned to him, and her eyes were clouded with fear. "My uncle and aunt, they're not good people. Even Ma said they were mean."

Thad hesitated for a moment, then he said, "Two days ago I found, in the book of Mark, Jesus talking about a mountain: 'Be thou removed, and be thou cast into the sea.'"

"You can't talk to a mountain!"

"If Temperance believes that the Bible is true, then it's got to be so." He stroked his chin thoughtfully and then he smiled. Her eyes were fixed on him steadfastly. Suddenly she threw her arms around him and gave him a hug, then whirled and ran down the deck. He watched her go and was filled with concern for her, and for Bent and Bess. He shook his head, for this had not been his attitude when he had first met the children they had brought from Walla Walla. He had known very little about children, as a matter of fact, but all that had changed. Now as he stood on the deck of the *Memphis Queen*, with thoughts running through his head, he looked up and saw Quaid coming toward him. An impulse had been growing in Thad for some time, and now he knew it was time. "Quaid, I need to talk to you."

Quaid stood before him. "What is it, partner?"

"I acted like a fool—over you wanting to marry Temperance. Well, to tell the truth, I wanted to marry her myself. I had this crazy idea that God said she was for me. She deserves a better man than me, so I'll be happy for you and her if you get married."

"This isn't the Thaddeus I knew," Quaid said finally. "You would never have given up in the old days."

"She'll make you a good wife." Suddenly Thad could not bear to speak of the two, so he said, "Good night. I'll see you in the morning." He left the deck, and Quaid stared after him, a puzzled expression on his face.

THE DOCK AT BATON ROUGE was full of boats, some loading and some unloading. Temperance had watched as the boat docked and then returned to her cabin. She was getting ready to disembark when she saw Quaid coming toward her. "Well, you made it to Baton Rouge," he smiled.

Temperance asked, "Aren't you getting off?"

"No, I'm going to New Orleans, Belle and I." He saw the surprise in her face and smiled. "I'm a good man, but you turned me down. You can't get everything you want."

Temperance was surprised that Quaid Mitchell was giving up. She thought many times about his proposal. At times she thought she had been a fool to refuse him. Not many women would do that! "Thank you for all you've done for us."

Quaid thought for a moment and then forced himself to smile. "I'll get settled and then I'll buy that plantation. I'll think about you when I'm sitting on my veranda, drinking my mint juleps. I'll give you my address down here, and if you need me, you can write. Even if you don't need help, write me, Temperance, and let me know the end of your story." He took her hand and then surprisingly kissed it. "I hope it ends like those romances in the books."

Belle joined them, and Temperance said, "I'll think of you, Belle. I hope . . . you'll find happiness."

Belle said, "I guess I won't change, but I'll think of you."

There was no time for long good-byes, for the passengers were disembarking quickly. Temperance hugged Belle and impulsively hugged Quaid, too, then hurried off the ship, carrying Bess and leading Rena and Bent. She waited until Thad had gotten the baggage ashore. It was a considerable amount. He turned to her. "I guess we'd better get a carriage. You got that address where these people live? What's their name?"

"Ed and Maude Slaughter. Here's the address."

Taking the slip of paper, Thad saw a large carriage with a dark-skinned, young man leaning on it. He asked, "Can you take us to this place?"

The driver said, "Sure. I take you there. It's a long way. Cost you a lot."

"That's all right. Here's the luggage over here."

Thad helped him load the luggage and put the children in the second seat; he and Temperance got in the front seat beside the driver. "Why you want to go to this place?" the driver demanded.

"It's where we need to go," Thad said. "What's wrong with it?"

"Not a good place to go."

Thad exchanged glances with Temperance. She had a worried look. "What's wrong with it?"

"Bad part of Baton Rouge. You want to go to a hotel. Don't stay there. I'll take you to one."

"We have to go there first," Temperance said.

"No skin off my nose," the driver said cheerfully.

The trip from the wharf to the address was from the acceptable to the terrible. The neighborhoods kept getting worse until finally they had to be in one of the worst sections of Baton Rouge. Every other building seemed to be a saloon, and people they saw in the streets were either drunks or harlots from the look of them.

"This is terrible, Thad."

"It doesn't look too good," he agreed, "but we've got to go through with it."

Finally the driver pulled over and waved his whip. "That's the place. You want me to wait?"

"Yes, please," Temperance said. Thad leaped out and helped her down, and she took Bess while Rena and Bent got out.

"This place is awful," Rena said. "Do we have to go here?"

"I'm afraid so," Temperance said. Her lips grew tight, and she shook her head. "It's sad." She started toward the door, carrying Bess. She knocked, and there was a long wait. Finally it opened, and a huge, slatternly woman wearing a filthy dress stepped out. She had a broad face, flushed, and the scent of strong alcohol was in the air. "Who are you? What do you want?" she demanded.

"I'm looking for Ed and Maude Slaughter."

"I'm Maude. What do you want with us? You're not the law."

"Oh no. My name is Peabody."

The woman stared at her. "Oh, yeah, you're the one that wrote the letter about Sadie's kids."

"Yes, Mrs. Slaughter. Could we come in?"

"Is them the kids there?" the woman demanded, waving a meaty hand at the Overmeyer children.

"Yes, they are."

"Well, come on in." Temperance followed her, and Rena and Bent came behind. Thad came in and shut the door. The room was a disaster, filthy in every way—dirty dishes were everywhere, flies swarmed around a table, and there was a terrible odor of urine, cabbage, and open drains.

"My husband, Ed, ain't here," she said. She studied the children and shook her head. "I don't know what Sadie was thinking, sending the kids here. This ain't no place for them."

Temperance was speechless. Thad said quickly, "What time will your husband be back?"

"I don't know. He just got out of the jail yesterday. I expect he's in one of the saloons." She scratched vigorously and shook her head. "He didn't want them kids coming here, but I talked him into it. What's your name?" She got the names from Rena and shrugged. "Well, you two are big enough to work. I don't know what we'll do with that baby. She'll have to get by the best way she can. You bring their clothes?" she demanded abruptly.

"I'll get them," Thad said quickly. He stepped outside, took a deep breath, and sorted through the baggage. When he stepped back in, he saw that Temperance's face was pale and Bent and Rena were speechless. The woman was speaking. "My man ain't easy to get along with," she said. "Just don't you two cross him."

Thad put the baggage down, and then Temperance turned to Rena. She put her arms around her and kissed her. She was so overwhelmed for a moment she could not speak and then she said, "Good-bye, sweetheart."

Rena was fighting to keep the tears back. She took Bess while Temperance bent over to hug Bent. "You behave yourself and be good."

"Don't leave us here," Bent whispered.

"We've got to go, honey. I'm sorry." She stood up quickly and left the room. Thad went over and placed his hand on Bent's head. "Hang in there, partner. It'll be all right." He turned to Rena. "You remember what I said about the mountain."

He hugged Rena, and she whispered, "I ain't forgot about the mountain, Thad." He hesitated, feeling her hanging on to him for dear life. He finally pulled her arm away, quickly turned, and walked out the room. Temperance was standing by the carriage, her face turned away. He came forward and said, "I guess we'd better go." He saw that tears were gathering in her eyes, but he couldn't think of any comfort. He helped her in, got in after her, and said, "Take us to a good hotel, driver."

"I take you to a good one."

Neither of them spoke on the way to the hotel. They got out, paid their fare, and went inside. They registered, and when it was time to go to their rooms, Thad turned and said, "Temperance, I feel sick."

"So do I—but there's nothing we can do." She left quickly. He watched her go and then went to his room. He washed his face and hands and was astonished to see his hands were unsteady. He stared at them and shook his head. "I didn't think anything in the world could do that to me." He lay down on the bed fully dressed, but there was no peace to it. Finally he got up, left the room, and for the rest of the afternoon walked the streets of Baton Rouge. He had never felt such uneasiness in all his life even though he had been in many hard places. Finally he went back to Temperance's room and knocked on the door. "Who is it?" Her voice was muffled.

"Let's eat something."

"I'm not hungry."

"You've got to eat, Temperance."

"Just leave me alone, Thad."

He hesitated for a moment and then muttered, "I know how you feel." He went to the dining room and tried to eat, but he could not get the food down. Once again he went out and walked the streets of Baton Rouge, and as he did, he prayed in a strange way. He found himself almost accusing God. *God, I don't understand You. You can't want those little kids to be in a place like that. It's the worst thing in the world for them. You've got to do something.*

He felt ashamed of himself for challenging God, but then he finally returned to the hotel and spent a restless night.

WHEN THAD KNOCKED ON Temperance's door, she was there almost at once. There were hollows under her eyes, and her face was pale. "You look terrible, Temperance," he said.

"I know it. I feel terrible. That's an awful woman, and the man's probably worse."

Thad suddenly made up his mind. "Come on. I'm going over there."

"Why? What good would that do?"

"I don't know. I'm just going, that's all. You can stay here if you want to."

"No, I'll go with you."

The two of them left the hotel, got a carriage, and drove back to the Slaughters' house. When they arrived, Temperance was frightened. "I don't know what you're going to say."

"I'm going to talk about how kids ought to be treated. Somehow I got the idea that Maude Slaughter doesn't have much notion of that."

"You can't take them away."

Thad didn't answer. He knocked on the door and for a long time there was no answer. Then it opened, and a huge man filled the doorway. He hadn't shaved in days and he spilled out of his clothes.

"What do you want?"

"I'm Thad Brennan. This is Miss Peabody. We brought the children here yesterday."

"Yeah, well, they're here. What do you want now?"

"I thought I might leave some money here to help with the board."

"Well, hand over the cash."

"I'll give it to them," Thad said carefully.

For a moment Ed Slaughter seemed about to shut the door, then he said, "You can give it to them, but I'll get it sooner or later." He stepped back.

Thad took that as an invitation to enter. He stepped inside and saw Maude Slaughter with her back against the wall. She had bruises on her face and was obviously terrified. "Don't you do nothing, Ed," she said. "You don't want to go back to that jail."

"Shut up," Slaughter demanded. "Come here, girl. This man's going to give you money, and you're going to give it to me."

Rena and Bent had been standing as far away from Slaughter as they could, with their backs against the wall too. Both of them were still wearing the same clothes they had worn yesterday, and they had obviously been slept in.

Thad reached into his pocket for money and then suddenly he saw that Rena was turning her face away.

He reached out, asking, "What's wrong?"

"Nothing."

He took her chin, gently pushed it away from him, and saw a huge, blue black bruise on the side of her face. "Who did this to you, Rena?" he said. His voice was very soft, but anger raged through him.

"I did it to her," Slaughter said as if proud of it. "She's got a smart mouth."

"He—he beat Bent and he put his hands on me."

Temperance could stand it no longer. "Get your things. You're not staying here."

Slaughter turned and faced her. "Keep your mouth shut! You're not taking these kids anywhere. Get out of my house!" He caught Temperance by the arm and shoved her toward the door.

Instantly Thad stepped forward. "Take your hands off that woman, or I'll break your neck."

Slaughter roared out a vile curse and threw his massive fist toward Thad. The blow slashed Thad on the cheek, causing blood to run down his face, but Thad ignored it. He stepped under it and with all his might struck Ed Slaughter far below the belt. It was as hard as he had ever hit a man in his life, and he got an intense satisfaction when Slaughter suddenly screamed like a woman and fell to the floor, holding himself in a fetal position. Thad stared at him for a moment. "I ought to kick your head in, but I'm letting you off easy." He turned and smiled. "Bent, get your things; we're leaving."

Bent ran into the adjoining room. "Help me, Rena!"

Temperance quickly took Bess. "Help him get your things, Rena. You're not staying here."

Rena's eyes were shining. She disappeared, and soon the two returned carrying their clothes and suitcases.

Slaughter had struggled to his feet, and as the children moved toward the door, he began screaming, "I'll have the law on you! You can't—"

He broke off suddenly. In one smooth movement Thad drew the Navy Colt he had stuck inside his belt under his coat. He rammed it into Slaughter's mouth, grabbed the man's hair, and held the Colt steady. He pulled the hammer back, and it made an ominous click. "Shut your mouth, Slaughter! I've got a mind to pull this trigger right now." Slaughter began moaning and trying to talk, but Thad shoved the gun even farther against the roof of his mouth. "You let me hear one word of complaint out of you, I promise you'll get this slug right through your brain." He jerked the revolver out, loosening several of Slaughter's teeth. He waited to see what the man would do, backed to the door, and stepped outside. He put the gun back under his belt and noted that the carriage driver was watching him cautiously. "That's Ed Slaughter," he said. "He killed one man."

"He looks like a sissy to me," Thad said. "Now, take us back to the hotel." He helped Temperance into the back seat with the children and saw that she was holding Bess and had her arm around the other two, holding them tightly. He looked at Rena and said, "I'm sorry you kids had to go through that."

"It's all right," Rena said, and then she reached out and touched his face. "You moved a mountain, Thad. You did it!"

Chapter Twenty-five

"WE'VE GOT TO GET you cleaned up, Thad."

They were in the lobby of the hotel, and Thad dabbed at the blood on his cheek with his handkerchief. "It's not too bad," he said.

"No, we need to take care of it. Come to my room."

She led the way and told him to sit on the bed while the children watched. She began to clean the wound, and fishing into one of the bags, she found a bit of sticking plaster. She put it over the cut. "There. That ought to do."

Rena had kept quiet as long as possible. "What are we going to do? We're not going back to that place, are we?"

"No, you're not," Thad said. "What are we going to do? We're going to go eat breakfast." He led them down the stairs, into the dining room, and ordered a monumental breakfast for all of them. They were all hungry, it seemed, for Bent and Rena had had nothing to eat. They had eggs, pork chops, and biscuits. Thad kept his eye on the children and saw that they were worried, and finally he looked up and said, "I'll tell you what we're going to do. We're going to stay in this hotel for a few days. I've got a little business here, and we're going to see all the sights of Baton Rouge. Maybe go to a theater. Go see some of them fancy show girls I've been hearing about."

"We're not going to see any show girls," Temperance said. "Maybe there'll be a concert."

"Whatever you want. We're just going to enjoy life."

"What if Mr. Slaughter comes after you?" Bent said. "They say he's mean."

"I don't think he'll do that. If he does, I'll clean his clock for him. Temperance, why don't you take the girls with you in your room? Bent can stay in mine. How's that sound?"

Temperance was immensely relieved. She had no idea under the sun what to do. Her plans had fallen apart, and now she was glad Thad had taken charge. "It sounds wonderful to me."

"Good. You all hang on to your Uncle Thad here, and I'll show you how to have a good time in Baton Rouge, Louisiana!"

❧

THE NEXT THREE DAYS passed, and it was the best time in the lives of any of them. The children had never had anyone pamper them, and Thad set out to do exactly that. He took them to see the sights, bought them trinkets, and spent time with them.

Temperance felt as if a mountain had been lifted from her shoulders. Somehow Thad had become responsible, and although she had no idea about the future, at least she was enjoying the present. She saw a side of Thaddeus she had not seen before—a lighthearted, easy-going side—but she also noticed that the children were able to talk him into nearly anything. He spoiled them, but he could be stern when he had to. But they adored him, and this pleased her.

They were sitting in the park, feeding stale bread to the ducks late one afternoon, and finally Rena said, "We can't stay here and feed ducks the rest of our lives. We've got to go live somewhere."

"That's right," Bent said. "It must cost a lot of money to stay in that hotel."

"I'm afraid you're right," Temperance said, "but I don't know what we can do."

Thad was whittling at a piece of cedar he had found, carefully peeling off long slivers and watching them curl up. "You can't whittle the rest of your life, Thaddeus," Temperance rebuked him.

"Why, God's going to take care of us. Isn't that what you're always saying?"

"I know, but—"

"I know what we can do," Rena said. She turned to face Temperance and Thad. "You and Thad can get married, and we'll be your kids."

Temperance's face turned scarlet. She could not speak for a moment and then she sputtered, "Why, you—that isn't—"

She was interrupted when Thad suddenly looked up, his eyes dancing with delight. "Now, that's a fine idea, young lady. I don't know why I didn't think of that myself."

"Don't you be ridiculous, Thaddeus!"

"Nothing ridiculous about it. Just look at the economy of it all."

"The economy? What in the world are you talking about?"

"Well, you ever stop and think about how much it costs to raise three kids like this? You got all the expense of buying clothes and diapers and then there's doctor bills. Oh, all kinds of expense. We'll skip all that. They're mostly through diapers anyway, and I don't have to go through the trouble of living with a big, swollen-up wife for nine months for every youngun. Why, it's wonderful!"

Temperance had become accustomed in the past three days to his mild teasing, and that was how she saw this. She got up and stalked away, saying, "I refuse to listen to such nonsense." She walked to the water and stared out over the lake.

"Thad," Rena said, "you've got to talk romantic to her."

"Why, shucks, I don't know how."

"Yes, you do. Tell her how pretty she is and how she smells good and how you love her to death. Stuff like that."

"I don't think I can change her, Rena. She's stubborn."

"She wants to hear things like that," Rena said fiercely, "and she loves you. I know she does. You're just too blind to see it."

Thaddeus stared at the young girl and said, "Well, you may be right. She's too mad to talk right now, but later tonight I'll give it a shot."

ॐ

TEMPERANCE HAD REFUSED TO eat dinner with the others in the restaurant and had gone straight to her room. She felt humiliated that Thad would make such talk about marriage to her. It was getting late now, she knew, and she wondered where Rena and Bess were. They should be coming in. A knock came at the door, and she assumed they were there. When she opened it, she saw Thad. "Where's Bess and Rena?"

"They're down in my room. I had to talk to you. Can I come in?"

"I don't want to talk to you, Thaddeus. Go away."

He stepped inside and shut the door, ignoring her. She stared at him and said, "You'll never know how you hurt my feelings, talking like you did. You don't know how a woman can be hurt, Thaddeus, about—"

"About what?"

"I've never had a man. No man ever wanted me, and here you make all those jokes about getting married and saving money on kids. Oh, it was humiliating."

Thad moved toward her, and she twirled and started away, but he caught her by the shoulders and turned her around. He held her firmly. His face was totally serious. "I don't know how to go about this, but I have to tell you three things. If you want me to leave after that, I will."

"What three things?"

"Well, one thing is I love those kids. You don't know it, but that's a miracle. I've never been around kids. I thought they were pesky, but these have gotten to me. I couldn't love them any better if they were my own blood. Can't bear the thought of anything bad happening to them."

"That's—that's a good thing, Thaddeus."

"Well, I'm glad you believe that, and I hope you'll believe this." He hesitated and cleared his throat, and his hand tightened on her arm. "The second thing is I love you, Temperance." He watched her face. He pulled her forward, kissed her gently, and ran his hand down the back of her hair. "That's the second thing. Do you believe it?"

And suddenly Temperance Peabody knew that this man, so hard in some ways, who had struggled for his whole life, meant it—that he did love her. She had never had a man say this, and it seemed to sink into her inner depths. "Yes," she whispered, "I believe you. What's the third thing?"

"Well, the third thing. I want us to get married. I want us to go on a honeymoon."

"A honeymoon? What are you talking about?"

"I want to take passage on a ship all the way around the cape to Africa. I want us to take the kids with us. They'll be our kids, yours and mine. I want to change their names to Brennan. We'll be Mr. and Mrs. Brennan. We'll go to California. I always had a hankering to go to Santa Fe and get into the freight-hauling business. You can sell your farm and give me all the money. You can be a silent partner."

"But what about the man you shot?"

"Oh, that's the business I had here. I've been saving it. I sent a wire to Joe Meek the day we got here. That fellow Simons got well. Meek pulled some strings with his senator daddy, made a deal somehow. He said I'm a free man."

Suddenly joy filled Temperance Peabody. She smiled broadly and put her hand on his cheek. "You won't be free with a wife and three children."

"Oh, it won't be three for long." He winked lewdly at her, and she laughed but shook her head. "I'm too old to have children."

"No, you're not. I want at least three more. Now, you can do it any way you please," he said and pulled her closer. "You can have them one at a time, or you can have a single and a double, or you can have a triple. It makes no difference to me."

"You fool! That could never happen!"

"Anything can happen when you're on God's side. I found that out about moving mountains."

Temperance Peabody put her arms around his neck and pulled his head down. She kissed him and felt a freedom and a joy she had thought would never be hers. When she pulled her head back, she said, "Oh, Thaddeus, can we really do it?"

"Can we do it? As sure as a cat's got climbing gear!" He laughed and then turned her around. "Come on, let's go tell the kids they've got a new mama and daddy." He opened the door but kept his arm around her as he closed it.

Augustus the cat had come all the way from Walla Walla. He felt neglected lately, and now he looked up from the bed where he had been lying as the two left the room. Gus stared at the door, yawned, and stretched out on the bed, digging his claws into the coverlet. Then his eyes closed, and the sound of his purring filled the room.